"A solid and provocative collection
one Jewish community north of Tor
jam-packed with scrappiness, turm
——TAMARA FAITH BERGER, *author of* Yara

"The stories simultaneously ground themselves in the immediate, lived
experience of the Jewish community in Toronto and leap beyond it into
possible futures, following flights of imagination that curl back on the
present, revealing its hidden dimensions. Rubble Children *breaks what
is essentially new ground for the Canadian short story. Urgent, topical,
and contemporary, it makes for genuinely exhilarating reading."
——AARON SCHNEIDER, *author of* The Supply Chain

"What if the worldview you were raised in turns out to be monstrous?
In the stories that form Rubble Children, Aaron Kreuter examines a
Jewish community in flux, caught between its historical fealty to Israel
and a growing awakening and resistance to it. Rubble Children *is
a book of great range: at once political, communitarian, empathetic,
funny, revolutionary, touching, and hopeful. This is a work that is
essential for our moment."
——SAEED TEEBI, *author of* Her First Palestinian

Also by Aaron Kreuter

*Leaving Other People Alone: Diaspora, Zionism, and Palestine
in Contemporary Jewish Fiction*

Shifting Baseline Syndrome

You and Me, Belonging

Arguments for Lawn Chairs

UNIVERSITY
of **ALBERTA**
PRESS

Aaron
Kreuter

Rubble
Children

SEVEN AND A HALF STORIES

Published by

University of Alberta Press
1–16 Rutherford Library South
11204 89 Avenue NW
Edmonton, Alberta, Canada T6G 2J4
amiskwaciwâskahikan | Treaty 6 |
Métis Territory
ualbertapress.ca | uapress@ualberta.ca

Copyright © 2024 Aaron Kreuter

LIBRARY AND ARCHIVES CANADA
CATALOGUING IN PUBLICATION

Title: Rubble children : seven and a half
      stories / Aaron Kreuter.
Names: Kreuter, Aaron, author.
Identifiers: Canadiana (print) 2024032708X |
      Canadiana (ebook) 20240327098 |
      ISBN 9781772127720 (softcover) |
      ISBN 9781772127812 (EPUB) |
      ISBN 9781772127829 (PDF)
Subjects: LCGFT: Short stories.
Classification: LCC PS8621.R485 R82 2024 |
      DDC C813/.6—dc23

First edition, first printing, 2024.
First printed and bound in Canada by
Houghton Boston Printers, Saskatoon,
Saskatchewan.
Copyediting by Kimmy Beach.
Proofreading by Mary Lou Roy.

A volume in the Robert Kroetsch Series.

This is a work of fiction. Names, characters,
places and incidents either are the products
of the author's imagination or are used
fictitiously, and any resemblance to actual
persons, living or dead, business establish-
ments, events, or locales is entirely
coincidental.

University of Alberta Press is committed to
protecting our natural environment. As part
of our efforts, this book is printed on Enviro
Paper: it contains 100% post-consumer
recycled fibres and is acid- and chlorine-free.

University of Alberta Press gratefully
acknowledges the support received for its
publishing program from the Government
of Canada, the Canada Council for the Arts,
and the Government of Alberta through the
Alberta Media Fund.

Canada   Canada Council   Conseil des Arts
for the Arts   du Canada

Alberta Government

For My Parents, Cathy and David

Contents

Mourning Rituals

WHEN OUR FATHER DIED, one by one we took every piece of our life, shook it, threw it against the wall, screamed at it, discarded it, tried to move on. It started while he was sick and dying in the hospital, reached its height during the last few weeks, the coma—and once he died, it peaked, the grief and anger, with the power and force of a flooding sea, washing everything away, leaving us clean, unencumbered, clear-eyed, vulnerable.

Our father died, and there was suddenly nothing left to hold us in place.

⦂ Tamara and Joshua sit at the shiva, brother and sister. Shelly was there too, of course, but she was twelve years younger, another generation, still in university. They had never been close: she was more of a cousin than a sister, had, from a very young age, made her own way in the world, with one rebellion after another, each new identity dug into with more abandon than the last; after a few years Joshua and Tamara had stopped trying to stay involved, busy enough making their own lives. Tamara was still wearing her funeral outfit: black skirt, boots laced up to her knees, black makeup; Joshua had torn his suit off as soon as he got to his father's house, put on jeans and a grey top. Guests came up to them one by one, said something, asked a question, told them something about their father; they smiled and nodded, smiled and nodded, smiled and nodded.

Tamara had given the eulogy. In her blunt, no-nonsense style, she narrated Sherman's life: growing up in the Annex, nightly pickup games of basketball at the JCC, meeting their mother at the Young Judea meetings amid trays of deli and white-and-blue flags and basic conversational Hebrew, moving to Israel together, having two children, moving back to Toronto in the eighties. Their mother's death, hilariously tragic, tragically hilarious, leaving Sherman with two teenage children and the infant Shelly. Sherman never remarrying, though there was always a female friend or two to help out with the kids, lend temporary companionship. The stoicism with which he faced the cancer. Afterwards, a group of women from Kol B'Seder made a circle around Tamara, hugging and crying (it was these same women—the "shiva crew" Sherman would have called them—that entered their dad's house like a storm the day before the funeral, bringing tablecloths and coffee carafes and paper plates and rubber mats for shoes and white foam to block out the house's mirrors). The most important part of the seven days of mourning was to keep the mourners occupied, distracted, fed, loved, grounded to something tangible, and these women took to the task with determined zeal.

Tamara and Joshua were surrounded by family, neighbours, Sherman's friends from work. The majority of the mourners and well-wishers were from Kol B'Seder, the Reform synagogue Tamara and Joshua's parents belonged to since they returned from Tel Aviv, where community and ritual allowed Sherman to survive their mother's death, focus on Tamara and Joshua, raise six-month-old Shelly. Norman Greenski told Tamara he thought her eulogy was very well done, by which he meant he was relieved Tamara didn't live up to her reputation as a Marxist shit disturber. Sheri Teitelbaum fawned over them, repeating what a special, special person Sherman was. Tamara managed to hold her tongue, though Joshua knew what she was thinking. Stefan Lemieux, a kind older man Joshua always suspected was gay, was crying, said something to them in French as he held their fingers in his soft, wet hands. David Krasner squeezed Joshua's hand, could barely get out a word for the emotion breaking on his large face, his wife Geri mussing Tamara's cropped hair, *it's about time you cut those dreadlocks off*. They sat there, in low wooden chairs supplied by the funeral home, and made their mouths smile.

"All these men and their bank accounts, their wars, their hubris," Tamara said a little later. For the moment, it was just the two of them, still sitting in the wooden shiva chairs in the living room; David Krasner was at the dining room table with the other men, talking loudly about tax breaks, creeping socialism, raging Islamism. Tamara had held herself back for long enough and had returned to her preferred mode: brimming with life, with subversive anger, more than comfortable enough in the world to want to impose herself on it. "I can't stop thinking of them in the bathroom, shitting, that smell of suits and newspapers and human waste."

"Even great men shit," Joshua said in a British accent, on autopilot.

"When did all of our parents' friends become so right-wing? Lower taxes, stop immigration, support Israel at all moral, financial, or humanitarian cost!" she said, imitating the majority of adults in the room in a deep, ridiculous voice.

"Jews being conservative is the millennium's new blackface," said Joshua, warming slightly to the conversation, "it allows them to continue fitting in with the dominant group."

"Thank god Dad didn't live long enough to go right-wing on us."

"Would he have? Not Dad."

"Israel would've flipped him. Israel was days away from flipping him."

Joshua didn't say anything. Till the moment Sherman died Joshua had shared his father's liberal Zionism—two states, two peoples!—but, like everything else, that too was being put through the existential grinder. It's true that their parents had left Israel because of the disaster of the first Lebanon War, but that hadn't stopped them from holding out hope for the possibility of a just ethnic democracy—maybe Tamara was right, maybe in the face of all the evidence (evidence Joshua was having trouble not obsessing over ever since Sherman got sick), there would have been no choice but for their father to veer to the right in order to continue supporting the Jewish state. Either that, or give up on the dream, which Joshua, however much he respected his father, didn't see in the cards. Past tense.

"I broke up with Obinze last week," Tamara said.

"I was wondering where he's been."

"I deleted my Facebook account."

"Permanent delete?"

"Permanent delete."

Joshua sighed. "I put all of my Grizzly and Phish CDs, my Dead tapes, into two dozen wine boxes, left them outside of Rotate This! in the middle of the night," he said.

"Should've given them to Jerry."

"I gave Jerry all of the posters."

Tamara paused. "I quit my job," she said.

"Me too," Joshua said after a pause of his own.

For the first time since their father died, they looked each other in the eyes.

Only two days ago they had buried him. A mild spring day at the sprawling Jewish cemetery north of Toronto. His coffin was lowered into the ground, and Joshua was the first to lift a shovel of dirt and to drop it crumbling and pocking onto the lacquered walnut. He had dropped another shovel-load, and another, and another, moving into the key of furious, sweat mapping his forehead, a hundred people watching, another shovelful, another, another!—till Tamara put a hand on his pistoning shoulder and he thrust the shovel into the giving mound of dirt, to let another mourner rack up points with their god for helping ease the erasure of the dead.

⋮ That evening, the adults praying in the living room, facing east, worn blue prayer books brought from Kol B'Seder in their hands, bending and calling out, Joshua and Tamara sat with their cousins in the family room in half-tense silence. Simon in his Israel Defense Forces uniform, Clarissa, her hair in a high bun, sweatpants tucked into woollies snug in Uggs, bent over her phone, thumbs dancing. Shelly, cuddling with Andre, her new boyfriend; he looked lost, out-of-place, the Hebrew rising and falling from the front of the house registering on his face as alien, off-putting cacophony.

Joshua was staring at the rug, the day's bottomless allotment of grief having finally tipped his meagre watercraft. Simon was looking around the house with detached, distant arrogance. His head was smooth, his skin tanned deep brown, his cheek shaven by a naked blade. He'd made aliyah two years ago. Tamara was staring at him, her face souring with each passing minute.

She bent over to Joshua.

"It looks like Simon's itching to pick a fight," she said into his ear.

"Hmm..."

"He's holding his babka like a semi-automatic."

"He probably just misses his gun."

"He'd rather be with his unit, riding a tank through the desert at dawn, trashing the house of a Palestinian family because the father looked at him funny."

"Tamara, not now."

"...I might just oblige him."

Simon must have known they were talking about him.

"Sorry for your loss," he said to them from across the room, the first thing he'd said to them since arriving. Tamara smiled sarcastically.

"How's Panem?" she shot at him. "Get out to the districts much?"

Simon looked startled. "Pardon?" he said. He was affecting a slight Hebrew accent.

"Tamara!" Shelly shouted. Tamara looked at everyone in turn, the flourishes of prayer fluttering through the house. She was in her element.

"What?" she said, feigning innocence. "What? He chose to go over there and play-act as a colonialist, comes here to this house of mourning dressed in his uniform, and we're supposed to sit here smiling like idiots?"

Now it was Joshua's turn to put a hand on Tamara's shoulder, to push pause on the coming confrontation. She shrugged it off but didn't continue. It was too late, though: the floodgates were open.

Simon smiled. "What, you don't approve of my joining the army or something? Shit, my dad's right about you: you're too far gone to the left to even see reality. I know your dad just died, and, like I said, I'm sorry about that, but do I really have to tell you that if we weren't keeping the Arab hordes at bay your little North American hippie-dippie pacifist hacker existence would become ancient news?" Simon turned to Joshua now, who was trying not to look at anyone, trying to not get involved. "I hope you haven't followed your sister to the dark side, Joshua. Especially you."

He had no choice but to look at Simon. "What's that supposed to mean?"

"You know what it means. Israel is the only country in the whole Middle East where you wouldn't be stoned to death for your, for your...lifestyle."

Joshua laughed, to himself, like he had had a private revelation. Tamara, though, Tamara's mouth was agape. She was gathering her wits for a full-frontal assault, but Clarissa beat her to it, pivoting from her phone for the first time since she arrived.

"You know, Simon. I wasn't going to say anything because I was raised better, but you've really become an asshole. And, I'm sorry, I've got to say it: why is joining the Israeli army, like, given a pass? You know how our parents would react if one of us joined the Canadian army? The Canadian army is for people from

Saskatchewan! And the American army, oh, you're a misguided, bloodthirsty imperialist! But the Israeli army! Ooooh, the Israeli army! Why, then, you're fighting for the Jewish nation! You're a hero! You're rewriting the history of a blighted people! How does it not, like, ring terribly false? Hero! What total horseshit!"

Everybody was silent, stunned, in the wake of Clarissa's outburst. Later, Joshua would tell Tamara how surprised he was that Clarissa had thoughts or feelings like that. "The last serious conversation we had was five years ago, when we debated which Backstreet Boy we'd rather went down on us."

Somebody hiccupped and all eyes turned to Shelly. She was crying. Andre was stiff beside her, stuck between wanting to comfort his girlfriend and wanting to get out of this house of strange Jewish customs and head-on battles. Feeling the attention, Shelly looked up. "How could you say those things, Clarissa? And during my Aba's shiva! Don't act like you don't remember how proud he was of Simon when he made aliyah! He *is* a hero, out there all alone protecting the homeland!" She jumped up and ran to her room, her stomping feet on the stairs echoing through the house.

Tamara and Joshua looked at each other. Andre looked like he had just found out that *his* father had died. Simon swept a triumphant scowl across the room, stood, smoothed his uniform, and went up the stairs after Shelly, not making a sound as he ascended. Clarissa shrugged, went back to her phone. The steady chatter that rose from the other room and permeated the house meant one thing: the prayers were finished. Soon the house would empty out, and, tomorrow, it would start all over again, the pattern repeating for four more days and then—just like that—ceasing, leaving the mourners alone with their grief, with nothing but time to do what it will.

: A month later Tamara and Joshua met for coffee in Kensington Market. The whole city was abuzz with what was going on in the

Middle East (or did it only seem that way to those whose heads were tortuously ahum with it?): the kidnapping, three dead settler children, aggressive words, burned Palestinian teenagers, missiles, threats, Operation Protective Edge, the Israeli airforce flattening Gaza, confident Israelis doing damage control on CNN.

Joshua was already sitting at a small table in the back of the busy café, a soccer game on the small television, when Tamara burst in, sat down at the table. She had shaved off her hair.

"Taking a page out of Simon's book?"

"Fuck you!"

"It's good to see you too. I ordered you a latte." Joshua could tell something was upsetting Tamara, not from anything she said, more a sense, a feeling. He wouldn't prod; she'd tell him if she wanted to.

"Thanks. Speaking of Simon, did you know Shelly hooked up with him?"

"What?! No! Tamara! He's our cousin!"

"I think she told me just to piss me off. How soft and loving Simon is when he's alone with her, how he confides in her. He told her how lonely it is being a lone wolf in the army, how it's the little things that make him feel foreign, removed, but it just makes him want to try harder, fight harder. Ha! I wanted to hurl! She says he reminds her of Aba. Shows how delusional she is. Anyways, it's only cousins through marriage, not blood."

"Yeah, but still…"

"Hey if you believe the narrative, all of us Ashkenazi Jews are cousins," Tamara said.

"Bullshit."

"Poor Shelly. She's never been able to stay with a guy for more than six weeks."

"She has shitty role models, I guess."

"How's the new bartending job?"

"It's alright I guess, better than serving coffee. How's being one of the more sought-after coders in Toronto?"

Tamara smiled, not one to brag. "Anyways, Josh," she said, veering into more exciting territory, "you still willing to defend the Jewish state like the last time they bombed the shit out of Gaza?"

"To tell you the truth, no, not really at all. I feel sick for ever having wanted to justify what goes on over there." Joshua paused, took a long sip. "But what am I supposed to do about it, Tamara? I'm not like you. I can't just confront everybody I know, alienate our whole family, just because—"

"Because they're brainwashed?"

"I feel stuck. I wish I could just leave the whole thing alone, but I can't. Not since..." Joshua tapered off, drank his coffee. Tamara watched her brother. He took another sip, his face turning defiant. "Imagine, imagine if we were Palestinian children, born in Gaza, what would we think?"

Tamara smiled. "We'd think that every Jew is a monster, worse than a Cossack."

Another silence. "What are we supposed to do? Look at Shelly, veering in the exact opposite direction."

"Shelly's just acting out."

"Maybe I should give her a call. We don't give her enough attention. She's lost."

"Shelly's been lost since she was six months old."

The soccer match ended, and the news came on. The lead story: bombs exploding over Gaza. Tamara and Joshua watched the screen. "Fuck this. Let's get something real to drink," Tamara said. They left the café and went to a bar across the street, started with a shot of whisky, moved on to beer. After the second beer Joshua told Tamara about a guy he had been seeing, mostly sex, but it was alleviating the entropy of his sorrow. As it turned out, though, he was totally on board with the Israeli side of the conflict, and Joshua didn't know what to do.

"I just don't have time to pretend politics isn't important," Joshua said, slamming back another whisky shot. The sun hadn't even set and he was sloshingly drunk.

"You should break up with him."

"Maybe I'll just stop returning his text messages. It's already been three days."

They drank through the evening, ate fish and chips, got louder and more boisterous as the night went on. Around 9:00 two women with classical guitars took the stage, started covering Neil Young and Joni Mitchell tunes, taking turns singing and soloing. At 11:00 the drunken joy fallowed into drunken grief; without needing to say anything, they spoke of their dead father, the cancer still eating his body thirty kilometres away, their dead mother, taken from them at the height of her life for the stupidest of reasons. At midnight a drunk man started hitting on Tamara and she viciously told him off, Joshua watching her, nothing but love on his face for his wild sister.

They were walking up Spadina now, through Chinatown. When they left the bar Kensington was empty, silent, the fish and cheese and bulk shops shuttered. It was after 1:00, the greys and blacks and lights of the city heavy, fluid. Spadina rose at a slight incline, capped by the Gothic turrets of 1 Spadina Crescent, sharp against the night sky.

"Speaking of confrontation," Tamara said, almost screaming, as if continuing a conversation that had only been paused momentarily, "I got into a huge fight with my old high school girls."

"Shit, Tamar."

"What? Yeah, I grew up with them, yeah I love them like sisters, yeah they know things about me not even YOU know, but when they start spouting racist nonsense I'm not going to hold my tongue." She was yelling now.

"How'd you leave it?"

"Not good. Hailey said she never wants to talk to me again. Suzanne called me a terrorist sympathizer."

"Yikes. What'd you say to that?"

"I said you could feel sick when someone blows themselves up on a bus but still see that violent occupation breeds violence.

Anyways, fuck them! They've all drunk the Kool-Aid. If this is what being Jewish means right now, fuck you very much, I want out."

Joshua didn't respond. He would never be able to do that, to stand up to such firmly held community beliefs, to take such a public stand.

"What would have happened if Ema and Aba hadn't left Israel?" Tamara asked, switching into a philosophical mode, light, playful.

"Ema'd still be alive, I guess. Aba would probably still be recently dead from cancer."

"Would I be a military wife, watching with dread as my little boys approached the army?"

Joshua laughed. "Tamar, I don't think, no matter where you grew up, you would ever have become a military wife."

"Oh Joshua, my heart!"

"Hopefully, if we had stayed, we wouldn't be sitting in lawn chairs on the beach, cheering every bomb that hit a hospital in Gaza City."

"My god. If this isn't enough to turn us off ethnic nationalism, what will be?" The closed stalls and dimly lit restaurants of Chinatown started to give way to the bars and storied rock 'n' roll venues of College Street.

"That's what I can't get past," Joshua said, skirting around a group of drunken teenagers cloaked in skunky marijuana. It felt good to talk about what had been causing such internal turmoil. "We thought we were so much better than everyone else, so different, so long suffering. Perhaps we were, somewhere, back there. But then we got a state, and guess what? We're just as violent, just as corruptible, just as power-hungry as everybody else."

"It's amazing how deeply we've been lied to."

They crossed busy College in silence, started up Spadina Crescent, the street splitting in two, parting ways to encircle 1 Spadina Crescent, the old building covered in scaffolding and opaque plastic sheeting. As soon as the street split the noise and drunkenness of College vanished. They stayed on the east side, walked along the curving sidewalk, the university buildings on their right, the moon hanging over the turrets of the under-construction building on their left. A streetcar bended screechingly past them, drunken nighttime faces floating in the windows.

"I can't stand this city anymore," Tamara said once it passed. "I'm taking off for a while."

"Where you going to go?"

"Who knows. For now, anybody but here." Joshua looked at Tamara, decided not to correct her. "I see Aba everywhere I look," she said.

Joshua nodded. Should he tell Tamara he didn't know what he'd do without her, without knowing she was somewhere in the city? "Out of all the memories I have of him, since the war started, one keeps coming up," he said instead.

"Tell me."

"I must have been eleven, twelve. Ema had just died. I was following Aba around everywhere, remember?"

"I was sixteen, dropping mushrooms every three days, hanging out on hacker chat rooms, avoiding the guilt I felt every time I was near Shelly. I was barely home during that time. So, no, I don't remember."

"Aba and I would go to Torah study at Kol B'Seder Sunday mornings. Rabbi Koffee, Daniel Koffee, the Levines, the Glassmans, Terri and Stew, Chaim Greenski, there was a regular group of us. David Krasner would come whenever he was in town. We'd meet in the boardroom, have bagels and cream cheese, thin coffee."

"I had no idea."

"I really was drawn to it then. I was obsessed with the idea of God, an ultimate being who has the power to judge. You know, even with what happened to Ema, maybe because of it, I thought I might become a rabbi."

"What?! No! Joshua!"

"Daniel Koffee was going to follow in his father's footsteps, I thought I might too."

"Daniel Koffee. He was so hot. I wonder what happened to him."

"He was the first boy I kissed."

"Shut the front door!" Tamara exclaimed. They were on the other side of the crescent now, Spadina once again two-ways. The university was still on their right, townhouses on their left, the avenue bisected by the streetcar tracks.

"Anyways," Joshua continued, "at one particular Torah study, I remember it as if it was yesterday, sitting in those fancy swivel chairs, the big mahogany table, the photocopies of the passage under consideration, fall sunlight streaming through those big windows. It was the part of the book of Joshua—"

"Your namesake!—"

"—where God tells him to destroy the city of Jericho, to kill every man, woman and child. 'Is the god of the book of Joshua a moral god?' Rabbi Koffee asked in his squeaky voice. 'Yes,' Beth Mitzcovitz said, 'God promised the land of Canaan to the Jews, his chosen people. They had a right to remove who was there before.' 'No,' said Sarah Hoffman, 'murder is never justified.' Then Aba gave his response. 'What does it matter if the god of this book or that book is a moral god? What matters is if *we* act morally. Putting it off onto God completely misses the lessons of Jericho.'"

"Hah. Sounds like Aba."

"Yeah. At the time, I disagreed with him. But now, I see how right he was. Righter than he knew. Why put people in Jericho at all if they were only going to be massacred? It's total nonsense."

"Because there is no god, Joshua," Tamara said. She skipped around him, started humming one of the Joni Mitchell tunes the folk singers had performed at the bar.

"Anyways, Koffee started talking about how killing when you're in the army isn't murder per se, then Beth brought up the

Holocaust, effectively bringing an end to the discussion. Aba and I went for pizza after."

Tamara sung, loud and fierce, into the blue Toronto night. "They repaved paradise, and put up a Holocaust museum." The words didn't fit the syllable count, but she forced them through all the same.

They were at Bloor. They stopped and sat down on a bench on a small hill of green across from the Jewish Community Centre. The city was full of life again. They watched the traffic lights change, change again. Drunken revellers, university students, Annex dog owners crossed Bloor, crossed Spadina, in timed bursts. A little south of them a streetcar exited the tunnel with a slow mechanical groan. The night changed moods in its swift and blustery way, slipping into its cold apex—the hollow centre where it feels like morning would never come, mourning never end. Joshua, as if suddenly waking up, looked up at the City of Toronto sign, remembered where they were: Matt Cohen Park. He started to cry. Tamara put her arm around him.

"It's alright, Joshua," she said. "It's okay. Everything is alright. Everything in the universe is alright." They both knew she was lying, but it didn't matter. For the moment, it felt like it could be true.

⦂ Exactly a year to the day later, Joshua was at the airport, waiting for Tamara's plane to land. He had gotten bored of waiting in the cellphone lot, sitting on the hood of the car he inherited from his father, alone with his thoughts and the tall grass growing where asphalt met barbed wire, so he was testing his luck at Arrivals. He watched everyone coming and going, parked illegally, one eye looking out for airport security. He let himself be soothed by the comforting pull of the non-space of the airport, that portal, that time machine, that blender, reconnecting, breaking apart, pushing, pulling, shuffling, reinterpreting—he could slip into its space-time distortions as easily as anybody, but where would he go? He watched a South Asian family hug and kiss, load into three different cars, their saris and head scarves bright with colour. He watched four young women, each with a half-dozen large suitcases stacked precariously on Air Canada trolleys. It wasn't hard to imagine all of their earthly possessions in those battered husks. When Tamara emerged from the airport's sliding doors, crossed through the three lanes of idling taxis and limos, shaking her head at the milling drivers offering rides, he almost didn't recognize her: the towering rucksack was the same, but Tamara's hair was almost down to her chin, and her face was bright with health, her eyes radiant.

"You look like shit," she said to her brother, getting into the car. It was true: Joshua's face was thin, his skin pale; he obviously had not been sleeping or eating well.

They hadn't seen each other in eleven months.

"It hasn't been the best year," he said, merging and turning and merging again to escape the black hole of the airport. "It's good to see you."

"You too."

"A year in South America," Joshua said. Tamara ignored him, not ready to talk yet.

"Did you hear what happened to Simon?" she asked instead.

"Nope."

"He broke his leg in some training exercise in the Negev. He was boasting about it all over the internet."

"'In Valhalla, you will ride eternal, shiny and chrome,'" Joshua muttered towards the window.

"What's that?"

"Nothing."

"Whatever. Have you seen Shelly much?"

"Not really. She's got a new boyfriend. Yaniv. An Israeli. Doctor-in-training. Semi-religious. She's on her way too. She's leading a

March of the Living trip with him right now. A week touring the ghost shtetls and death camps of Poland followed by a week in sunny, Jewish Israel."

"I know, she sent me a long, rambling email after they had gone to Auschwitz. All about the horrors of life in the diaspora, how she's blessed that she was born in Israel, how she can't wait to get back there, how she's never going to leave. How her life in galut has been a waste. This is what we have been chosen for. A light unto the nations. A citadel on the hill. A bridge between East and West—or was it a bulwark? A pillar of democracy in a political and cultural wasteland. On and on. Am Yisrael Chai written in all caps."

"What the fuck? Shelly wasn't born in Israel!"

Tamara laughed, like she had forgotten that they had been in Canada for a decade before their youngest sister was born, that only six months later their mother would die, hit by the Hanukkah van that had run a red light, the driver rushing to get home for the Sabbath, which also happened to be the last night of the holiday, every bulb on the huge menorah bolted to the top of the van lit up, soon to be joined by the swinging lights of the ambulance. "No, she wasn't, was she. Shit, I hope she sees something in Israel that snaps her out of this."

"'You know hope is a mistake,'" Joshua said in a pensive growl.

Tamara smiled. "'Who killed the world?'" she asked in a spot-on Australian accent.

Joshua shot Tamara a look of surprise.

"What?! They have movie theatres in South America, Joshy."

Joshua nodded. They drove in silence for a while.

"Let's go to Dad's house," Tamara said, as if she had made a momentous decision for the two of them. Joshua didn't say anything, but he changed lanes, signalling for the next exit. They didn't speak again till they were heading north, towards the suburbs.

"So, tell me about your trip, Tamara. Any revelations, epiphanies, life-changing encounters? Any torrid love affairs?"

"A few here and there, nothing to write home about. Anti-austerity marches in Chile, fell in with some left-wing Jewish computer programmers in Peru, so loose and loving and physical, had a threesome, a Passover Seder in Buenos Aires—"

"—How was that?"

"Loud, warm, full of Eastern European food and two-hundred-words-a-minute Spanish argument. What else? Got kicked out of a Hillel Friday night dinner in Rio de Janeiro. Spent a few weeks with an Iraqi heart surgeon in the Bolivian jungle."

"Really? How was that?"

"Good at first, then weird. He'd actually been to Israel, supports the occupation, loves America."

"Weird."

They entered the familiar suburbs, turned off the main street, drove past their high school, pulled up to the curb in front of their dad's house (once their parents' house, once their house). The grass was trim, there was no garbage or old newspapers on the lawn, nothing to signal that the house was uninhabited.

"George's been coming by to do the lawn, get the mail," Joshua said, turning the key, "says it keeps the property value up."

"I haven't been here since the shiva." The front hallway was full of boxes, some taped shut, others still open. The dining room table was piled high with books, file folders, documents. The kitchen was sheened in dust. The house smelled of cardboard, must, vinegar.

"I've been up a couple of times the past few months," Joshua said, "trying to sort through everything. I never realized how many books were in this house." He pushed one box with his foot. "This one is all of his Matt Cohens."

Tamara bent down, picked up a worn Romantic poetry anthology from a half-full box. "He used to read to us all the time from this," she said, following Joshua up the stairs into his old room. "'An old, mad, blind, despised, and dying King,'" Tamara orated from memory, dropping onto Joshua's bed. Joshua's room hadn't changed much since he had moved out: twin bed with dark grey comforter, posters of Marx, Che, Garcia, and Trey Anastasio, the dresser, night table, and desk the same chipped blue set Simon's parents had bought for Joshua when they first moved back from Israel. Joshua's suit was still crumpled on the floor, where he had left it after Sherman's funeral.

Joshua opened his desk drawer. "Look what I found last time I was here," he said, pulling out a joint, passing it to Tamara. It had on it, written in careful blue pen, THE LAST JOINT I WILL EVER SMOKE. "I rolled it in high school, to keep till I was ready to not smoke ever again. I was smoking a lot I guess, was afraid I would never stop. It made me feel like there was a way out. If I needed one."

Tamara laughed, a wave of tiredness rinsing through her. Now that she had stopped moving, the thirty-six hours of travel—the eleven months of non-stop movement, of nomadism—were catching up to her.

"So. Are you ready?"

"Seems like the best time." He opened the window, and they climbed out onto the slanted kitchen roof. Unlike the front yard, the backyard showed the house's vacancy. The lawn was over-grown, the drained pool splotched with brown, littered with crushed beer cans, used condoms, pizza boxes. It looked like someone had been having campfires on the grass behind the pool.

"George and Beth are on me about the house," Joshua said, lighting the joint, the decades-old paper crackling and popping in the flame, "they want us to sell."

Tamara lay down on the shingles. "How much are we going to get for it?"

"I don't know. A lot. Probably almost a million. More. Split two ways."

"Three ways."

"Oh, yeah, right. Three ways."

Tamara closed her eyes, breathed in deeply. "Let's hold on to it for a while longer," she said. Joshua passed her the joint. "So. What have you been up to?"

"The usual. Nothing. Reading a lot. I had a job for a while, but it got ugly."

"Tell me."

"Well, after you left, I stayed here for a few days, couldn't take it, went down to Jerry's. I was unemployed, the money from Dad hadn't come through yet, I had no drive, no desire to do anything. The grief came back, hard. I'd pick up Jerry's guitar, strum a single chord, feel disgusted, exhausted from the exertion. I couldn't read, I couldn't watch a movie without going to the bathroom, outside, anywhere, for half an hour in the middle, leaving a hole in the narrative. That lasted a few weeks, maybe more. I bounced around the city, slowly started being able to get through more than one sentence at a time. On the winter solstice I had a burst of energy, signed up for a temp agency. In January they placed me at a corporate headquarters up near Downsview for a six-week contract that turned into an open-ended position. I worked in the mail room, in the headquarters' massive basement, stuffing boxes, running packages to higher floors, helping with the printing and stuff like that. I was doing well, was adjusting, had a flirtation going with a blond Australian weightlifter in accounting. In the spring, I signed up for a grief management group that I saw advertised in the lunchroom—can you imagine me doing something like that?! That's how recovered I felt, how ready for a serious life change. Everyone at each meeting had an opportunity to speak, no interruptions. I hadn't spoken yet, but was feeling almost ready to, when, it was right after Netanyahu gave that ridiculous speech at the UN—did you hear about it?—when Dale, this young guy, friendly, we'd chatted a few times, he worked in the cafeteria, always wore a backwards hat, his sister and her whole family were killed in a pile-up on the DVP, just went on a horrible antisemitic rant."

"Shut the front door!" Tamara took a long drag on the joint, started coughing, passed it to Joshua. Her mouth tasted like the leached contents of Joshua's desk drawer: long-dead elementary school calculators, paper clips, pennies and nickels and dimes.

"You should have heard the shit he was saying. 'I don't condone what the Nazis did, but I understand where they were coming from. The Jews own the banks, own the newspapers, own the movie theatres. Do you think it's a coincidence that they supported civil rights here in North America, but don't in Israel? It's all part of their plan to take over the white race and then, the rest of the world. A history of duplicity, of trickery. It always comes down to money for them, always. I wouldn't mind seeing the Arabs knock them down a peg or two.' Just all of the stereotypical stuff."

"What did you say?" Tamara asked, her eyes glassy—this was the kind of confrontation she excelled at. She was jealous.

"What did I say? Nothing. I was quaking with anger, but I said nothing. I stayed till the end of the meeting, got plastered, went back and quit the next day, that's what I did. Hid out in Jerry's second bedroom for a week."

"Oh Josh."

"I seriously considered taking after Simon, making aliyah, moving to Israel, giving in, running into old classmates in the basement grocery store at the Dizengoff Center. Buy the narrative, drink the Kool-Aid. I was honestly this close. I had the plane ticket up on my computer and everything. Imagine how easy it would be."

"Just because there are still antisemitic fucktards festering all around us is no reason to give in. Actually, it's the exact reason not to give in."

"It's so hard, Tamara. The hatred, the lies, the violence. We've turned into a people of propagandists. It wasn't long after that that I started my first Facebook argument."

"Oh Josh, my sweet little brother, what are we going to do."

"What are we going to do."

"We could learn Arabic, for a start."

"Before or after we learn Yiddish?"

Tamara started coughing, sat up. "This weed tastes like shit."

"It's over fifteen years old."

Joshua sat up too fast, bringing on a flush of dizziness. They continued passing the joint. Tamara was ready to take a shower, sleep for three days, see what Toronto was ready to offer her, see what her girls were up to. She wondered if they were still mad at her; they hadn't spoken since the fight last summer. If they were (she had decided as Toronto came into view that morning, tall sharp buildings huddled against the lake), she would apologize. Joshua imagined himself going into his bedroom, taking out each of his old guitars, even the ones he had sold or traded over the years, and methodically tossing them off the roof and into the empty swimming pool, watching as they gave in to gravity, delighting in each twangy crash.

Instead, he tossed the roach, watched it spiral through the air, land near the barbecue. He closed his eyes. Tamara's were already closed; she might have been sleeping. Soon they would stand slowly, climb back into the house, shut the window. Decide what to do next.

⁞ Standing amid the boxes and books while Joshua was in the washroom, washing and washing his hands in front of the still-white-foam-covered mirror, Tamara noticed a pile of mail sitting on the front hall table. "There's a letter from Shelly here!" she said, pulling it out of the pile. Joshua came up next to her, and they contemplated the envelope. It was thick, heavy, its travel history marked in Hebrew and English stamps, addressed to them.

The return address was written in flowery Hebrew. What drew their eyes, though, was the big black-and-white face of David Ben-Gurion. Tamara and Joshua stared at the stamp of the first Israeli prime minister: the intense eyes, the Einstein hair, the face moulded into a mask of defiance, of purpose, of mission, ready to push himself and his followers into an unforeseen cul-de-sac of history. Such a deliberate choice, a stamp. Neither made to open the envelope. "Ah, Ben-Gurion! Ah, humanity!" Joshua exclaimed, moving away from Tamara and the letter, opening the front door.

"Ben-Gurion hated fiction, you know," Joshua said, closing the door behind them. "He claimed to have never read it, had none in his extensive library."

"No wonder his country ended up the way it did." Without discussing it, without a destination, they started walking through the old neighbourhood. They had left the door to their father's house unlocked. Tamara was still holding the letter.

Their words dried up. They walked in silence for ten minutes, twenty, thirty, forty. Almost every house had a memory, a trace, an attachment. When they were growing up, the area had been almost a hundred percent Jewish, but now they were happy to see a Chinese man watering his lawn, a brown family, the men in turbans, unloading groceries from a minivan, five teenagers, Black, South Asian, a lanky Jewish kid with a marijuana leaf–embroidered kippah laughing and shouting outside of the elementary school Shelly had gone to till she got expelled for flipping a desk at a teacher. After almost an hour, Isaac Babel Elementary, the Jewish parochial elementary school that housed Kol B'Seder, their old synagogue, came into view.

"Looks like we were drawn here."

"Our illustrious return to the homeland."

They went to the park behind the shul, sat down on a hill overlooking the property. "We used to get so high here before Hebrew classes," Joshua said.

"Too bad you're never smoking another joint again."

Joshua looked startled for a minute. "Oh yeah, fuck. Too bad."

From their vantage on the hill, things had changed at Kol B'Seder, but they had also not changed. The old wooden playground had been replaced. The parking lot had recently been repaved. There was an addition built onto the back of the school, grey brick and white siding. The red pines along the fence had doubled in size, were now much taller than the houses behind them. The big windows of the boardroom turned the sunlight into a curved silver ocean.

"Did I tell you about the trees I planted in Palestine?" Tamara asked.

"Nope."

"For a while I had been feeling horrible about all those trees I planted in Israel as a kid. I guess it started while I was flying over the Amazon clearcuts. Every T'bushevat we'd pay for another one to be planted, remember? How were we supposed to know that trees were being used as weapons? So anyways, shortly after I broke up with the Iraqi, an ultra-Orthodox anti-Zionist I met on a bus from La Paz to Lima—he wouldn't touch me, but he had plenty to say!—told me about an organization online that will plant a tree on your behalf in West Bank villages and towns. As soon as I could get to the internet, I bought thirty-seven of them, one for every year of my life."

"Sort of a carbon neutralizing of past tree sins."

"The funny thing is, while I was buying those trees in a darkly lit internet café in Lima, I never felt more Jewish."

"Fuck, Tamar! You're out there living your beliefs. What do I do? Nothing! I only just started disagreeing with people on Facebook, and I don't even do that very well."

"It's something, Joshua."

"Not enough."

A car pulled into the Kol B'Seder parking lot. They watched from their hill as Chaim Greenski got out, slowly started walking towards the building. Chaim was a Holocaust survivor, had spent sixteen months at Auschwitz before walking halfway across Europe, was a regular fixture at the shul throughout Joshua and Tamara's childhood. At one of the last Rosh Hashanah services they went to, when the guest rabbi gave a sermon about vanquishing one's enemies, in a thinly veiled reference to the Palestinians, Chaim had stood up and yelled, "Yasher ko-ach!," everybody cheering and whooping in agreement.

"Didn't know old Chaim was still alive," Tamara said, squinting to see him better. Her mouth still had the metallic tang of the joint.

"It was such a shock when I found out what a racist he is."

"Most of us are. He wasn't all bad though."

"What happened to us, Tamara?"

"For them, Israel meant something different, I guess. It meant: the Holocaust won't happen again, now that some Jewish boys are flying fighter jets."

"'In Valhalla, you will ride eternal, shiny and chrome.' What can you say to them? What can you say to that?"

"Nothing. We just have to wait for them to die. It's what old people do, right? They die."

"Yeah, but what about when those who replace them are not much—are not *any*—better than those they're replacing. Look at our friends, look at Simon, look at Shelly. Already so hawkish, so right wing, so ideologically constrained, where are they going to end up in middle age?"

"The ones who also have money will become total tyrants, I imagine. Not much different than our parents' generation."

"What monsters we are."

"Totally." Joshua glanced towards Tamara, noticed that she was still clutching the letter. Ben-Gurion staring, taunting.

"Should we open Shelly's letter?"

Tamara breathed out slowly. "No, I don't think so."

Joshua nodded.

"I've been having this, sort of, waking vision, I guess," he said. "When the full scope of what's been done in our names over there comes crashing into view. The nightmare over, the mass Jewish hallucination lifted. The possibility of a new morning."

"Tell me," Tamara said. Tell me.

Joshua was overcome with tiredness. He wanted to lie down on that green hill and melt into it, melt away, never come down. "Later, later," he said.

"At least Aba won't be around to see it, whatever happens."

"I realized, waiting for you at the airport today, that he's been gone for over a year."

Tamara nodded. "I think I've finally gotten out from under the grief. The worst of it, at least."

Joshua didn't say anything for a minute. "Should we say a prayer or something? You know, to end the traditional mourning period?"

"Do you remember any of the mourner's kaddish?"

"Not really."

"Me neither."

"I remember the prayer for reading the Torah."

"That should do."

Joshua started to sing: "Bar'chu et Adonai ham'vorach." To Tamara's surprise, she responded: "Baruch Adonai ham'vorach l'olam va-ed." Joshua faltered. Tamara shrugged. They repeated the two lines of call-and-response again. It was something. It was enough.

: Joshua and Tamara sit on the hill, watch the evening light play on Kol B'Seder's flat roof, read the changeable silver ocean of the boardroom windows, Shelly's letter between them. They're waiting, waiting, waiting. Waiting for the sun to set, waiting for clarity, waiting for action, waiting for the oncoming catastrophe. Waiting for history to wake, stretch, shake off its all-too-brief slumber, resume its relentless charge.

It lurches. It shambles. It barrels towards us.

Temples

BEFORE WE WENT TO THE TEMPLE for the night, Vicki came over to get ready. We took over the upstairs bathroom with makeup, mousse, discarded outfits. Michael Jackson blared from the black-and-yellow shower radio I bought for camp last summer. We giggled and threw stuff as we danced and got dressed, continued the freewheeling all-directions-at-once conversation we'd been having since we were nine years old. Jeff's friend Gerald knocked on the door and we laughed harder. He grumbled something, and the bathroom shook a little as he went down the stairs.

"I can't believe we're going to this stupid thing," Vicki said, fixing her hair in the mirror, flashing her mouth of silver braces at different angles. I was sitting on the toilet, flossing.

"Why, didn't we have so much fun last year?" I asked.

"Yeah, but Sandra, we were *teenagers* last year. We're *adults* now!"

I laughed. We were fourteen. And even though Vicki had braces and I didn't—I was the *only* one of our friends blessed with perfect teeth—she felt like she was somebody much older. Most of the time.

"Oh, yeah right," I said. "So you're going to act all adult-like around Todd Millman?" I wanted to tease Vicki, because I knew that this was the most attention she would pay me the whole night. Looking at her reaction, though, I wished I hadn't mentioned Todd.

Vicki smiled with innocent mischief, threw a hairbrush at me.

⸭ Jeff gave us a lift to the shul, but first we had to pick up our cousin Ronald. Since Gerald was sitting up front with Jeff, after tossing his sleeping bag and duffel into the trunk, Ronnie had to squish into the back with us. While Vicki and I had dressed up like we were going to a bat mitzvah—me in leggings and a purple sweater, her in a black dress, the straps of her red bra showing—Ronnie was wearing sweatpants and a Led Zeppelin shirt that was much too tight. I could smell Cheetos and root beer on his breath. It was totally gross.

"Good evening, fellow Jews and Jewesses," he said. "Oh, and Gerald. Jeff and Gerald, a friendship attempting to once again forge an alliance between North American Blacks and Jews." We—and by we, I mean *everyone*—were used to Ronnie talking this way. Ignoring him was second nature. Still, as Ronnie pushed against me as he tried to force his seatbelt into its clip, I yelled at him a little, trying to impress Vicki.

"Ugh, get off me Ronnie, you're so fat!"

"You're not exactly a picture of health yourself," he said lightly. Though we'd been insulting each other like that since we learned to talk, his comment on my weight still stung.

Vicki wasn't paying any attention anyways. She leaned over the front seat and rested her head on Jeff's shoulder, her big hoop earrings dangling against the headrest.

"Hey Jeff, do you think we could stop at the LCBO and you could get us some vodka or something? Please? It's going to be *so* boring there." She really drew out the please.

I watched Jeff's face as he battled with a number of competing desires. I was ready to be disgusted.

"How old are you again, Vicki?" he asked, pushing her head out of his space, playfully but with finality. "I remember when you were an eight-year-old obsessed with Sailor Moon!"

"Sailor Moon? That chick was hot!" Gerald enthused, turning the radio up.

Vicki slumped back into her seat, her face pouty with disappointment. The new Beyoncé came on, Vicki's pout disappeared, and she started dancing and singing. Ronnie was eating a bag of Ringolos that had appeared from somewhere, was reading a worn sci-fi paperback. I shifted between the two, unable to get comfortable.

We weren't the first to arrive at the shul, but we might as well have been. The front doors were locked, so we knocked until Sherman, our adult chaperone for the night, let us in.

"Jeff's not coming?" he asked as he held the door open for us, watching my brother and Gerald drive away.

"Jeff? He's *much* too old for this," I said. We were following Sherman down the hall towards the Hebrew school classrooms.

"How can anybody be too old to spend a barely supervised night at their synagogue?" Sherman asked.

Vicki snorted. Sherman said gesundheit.

We dropped our knapsacks and sleeping bags in one of the classrooms left open for us. I scanned what was already there, placing objects with their owners. Ninja Turtle sleeping bag with the Game Boy on top: Billy or Jonah. The plain brown sleeping bags, the small library of history books, and the Canadian Tire survival kits obviously belonged to Betsy, Amanda, Sam, and Danielle. Such weirdos (the type of girls Ronnie would fit in with, if he had any interest to fit in with anyone). No skateboard, no marijuana leaf sleeping bag, no electric guitar case: Todd wasn't here yet.

As Vicki and I were on our way to the washroom, somebody screamed behind me. I spun around: it was Kate! I screamed, we ran to each other, jumped, hugged, screamed a little more. Kate was—along with Vicki—my best friend. We went to the same camp and so had that special camp connection that's impossible to describe to anybody who doesn't know, and that I knew Vicki was secretly jealous of (I've had to explain it to my non-Jewish friends countless times: Kate was a camp friend and a shul friend, Vicki was shul and school; the only people who were shul, school, *and* camp besides Jeff—who was now in high school anyways—was Ronnie. Ew).

"Hey Vicki," Kate said after we had finished screaming in greeting, "looking good." A year ago Kate came out, and she loved to tease Vicki about it. She had a serious girlfriend now, Brenda, who went to a fancy arts high school downtown. They had been together for three and a half weeks, but it felt like they had been married for four decades! Naturally, I didn't get to see her as much as I used to. Was I jealous? I was totally jealous.

We were still standing at the washroom doors, chatting and laughing, when Sherman let Todd and his brother Phil into the building. Vicki lit up; I wanted to light up, but instead my bulb, already dim in comparison, blew its fuse.

Sherman checked the brothers' names off on his clipboard.

"Everybody's here," he said.

: We all ate dinner together in the school's gym, basketball nets hanging from the ceiling, a raised stage along one entire wall, the shimmery black curtains closed. Dinner was delivery pizza and salad that Sheri, the acting chair of Jewish Education with a head full of tight copper curls, brought in two large clear plastic bowls. Before we ate, Rabbi Koffee came out of his office to give a speech. We sat at the tables, bored and hungry, eyeing the stack of white pizza boxes as the rabbi droned on and on at his usual slow tempo.

"When I first came to Kol B'Seder fifteen years ago," he said, "I was amazed at the high quality of the youth programming taking place in our little Reform community. You, the young Jewish men and women who are the promise of our movement, were, and continue to be, involved in every aspect of temple life. And I'm happy to say that since then, and thanks in no small part to people like Sheri, like Sherman, the youth programming and youth involvement of our community has only grown. This 'shul-in' is an important part of that programming. Spending the night with your chevra, in the building that is the geographical nexus of our community, growing and making insoluble connections to our Jewish past, present, and future. What better way to spend a Saturday night! And remember, if you were to take away one thing from tonight, let it be the knowledge that this is *your* building, *your* temple, *your* relationship to our dynamic and robust brand of Judaism."

The rabbi blessed the food, which I had never heard him do before (there were even rumours that he ate bacon, on *Saturdays*!), and we ate. Ronnie shovelled slice after slice into his mouth. Vicki ate and flirted with every boy in reach, flashing food-stuck braces in all directions. The younger kids made a mess. I held myself to two slices, spent most of the meal watching Todd. He was so beautiful, so effortlessly cool. Unlike everyone else, his braces and their bright yellow elastics only added to his irresistible cuteness. I was totally, unabashedly in love with him. (Unfortunately, so was everybody. Except Kate, of course.) When the dinner was over and we had all helped clean up, the rabbi led us in a Havdalah ceremony. We put away the tables, stood in a large circle in the gym, lowered the lights, and, as the rabbi strummed his guitar and led us in singing the wordless melody, we passed around the three-wick Havdalah candle, the spicebox. Together we said goodbye to Shabbat, and welcomed the new week. Havdalah always reminded me of camp and I flushed with nostalgia and excitement. This was definitely my most favourite part of being Jewish, of going to shul. Standing in a circle singing a wordless melody over minor chords really got to me. It was such a pretty, comforting song. I watched the braided candle go around the room, light up our faces one by one. What would happen tonight? Last year David Krasner chaperoned, and after yelling at us after catching boys and girls in the boys' washroom he had made us get into our sleeping bags, and we were all asleep by midnight. This year would be different, I could feel it; Sherman was much lighter on rules and regulations than David (who had all the boys call him Mr. Krasner, *sir*). When the spicebox came to Todd, he took a huge loud snort and pretended to be knocked backwards. Le sigh.

The song over, Sheri turned the lights up. We were back in the gym. The rabbi went to his office. I looked at my watch. It was 8:30. The next twelve hours were totally, totally ours.

⋮ Back in our classroom, we unrolled our sleeping bags, made our temporary nests. Vicki was on my right, Kate on my left. I neatly lined up my toiletry bag, my *Harry Potter*, and my shower radio at the head of my sleeping bag. We entered the boring part of the night. We lay sprawled on our sleeping bags, played cards, chatted quietly. Todd took his electric guitar out, spent twenty minutes tuning it by ear, his hair falling in front of his eyes. Kate and I went for a walk in the hallway.

"How are things, Sandra?"

"Pretty good. Excited for camp."

"I might not be going this year."

"What?! What do you mean?" I stopped, looked at her. Super thin, her light brown hair in a short bob, she looked sharp, fitted, exact.

"Brenda and I might go to Europe."

"Oh. Cool." I was trying to be peppy, but Kate knew me too well.

"Oh Sandra. Don't worry. Just because we don't spend as much time together as we used to, doesn't mean we won't always be best friends." I looked at Kate. Vicki might have wanted to act like an adult, but Kate actually *was* an adult.

"I can't believe you aren't coming to camp!" I mock-yelled, shaking her. "What am I going to do?! Who's going to sing to me when I'm constipated on the toilet?" We collapsed into our famous giggly laughter, a balm sugary-sweet.

Back in our classroom, Vicki, Ronnie, Todd, and Simon were playing cards. I sat down beside them to watch. They were playing Kent: Simon and Vicki were partners, and Todd and Ronnie. Until that moment I had no idea Ronnie had a crush on Vicki, but the way he was looking and talking at her, it was ridiculously obvious. Todd seemed to be getting annoyed with Ronnie, was talking to him like he was a misbehaving child, kept saying "dookie" over and over again. Part of me was happy that they were not getting along. Vicki theatrically swept her hand through her hair.

"Kent," Simon said triumphantly, Vicki squealing with glee as she lay down her hand: four queens.

"Shit, Ronnie, pay attention!" Todd yelled, throwing down his cards. Four threes. Ronnie shrugged. He didn't care. The normal social pressures didn't apply to Ronnie.

Things calmed down for a while. It was quiet enough that we were able to hear Sherman and the rabbi walk to the front doors, say their goodbyes. The rabbi was chuckling. "Got to get home before the first pitch," he said. It was weird to hear him talk about something so normal, so non-Jewish, as baseball. At the click of the door, Todd jumped up, said "I'm bored, let's go exploring." Vicki and I immediately agreed. I grabbed Kate's hand, was slightly disappointed to see that Ronnie was also tagging along.

Todd led us down the hall, away from the front doors, and opened the doorway to the southeast stairwell and motioned for us to go in. As we were heading up the stairs, Vicki turned to me and smiled wickedly; I was scared of going where we weren't supposed to, but the desire to be with Todd, and to keep an eye on Vicki, compelled me onward. When we got to the locked doors at the top of the third floor, Todd looked around, pulled a hairpin out of Vicki's hair, Vicki crying out coyly, and picked the lock.

"Where'd you learn to do that?" Ronnie asked, apparently impressed with Todd's ability to so easily unlock supposedly locked doors.

In response, Todd pushed the door open, and vanished into the darkness. We followed. There was another flight of stairs, so narrow that only one of us could go up at a time. There might have been a light switch, but we didn't think to look for it; the staircase was totally dark. We were tunnelling into the unknown. I was terrified, wished I was back in our classroom on my sleeping bag with all the other boring people, or alone in the kitchen eating cold pizza. At the top of the stairs was a door, which opened onto the roof. We spilled out into the cool spring night, and I instantly felt better. I had never been up there before: the roof was flat, carpeted in crunchy gravel. There were some camping chairs near the far edge, so that's where we headed. Todd pulled out a joint, a long skinny thing, and lit it. When it got to me I declined awkwardly, as did Ronnie. Kate placed it between her thumb and pointer finger and took two small, neat sucks, passed it on as if she smoked on roofs every evening, was only missing a glass of wine in her other hand. When it got to Vicki she sucked as hard as she could for twenty, thirty seconds, immediately started coughing and hacking. I watched her eyes go as red as her bra. I was once again terrified, my heart pounding so hard I could barely hear Ronnie going on and on about the Indigenous people, the Anishinaabe, who used to live here and were forcibly removed by the government.

"How do you know all this?" Todd asked dismissively. "Sounds like bullshit to me." Ronnie just kept talking. I looked out over the parking lot, the park behind the shul, the roofs of the suburban houses, each one of us corresponding to one of those roofs. Was it possible that a whole other world was here before all this? Before us? I'd never thought of it like that before, but it suddenly seemed more than possible, seemed likely, close enough to touch.

"Yeah, jeez Ronnie!" Vicki said. I felt like I should say something, but whether to dig into Ronnie or defend him, I couldn't decide.

When we returned downstairs, the night had shifted. We were full of beans, over-the-top silly, laughing as we ran and stumbled through the brightly lit building. We zoomed! We hollered! We careened! Vicki, Todd, Ronnie, Kate and I were a team, a unit, a pack on a mission, a disconcerting blur! We didn't move according to a plan, according to decision or desire, we just *moved*. (Even though I hadn't smoked, I imagined this is what it must feel like to be high, the sugary swell of adrenaline, the toppling excitement, the surprising lack of inhibition.) We ran down the hallway, cackling and whooping, Todd literally jumping off the walls in his squeaky skater shoes. We burst into the kitchen, grabbed all the chips and cookies we could carry, kept moving. We hurtled over Billy, Jonah, and Gul, the youngest boys there, playing with their Game Boys in the hallway. We streamed past Betsy and Amanda, who barely had time to look up from their history books and shoot us dirty looks. We were an unstoppable force, smashing boundaries, going where we weren't supposed to, the temple yielding its secrets to us like a Jewish Hogwarts. We ran through the sanctuary, past the sombre ark, the bima, the electric light that represented God and was supposed to never go out. We flew up the northeast stairs, through the school library, knocking over a book or two, out the other end, down the southwest stairs. We pushed open the heavy doors of the administrative wing and stopped cold. A woman was crying. Todd motioned for us to be quiet. His hair was in his eyes and his cheeks were red, his cuteness melting a hole in my heart. The crying petered out, and we heard a voice. It was Sheri. "I just don't understand," she said. "Why hold on to something that is gone, gone forever?" We all looked at each other. Ronnie, that oaf, took a step back and crashed into a desk, knocking everything over, shaking us from our momentary stillness. "Let's go!" Vicki yelled, and we revved up again, ran deeper into the offices, towards the boardroom. I had an instant to glance into the rabbi's office as we lunged past, saw Sherman sitting on the desk, his head in his hands, Sheri across the room sitting cross-legged on the same chair I sat in during the lead-up to my bat mitzvah, when I met with Rabbi Koffee to talk about the speech I would give relating my Torah portion to my life. Her copper curls were aflame in the light from the desk lamp. They were both too preoccupied to notice us. We ran into the boardroom and out the other door, back into the hallway.

Our final stop was the basement. Todd did his trick with the door to the storage room, and we pooled in. Suddenly the urge to keep moving dissipated, vanished. Here we were, in a dark and stuffy windowless room of boxes and furniture in the basement of the synagogue we were willingly locked in for the night, all of us breathing hard, ourselves again after the mad rush. Kate found a light switch, and we fanned out. The congregation's chuppah, bare pine and white cloth, was disassembled in the corner, waiting for the next wedding. Todd opened a box of yahrzeit candles, and I opened one of the kiddish cups they give everyone on their bar or bat mitzvah. Under a box of rolled-up handheld Israeli flags that were for Yom Ha'atzmaut, Ronnie found a bright yellow binder. For some reason, we all crowded around him. The label on the binder read "Reform Rabbis Speak." "Bo-ring," Todd said. Ronnie opened it anyways, started to read from the random page it had fallen on. "It's from the *Pittsburgh Platform*, from 1885. Whoa. Listen to this. Number five. 'We recognize, in the modern era of universal culture of heart and intellect, the approaching of the realization of Israel's great Messianic hope for the establishment of the kingdom of truth, justice, and peace among all men. We consider ourselves no longer a nation, but a religious community, and therefore expect neither a return to Palestine, nor a sacrificial worship under the sons of Aaron, nor the restoration of any of the laws concerning the Jewish state.'"

"What does that mean?"

"We don't expect a return to Palestine?"

"Wait—Reform Jews didn't always support Zionism?"

"I guess not."

"Did you know that, Ronnie?" Todd asked.

Ronnie slowly closed the binder. "Well, the ultra-Orthodox didn't support Zionism either, but for the opposite reasons. They thought it was going against the word of God, to set up a Jewish state before the coming of messiah." He so obviously *hadn't* known about the contents of the yellow binder, was just trying to cover.

It came as a shock to me. We spent every Thursday night and Saturday morning learning Israeli Hebrew, talking about the links between Canada and Israel; when we were younger we even watched the Israeli Sesame Street, *Rechov Sumsum*. Never, not once, did we hear anything about the Reform movement's earlier position. When did it change? Did Rabbi Koffee know? Did Sherman? Did my parents?

What else had they been keeping from us?

Down there in the basement with those artifacts, ritual objects, and buried paragraphs, starting to feel unmoored.

Totally strange.

⋮ An hour later we were all sitting on the library floor, except for the youngest kids, who were downstairs, dreaming peacefully. Paul Cohen had a flask of whisky and was passing it around. When the flask came to me, I looked at Vicki, looked at Todd—the both of them so ready and willing to do anything, seemingly fearless—and, as terrified as I have ever been, took a swig. It burned my throat and I tried not to gag. Ugh, yuck. I took another small sip and passed it on. Matt and his friends came down from the roof, stinking of marijuana. They were only twelve years old. Vicki started making out with Paul, Shoshana made out with Mitzy, I was only slightly surprised when Joshua started making out with Phil, Todd's older, less-cute-but-still-Toddish-in-some-undefinable-Todd-way brother. Everybody was making out with everybody. Would somebody try to kiss *me*? I looked around at the shelves of the library, trying to distract myself from the panic earthquaking up and down my spine. Think of anything else, Sandra. As usual, my mind moved towards *Harry Potter*. Hermione was always able to go into the library, find the right books, discover hidden truths. How many books here had secrets like what we had unearthed in the basement? How much counter to what we knew was hiding in plain sight?

I happened to be looking when Ronnie leaned in towards Vicki, and she inched away. I knew she was trying not to hurt his feelings, which for some reason made me angry. I had never felt anything but cousinly embarrassment for Ronnie, but now, suddenly, I felt cousinly solidarity. We were both on the edge of the social, of the desirable: Ronnie with his block head, greasy hair, lack of hygiene, and non-stop talk of history and politics (though Ronnie didn't come across as *political* in any way, it was all just stories, nerdgasms, knowledge), me with my chubbiness, my self-conscious shyness, second fiddle to the Vickis and Kates of the world. I caught Kate's eyes from across the room and she made a face at me and we fell into giggles. When I stopped laughing I realized Todd was beside me. He was leaning in, his mouth puckered. It's happening, Sandra. I moved my face through the terrifying air and we were kissing, we were making out! His hair on my face felt like sharp straw, his hand on my knee was burning hot, his tongue was like an iron poker in my mouth. Not knowing what I was doing, I pushed him off. He looked at me. "What's wrong?" he said, smirking. "I, I have to pee," I said, jumping up. I was sure everyone was staring, but as I slipped behind the shelves it looked like nobody had paid the slightest attention. My own head was flaming, and not in a good way.

I peed, washed my face, looked at my teeth. That was…not what I was expecting. It was like there were two different Todds. I went back to the group, sat down. They were going on like nothing had happened. Todd was back where he was before. I watched him brush his hair out of his eyes, say something that made Vicki laugh. I reached for the flask lying on the hard carpet and took a long bitter drink.

: Two in the morning. Matt and Paul pull out all of the office chairs from the boardroom start racing each other down the curved hallway, the rest of us cheering them on. Matt's chair slams into the wall, one of the wheels popping off, we yell and whoop deliriously. Sherman and Sheri find us, make us roll the chairs back into the boardroom though they don't yell (we laugh later imagining what would have happened if David Krasner had found us in similar circumstances). We help Kate sneak Brenda in through an open window; they go off to find an empty classroom. I know I won't see them for the rest of the night, and I tell myself I'm alright with that. We're sitting on our sleeping bags, Todd playing Green Day songs on his electric, singing along. I'm fighting sleep with all my might, but it's no use: I fall asleep for a hard split second, have a dream that Todd's head is lying in my lap and everyone's standing around us, the classroom a smear of sleeping bags and windows and doors, and I'm flossing Todd's teeth, carefully, lovingly, expertly, the floss an extension of my innermost self—I shudder awake, all excited, heart racing, awash once again with love. A rumour goes around that Joshua (Sherman's only son) and some of the other older kids have eaten magic mushrooms. Ronnie: If they're on mushrooms, we should be able to feel it, the psychedelic particles aloose in the building. Todd: I feel it, I feel it! Pretending to seizure. Vicki, her face concentrating hard, even prettier all scrunched up: I think I *do* feel something. Everybody goes to the roof to smoke another joint. Me: I'm going to stay down here, do some reading. I'm walking back from the bathroom, where I've changed into my PJs—white, with dozens of little dachshunds barking all over them—when I see Sheri leaving the building. She sees me too. Sheri: Enjoy the rest of your night, Sandra. Hold on to these, these, opportunities of being young. Is she crying? Back on my sleeping bag, I can't stay focused on Harry Potter—his problems, his world, however grand, seem far away, distant. It's not until everybody's back downstairs and we're standing in the kitchen trying to find food and they're all talking about Joshua and Tamara and Paul up on the roof, the older teenagers' eyes all pupils, speaking in tongues, that I notice that Simon has attached himself onto our group, follows closely behind Vicki, laughs at everything she says. Well, well. Another contender.

Three in the morning. Bored and tired, trapped in this building, the promise of our earlier pack heat a dashed dream, my feelings a splintery jumble. We wander onto the stage at the back of the gym. It's dark back there, we have to wait for our eyes to adjust. Vicki and I sit down at the piano and start to play. It's the oldest piano I've ever played on, with "Gerhard Heintzman, Toronto" across the front in gold letters. We both took lessons from the same Korean woman since grade two, she taught us everything from Beethoven to The Beatles to chordal improvisation (Vicki quit the lessons six months ago, and I soon followed; we haven't played together since). As always, I play chords for Vicki to solo on top of. It comes back to us so naturally, I don't even notice that everybody is standing around watching. I bring the chords to a crashing crescendo, Vicki up in the pentatonic heights, and we end together on a series of fading A minor chords ringing from all ends of the keyboard. Everybody's clapping. Todd: That was, like, really awesome! I didn't know you girls could rip like that! Ronnie: Music is the language of the soul, after all. I fill with promise, with hope, again. Todd opens the curtains to the empty gym, flooding the backstage with light, and we start going through all the costumes. The Purim show was two weeks ago and all of the masks are still out. Vicki and I dress up as Esther and Mordechai. Todd finds a Nazi costume from *The Diary of Anne Frank* the kids at Isaac Babel Elementary had staged last year, puts it on. We chase each other across the stage, screaming and playing. I try to flash my mouth of perfect white teeth at Todd whatever chance I get, lure him back. How could Vicki's braceface compete? Ronnie finds a mask for Haman: brown skin, turban, beard. He puts it on. Vicki: You *totally* look like a terrorist, Ronnie! Ronnie, his voice muffled behind the mask: Actually, in Israel, Purim often leads to Jewish violence against the Palestinians, ya know. Todd: Shut up man, we're just having fun. I'm taken aback. Believe it or not, I had never heard the phrase 'Jewish violence' before. Ronnie keeps talking, and even though I'm still pretending to play, dodging Todd's Nazi as he chases us with zombie arms, I'm listening intently. Ronnie starts talking about 1948, the expulsions, the four hundred destroyed villages. Does he know how fully he has my attention? It's the first time I hear the word *Nakba*. Nakba. I say it to myself in my head. Nakba. I say it aloud. Nakba. I take off the costume, jump off the stage into the gym, where, six hours ago, three lifetimes ago, we had stood in a circle singing Havdalah, start running around, calling it out, Nakba Nakba Nakba. I stop. Turn around. Everybody's standing on the stage, watching. Ronnie's smirking, the Haman mask in his hand.

I feel like I'm crashing and taking off all at once.

Four in the morning. The synagogue full of shadows, of secrets we have yet to penetrate. We wander into the sanctuary. Todd opens the doors of the ark, and we are face-to-face with the Torahs. As Rabbi Koffee constantly reminds us, one of these Torahs survived the Holocaust. We stare at the ancient scrolls in their fancy wrappings for a long minute, the complicated parts we're supposed to know the names of, before shutting the ark. They're the only objects in the whole building none of us makes to touch, to open, to spill. In the small coat room beside the sanctuary there's a photo of the Western Wall in Jerusalem, the Dome of the Rock golden on the Temple Mount. Ronnie: Back in the temple days, our whole lives would have revolved around that exact spot. Simon, in a hushed voice: What do you think it was like for the high priest, entering the holy of holies? Todd: It must have been like taking a thousand hits of acid all at once. Ronnie: Ya know, there's a secret group working around the clock to build the third temple.

I don't know about the others, but I feel the night change once again.

"No way!"

"What about the Dome of the Rock or whatever it's called?"

"Way. And if they succeed, we're all in a lot of trouble. Just like the first two temples, the third temple is going to have crazy omnipotent powers."

"Yeah, like what?" Todd asked. His tone when talking to Ronnie had transformed since the beginning of the night—he seemed genuinely interested in what Ronnie had to say.

"Oh, you know, the gamut of sci-fi terror. Nuclear capabilities, fusion energy, mind-control, the ability to bend space-time to its will. The terror and retribution of God manifest in Jerusalem stone and mortar." Ronnie sensed that we were listening intently, that he had, for once, a captive audience. It empowered him. "It gets worse. The third temple will have the power to find anyone, anywhere throughout history—past, present *and* future—who wasn't actively involved in rebuilding it, or who tried to stop it, and punish them. Total, unfiltered malice. What do you choose, then? Will you commit yourself to the third temple, the all-seeing eye, to the coming messianic age of submission and terror, that will rule over all without exception? Or will you tempt the wrath of an all-powerful being?"

"Stop it, Ronnie!" To my surprise (and ashamed delight) Vicki was crying. Todd looked terrified, like *he* had eaten mushrooms and had stumbled into a bad trip, or was standing unprepared in that most sacred chamber in the days of Solomon. Simon was staring at the picture of the Temple Mount, his eyes wide. We were all pretty spooked, I guess. Todd put his arm around Vicki and she melted into him.

"Why wouldn't the third temple be empathetic, understanding, forgiving?" I asked, the question coming out of me before I knew it was there.

Ronnie shrugged. "Don't ask me, that's just how it is. How it is written." I stared at Ronnie. I'd never thought of him as someone with power, but listening to him spin his tales—because, as late as it was, as under his spell as we all were, as taken in by the moment, a part of me still knew that's all they were, tales—I was seeing him in a whole new light.

"I gotta get out of this fucking closet," Simon said, opening the door, breaking the spell. We all tromped out after him.

⸬ Two hours later and I was walking the halls alone, drunk on tiredness, drama, emotion, new ideas, perhaps even whisky. We had all gone back to our classroom to lie down, but unlike earlier, sleep wouldn't come—I couldn't keep still, my mind was a building on fire. Was this what it felt like to be drunk? I was walking hallways I'd walked five hundred million times before, but everything was different, strange, both new and old. Matt was passed out near the front doors in black sweatpants and a black sweatshirt, his arms and legs splayed. He was covered in ash and green flecks of marijuana; asleep, he had the face of an innocent child. Two or more people were having sex inside the handicap washroom, grunting softly. I stood for a minute, listening, wondering who it was, before I moved on. Sherman was in the boardroom sitting at the end of the table, snoring. He was a good-looking man with a sad story; no wonder everybody was in love with him. I stayed standing in the doorway. It was in this exact room where, five years ago, playing during Saturday services under the large mahogany table, Kate told me about her sleepover camp, and I decided then and there to go next summer no matter what. By far the biggest decision of my entire life. Outside the floor-to-ceiling boardroom windows the world was dark blue. I could just make out the outlines of the spruce trees. Missing Kate, I went back to our classroom. Betsy, Amanda, Sam, and Danielle were sleeping in a pile. Danielle was hugging a thick book called *Inside the Third Reich*. Simon was passed out on a plastic chair. Where was Vicki? I thought with a sinking feeling, noticing Todd's empty sleeping bag. When I had left she had been fast asleep. I went to look for her. I had a dark premonition as I walked past the southeast stairwell. Someone had turned off the lights in there. I put my face against the glass. Two people were sitting halfway up the stairs, embracing. As my eyes adjusted, I saw that it was Vicki and Todd, making out hard. The straps of Vicki's dress were off her shoulders, and it looked like her hand was down Todd's pants. I continued to watch as Vicki swung her body onto Todd's before I yanked myself away. All the anger, confusion, loss that I had been keeping at bay throughout the night broke their barriers—I knew it was coming, but it still hit me like a barely controlled demolition. Not knowing what I was doing, not in control of my feet or hands, I walked down the hall to the northeast stairs, up all three flights, shoved through the propped-open security door, and climbed the narrow stairway onto the roof.

I pushed open the final door and emerged into the furnace of a new morning. The world was vibrant, messy, dripping with colour, mild yellows and furious oranges. The holy of holies, Ronnie would have called it. I walked to the edge, looked down at the parking lot, at the trees and playground behind the building, everything glowing with their own vital lights. Two hawks were circling high in the sky. I don't think anybody has ever seen the morning like I was seeing it then. The world was totally pulsing with life, bursting with possibility. Awash in it, I saw clearly that, no matter what we tell ourselves, it would always be people like Todd, like Vicki, that the world gravitated towards: made for action, hungry for everything, built with a magnet and a furnace in the hearts of their architecture. People like me, like Ronnie, were forever watching, waiting, trembling.

Or were we?

Ronnie had his mind, his stories, sources of his own secret power. And, apparently, so did I. I saw Ronnie's story of the third temple differently now. It wasn't the temple itself that had such powers—it never was and it never would be—it was what the temple housed, what people believed it housed. I thought of Ronnie's large head, his greasy hair, his fatness, his total lack of desire to be cool, fit in, have friends. The world oozing and breathing all around me, I made a decision. In all that voluptuous heaving it seemed right and true, crazy and beautiful.

I took in the morning one more time—so this was the benefit of not going to sleep!—and climbed back into the building.

I had to find Ronnie.

He was in the boardroom sitting at one of the chairs, reading a thick paperback, drinking a coke. Sherman was gone. The room was flushed and flushing with bright clear light.

I sat down beside him.

"Hiya," he said, not looking up. I read the title of his book: *A People's History of the United States.*

"Todd and Vicki are making out in the stairwell," I said.

"Oh yeah?" He still didn't look up, but I saw his response move across his face like a rolling blackout.

"I've been thinking," I said, the words careful and precise, language conforming precisely to my will. "If the third temple will be so vindictive, so spoiled, so, like, totally childish, why should I do anything for it, for its coming-in-to-being? Out of fear, out of self-preservation? Gross! I'm not going to let it speak for me. I'll work against it, with all my might."

Now I had Ronnie's attention. He looked at me. I knew he felt it too. "And how will you mount this attack?" he asked in a hoarse whisper.

I flashed my perfect teeth at him one last time before leaning in, kissing him. His open mouth tasted like Cheetos and soft drink and morning, but we didn't care.

⠇ We made out until Sherman found us. "Taking 'insoluble connections' a little too seriously, are we?" he asked. He wasn't angry or disgusted or upset, but whimsical, sweet, a little sad. Outside the windows, morning had fully arrived; it was time for breakfast. We followed Sherman to the gym, joined the others. No one spoke as we ate warm muffins and drank cold orange juice, the last twelve hours shadowed on our faces. Sleeping bags rolled up, belongings packed away, the temple was now just another building, a regular daytime building full of regular daytime things. We all gathered in the front hall and Sherman ceremoniously unlocked the doors and out we ventured into the world. The colours and splendour of an hour ago were gone, tucked into some hidden pocket for those of us lucky enough to know where the zipper was.

Brenda was waiting in her vw Bug for Kate. Ronnie's mom picked him up. I don't know what happened to Todd. Vicki and I started to walk home together. She didn't say anything about Todd, and I didn't say anything about Ronnie. In a friendship like ours, words were not always necessary. Our hands found each other.

I didn't think I would ever sleep again.

The Krasners

WHEN I THINK BACK to those days it is fear that I remember, fear that I keep returning to, fear that I cannot get away from. First there's the free-floating, general fear of adolescence: the fear of fitting in, the fear of saying the right thing, the fear of a body under revolt. And, for the most part, it wasn't on the school playground or the mall food court, but at Kol B'Seder, the Reform synagogue my parents joined when I was twelve, where the major battles against these fears were waged. I fell in love in those hallways, made friends during those Thursday evening and Saturday morning classes, tested boundaries, discovered limits, and, thanks to a liberal focus on the Holocaust, came face-to-face with the depravity that every human society is capable of. We read harrowing accounts of Jewish children from Germany, Poland, and Holland, had elderly survivors come speak to us every couple of months, and on Yom HaShoah, we watched the videos. All the kids would pile into the sanctuary—I would sit with Mitzy, Erin, and Stephanie, and sometimes Paul Cohen would leave his own friends and come join us—and we would watch archival footage of the camps, interviews with survivors, fictional retellings of the Wannsee Conference, of the Warsaw Uprising, of the Nuremberg Trials. How many years of watching tractors organize hills of bodies does it take to give you lifelong nightmares? Of course, the burn of the Holocaust was always immediately remedied with the balm of Israel: footage of the

Declaration of Independence, grainy news briefs on the pioneer-
ing Israeli spirit, the wonders of the kibbutz, the marvel of Tel
Aviv, the Jewish city built in the desert.

My shul life was separate, distinct, from my school one, a parallel narrative to my daily existence, a place where I could reinvent
myself, learn from my social blunders, try new things. My parents found what they were looking for too, I suppose: having
recently relocated from Montreal, and knowing nobody in Toronto,
they managed to find friends, connection, community. We were
invited in with open arms: Friday night potlucks, Saturday morning services that would end almost every week with a bagels-
and-tuna kiddish celebrating the most recent bar or bat mitzvah,
the holidays strung through the Jewish year like an uneven neck-
lace; there were retreats, clubs, brotherhoods, sisterhoods, youth
groups, Torah study groups, lecture series, sports leagues, cooking classes, and it was all ours for the admission price of
membership and the sacrifice of sitting through forty-five minutes of guitar-backed prayers most Friday nights.

But that's not what I'm here to tell you about; I'm here to tell
you about the Krasners. The Krasners were royalty at Kol B'Seder,
one of the original six founding families. David Krasner was
president emeritus, head usher, and a major donor and philan-
thropist, his name appearing regularly in both the Jewish and
city papers. He was a big man, with a deep, commanding voice,
and we were all terrified of him (as head usher he especially
picked on Erin, who happened to often be the loudest person in
the room). Geri Krasner was president of the sisterhood, second
soloist in the choir, and head of fundraising for the shul's annual
trip to Israel. Though unofficial, they had two seats reserved for
them in the second row of the sanctuary, where, unless they were
on one of their frequent family trips to New York City, they would
be found every Friday night, Saturday morning, guest lecture,
and holiday large or small. They had five children: Joanna, Neta,
Yoni, Daniel, and Stephanie. Joanna and Neta were older than us,

were both off in the States at small, expensive liberal arts colleges; Yoni and Daniel both played competitive hockey and were hardly ever around; Stephanie, who was a year older than I was, played guitar, wrote short stories about desperate people lost in grotesque urban environments, wore her sisters' hand-me-downs, and was as confident as you would expect a beautiful, rich, creative, sheltered fourteen-year-old to be. She was the only Krasner child to spend time with us. Does it even need to be said that I was in love with her? I don't know if I recall the first time we were invited to the Krasners' mansion, or if all of those early nights are jumbled in my memory (how my parents managed to ingratiate themselves so quickly into Kol B'Seder's inner circle I have no idea). What I do know is that in the fall of my thirteenth year, my bar mitzvah already receding into the past, we were there almost every Saturday night, along with five or six other families from the shul: the Brickmans, the Golds, the Cohens, the Mitzcovitzes, the Hoffmans, the Krasners, and us. They were raucous nights of food, arguments, unrequited teenage passion, discovery.

The Krasner estate was situated on two acres of forest off the Bridle Path, and still is, without a doubt, the biggest house I have ever been in. Though unbelievably large—not deep, but wide—it was old, unrenovated, and deeply lived in. The front door opened into a tiled foyer, the double-wide white-carpet staircase spiralling to the second floor. When the kitchen was built in the mid-eighties it must have been state of the art, and had a separate eating area and breakfast nook; the dining room table could easily sit sixteen; and the living and family room walls were adorned with David and Geri's various awards, commendations, and photos of trips to Israel and the family at their New York apartment. A door in the kitchen led into the mudroom, which was the size of our school gym, with big sliding doors leading out to the woods and ravine behind the house and three separate entrances to the three self-contained heated garages. Next to the mudroom was the indoor pool, next to the indoor pool was the old stables that Krasner had renovated into a floor hockey rink for the boys, complete with stands and a scoreboard. We never went upstairs.

The basement, accessible from an open staircase in the living room and a dark, enclosed one off the pool that used to lead to the servant quarters, was a long narrow hallway traversing the length of the house, with keypad-locked doors on either side. The only room in the basement we had access to was the entertainment room, which was where we spent most of our time. We could shut the door while we were down there, be as loud and silly as we wanted: mostly we would watch Arnold Schwarzenegger VHSes and listen to Adam Sandler albums, kill ourselves laughing at Paul Cohen's dirty jokes. Paul brimmed with sexual innuendo, Sandler-influenced voices, and what I guess I would call now teenage bravura; without his own friends around, Paul lavished us with attention. I would try to laugh just the right amount, be careful what I said, hope my absolute devotion to the seventeen-year-old Paul was not as obvious to everybody else as it was to me, and try to not break out in a sweat whenever Stephanie Krasner was on the same side of the room as me, strumming her guitar or reading one of her thrillingly dark stories. Regular nights in the life of a shy, sensitive boy.

⫶ There is one night in particular that I would continue to go back to again and again, as if to locate some sense of forewarning, of premonition. My uncle Menachem had joined the Montreal exodus, was staying with us for a few weeks before his visa came through and he could head to the coast, where he had some friends in a folk band that were going to take him on as guitar tech, and he had joined us at the Krasners' for Saturday night dinner. It was after we had eaten and everybody under thirty-five had already gone to the basement, but I was still sitting at the table, next to my mom. I was fascinated by my uncle, enthralled by the way he engaged with others. He just didn't follow the same social conventions of the other adults in my life: he would argue, he would cut, he wouldn't let hyperbole or hypocrisy or xenophobia pass him by. He wore his curly hair halfway between short and acceptably long, had shown up at our door with nothing but a worn banjo case and a suitcase full of old sweaters and threadbare slacks, and was vocally opposed to every single thing I was being taught to value: the Western world, the market economy, the eons-long persecution of the Jews. It was like nothing I had ever known, and to see him in the same room as David Krasner was worth missing out on whatever was going on downstairs.

As I knew they would, it was only a few minutes into their coffee before they got into it. They had been talking about the situation in Quebec, when Geri Krasner mentioned something about Israel. As I remember it now, I happened to be looking at my parents as a wave of worry passed over their faces.

"Israel? Israel?" Menachem said, as if on cue. "I don't see what Israel has to do with any of this." My mother and Menachem grew up in a strict religious household; their father, my grandfather, was a famous rabbi of some kind, he wrote a treatise on some arcane Talmudic matter that was still required reading to those who read treatises on arcane Talmudic matters. When he died everything religious in their household disappeared, which included my grandfather's fervent Zionism. Joining Kol B'Seder was the first non-secular thing my mother had done since she was a teenager, and for the month he was with us Menachem never tired of making fun of her for it.

Geri looked personally hurt. "Israel has *everything* to do with it," she said. "Israel is what keeps us safe."

"Safe? Safe?! I can tell you, I don't feel safe knowing that, as it turns out, when you give Jews an army and a nuclear bomb they mistreat it as readily as anybody else. The state of Israel was supposed to be a bastion of ethical power, a light unto the nations, and look what they've done with it! Oppression, occupation, racism, all backed—not to mention—by US money and warplanes!" Menachem was talking animatedly, using his hands for emphasis, his curls bouncing against his forehead.

"You're a very strange man," Geri said, barely controlling her anger. "How can you say these things, with the way the world is going right now? With what's happening in our own country for Christ's sake?!"

"I still feel safer here, knowing I'm not a part of the machinery of occupation. Sometimes it's better to be the powerless one."

At this, all eyes turned to Krasner. David, unlike my uncle and Geri, was calm, collected, quietly sipping his coffee. We all knew his story, he came once a year to religious school to remind anyone who could possibly forget: his parents were born over there, in Europe, were survivors. They had lost three children, David's ghost siblings, as well as their entire extended families; the climax of David's harrowing familial saga, which he would always build to with exquisite suspense, centred on his mother's white gold engagement ring, which she had kept hidden, with great difficulty, until, in 1944, she traded it for the roast chicken and civilian clothes that ended up saving their lives. After spending two years as DPs in Europe they had come to Canada with absolutely nothing, spent the rest of their lives working and building a life for David. When Krasner Sr. died, the young Krasner took over his father's small factory, and within ten years had turned it into the international company it was today (for the life of me I can't remember what it was the Krasner family factory actually made, and now, of course, there's nobody around to ask). David's talk to us would always end with him imploring us to not grow too complacent: "It could happen again, even here, even in Canada," he would intone in his most stentorian voice. Imagine unloading that on a bunch of children. The last time he had spoken, Stephanie had raised her hand (is it any wonder Stephanie's stories were so bleak?). "Daddy," she asked, "what are *you* doing

to fight against complacency? We seem pretty complacent to me."
As in love with her as I already was, now I was in awe of her—
pushing back against the most feared man at shul, no matter
that it was also her father. "Don't underestimate your old man,
Stephy," Krasner had said, causing some cautious laughter from
the audience, "I'm in a constant state of preparedness. Nothing
is going to catch us off guard. Trust me." But I'm getting away
from the story. Back to the kitchen table: surely David wouldn't
let Menachem's comment slide, and it looked like he was getting
ready to speak, but Menachem beat him to it. The slight pause
in conversation had pushed him into an even higher level of
agitation.

"I can't believe a smart woman like you would fall for their
propaganda. Some Jews get some guns and we're all supposed
to bow down to them, let them do whatever they please in our
name? That's not how the world works. Wrong is wrong. The
abuse of power is the abuse of power, no matter who's committing it in whose name! We are not the only ones who can be
victimized!"

"Now, Menachem," my father said, attempting to neutralize
the situation, "be reasonable."

"I *am* being reasonable. It's these sheeple that aren't being reasonable!" Watching Menachem on the offensive I couldn't help
thinking about how that very afternoon I had walked into our
family room to find him sobbing to the international news, his
half-strung banjo forgotten in his lap.

My mother, who usually let Menachem go on without pushing
back, got involved. "Do you think Israel has the right to exist?"
she asked, softly, as if afraid of the answer.

Menachem grinned. "As much as any other nation state has
the right to exist. So, not so much."

Everyone started talking over each other at this point, until
David cleared his throat. It was as if we were at shul and he told us
to stop being so loud in the hallway during services: the adults,

even Menachem, his hands frozen mid-gesticulation, stopped yelling and turned to him.

David took his time before speaking. "So what you're saying, Menachem," he said finally, "is that if, god forbid, our little project of western democracy cracks apart, and fascists—or only-god-knows-what-worse—come into power, and start targeting Jews again, you wouldn't accept Israel's protection, be first in line to board one of their planes?"

Menachem looked like he had been hit in the gut. He sat for a minute, slumped in his chair, his face full of anguish. Unlike the right-to-exist question, he was apparently unprepared for this one; I don't think the problem had ever been presented to him like that before. A different kind of person would have pretended to be unfazed, but not my uncle. He would never lie, even to people like David Krasner, who he detested with the unique fervour of the anarchist, pacifist guitar tech that he was.

"Oh, I would go, why not? I don't have a death wish. But I'll tell you one thing, Mr. Krasner. I wouldn't sit idly over there in your 'promised land.' I would join the fight for social justice, for peace, for equal rights. One barbarity does not legitimate another." He said the last sentence again, quietly, to himself.

David laughed softly, sipped his coffee. It was obvious that as far as he was concerned, he had won. "Did you hear the latest from the US Congress?" Geri said, changing topics, "these are truly dark times."

Soon after that the room slipped back into its usual chatty noise and I escaped downstairs.

It must have been soon after that night that we broke into the Krasners' house for the first time. Menachem had recently left, the whole family seeing him off at the airport, but what I remember far more vividly than what would end up being the last time any of us saw Menachem, what I still see when I wake up in the morning, is the look of surprised joy on Paul's face when the window to the indoor hockey rink he had unlatched the night before swung open from the outside. Paul climbed through and opened the door for us, still grinning. The Krasners were in New York City for the week, so we knew the house would be empty. We walked through the dark hockey rink, the cavernous pool room, and took the back staircase into the long basement hallway. I was terrified, but not more terrified than when I had to play baseball during gym, or whenever I was talking to Stephanie Krasner, or any other number of social situations I found myself in on a weekly basis. With Paul's infectious confidence it was hard to stay afraid.

Every door in the basement was shut, but Mitzy knew the code to the entertainment room. The first few times we broke in, we would just hang out, play video games, listen to CDs and watch movies. It was like a regular Saturday night there, except unsanctioned, except without any adults. Except without Stephanie. On our third time, with Paul's urging, we ventured upstairs, and I got my first look at Stephanie's bedroom. It was everything I imagined it to be: thick warm carpet, guitar cases neatly stacked by the window, camp photos, necklaces, a four-poster bed with a heavy white duvet, a white desk with a red typewriter centred perfectly on it. The door to the walk-in closet was slightly ajar, and there was a pair of red underwear caught on the lip of the wicker laundry basket next to her bed. I didn't dare touch anything; this was sacred territory to my hormone-addled mind. I lagged behind for a few minutes before catching up to everybody in the master bedroom. We jumped on the bed, which must have been a triple-king, Erin had us all in stitches as she pretended to be Geri singing in the shower, turning on one of the three heads and soaking Mitzy, Paul pretended to stick various items into various holes.

Eventually we towelled the wet bathroom floor, smoothed the bed, and left the way we came, Paul carefully closing the hockey rink window behind us. That night we drove back to the suburbs and went for burgers and fries. Erin put the jawbreaker she had been working on all night on the table before picking up her burger. I was revelling in the intoxicating effects of belonging, of being with Paul as he grinned his way through his burger, but when I saw that Erin had a bracelet on her wrist that an hour ago was most definitely on Stephanie's night table, the high I had somewhat diminished, though not enough to stop me from going back to the Krasners' the night after, and the night after that.

The Saturday when the Krasners were back from NYC we were all there, as usual. After dinner, all the kids went down to the basement, but the door to our usual hang-out wouldn't open.

"Daddy must have changed the code again," Stephanie said. She went to the stairs and started calling for her father.

"Steph, Steph, it's all right, I have a master," Yoni, who had sprained his wrist and so had to miss practice that night, said. He pulled a tiny, shiny key from his pocket, and inserted it into the bottom of the keypad. The lock clicked open.

"How'd you get that?" Stephanie asked as we spilled into the room.

"Dad made a new one when he thought he lost this one; I found it at the bottom of the pool," he said. "What? Don't make that face! This is *our* house, after all!"

"Why is your dad so obsessed with keeping all these doors locked?" I asked Stephanie after we sat down on the couch. Paul, Mitzy, and Yoni were loudly playing video games, shouting out insults and knocking controllers out of hands. I would never have been able to ask Stephanie such a complicated question even a week ago; breaking into the house had empowered me—I had a secret.

"Oh, Daddy's just weird like that."

"What are in those other rooms, anyways?"

Stephanie smiled at me and my heart stoppered in my throat. "You don't want to know," she said.

"Maybe it's bodies!" Erin said. I hadn't even noticed her sit down next to us.

"Just like one of your stories," I said, turning back to Stephanie. She laughed, almost shyly, and my heart popped out of my throat and anchored in my stomach.

⁞ A few weeks later, a Wednesday night, the Krasner family back in NYC for some Jewish leaders gala, I got a text message from Paul: "come outside." I grabbed my shoes and coat and went out to Paul's idling car; Mitzy was riding shotgun, the latest Smith and Wesson catalogue in his lap, so I got into the back, next to Erin. "Show him Mitz!" Paul called as he pulled away from my house. With a flourish, Mitzy produced something out of his pocket: the Krasner master key. I laughed uncomfortably.

"What are we going to do with that?" I asked.

"What'd you think we're going to do little buddy?" Paul asked. I looked out the window. We were leaving the suburbs.

I opened my mouth to protest—who knows what would have happened, what would have been different if I had said something?—but at that moment Erin grabbed my hand. I was so startled it was as though my life rebooted and started over again at that exact instant. After ten minutes of us holding hands, I stole a glance at Erin. She smiled at me, her jawbreaker pushed into one cheek. I was so infatuated with Stephanie that I had never really given Erin much attention before, she had just always been there—how had I not noticed her mischievous eyes, her scrawniness, her cropped hair, her cheeks aglow in the swiping streetlights? I don't think I took a breath on the thirty-minute drive to the Krasners'.

We parked at the end of the street, walked casually along the sidewalkless road until cutting across the lawn and sprinting into the back of their property. Paul scampered through the window and let us in. Five minutes later we were standing at the end of the basement hallway. All those doors; all those possibilities. "Fuck it, let's eat," Paul said, and we began.

We worked our way down the hall, each door opening with the click of the key in the lock. We discovered: a darkroom, shelves of film, stations for the various washes, the intoxicating chemical stink; a workout room, benches and weights and a wall of mirrors; a wine cellar; a whisky cellar; a room of VHS tapes organized and labelled on floor-to-ceiling shelves; a dusty library; and, behind the second-last door on the right, a room full of gold.

How many people get to experience entering a room that is full of gold? Well, we did. It was the smallest room we had been in so far, grey carpet, bare white walls, and, piled neatly in the middle, there was a pyramid of dull gold bricks, about as tall as I was. The looks on our faces must have been priceless; Mitzy looked like he had ascended to heaven. "Look at all that gold!" Paul shouted in his goofiest Sandler voice. We didn't get any further than that room, but oh, did we celebrate, dancing around the gold, yelling with adrenaline, holding the bars above our heads, though they were heavy enough that I couldn't keep one up for more than a minute.

Somewhere in the revelry Erin grabbed my hand. "Come with me," she said. We went down the hall and into the entertainment room. I had never been in there with only one other person before and it seemed unnaturally large. Erin pushed me onto the couch. "Kiss me," she said, her sugary-sour breath on my face. I kissed her, and we fell onto the floor.

: The next day Paul was waiting in the parking lot of my elementary school, something he had never done before. I happened to be leaving at the same time as the vice principal, and I watched as she gave Paul, who was sitting on the hood of his car smoking a cigarette, a dirty look as she got into her car; I waited until she had pulled out of the lot before going over to him. I sensed right away that something about Paul had changed: he looked up at me with eyes that had been bent to a single purpose. "We're going back tonight," he said, as we drove the suburban streets, the newscaster on the radio talking about the emergency meeting just called at the UN. "Mitzy got his older bro to rent us a van. And Erin had a great idea."

This is always the hardest part of the story. Sure, I can tell you about my doubts, the debate I held in my head. But the end result will always be the same: I went along with it.

We stole eighty-five gold bricks from the Krasners' basement that night. My arms were sore for a week (a few days later when we gave the first bars to the launderer Paul had somehow found, we learned that they were Good Delivery regulation bars, 12.4 kilograms, 400 troy ounces, exactly eleven inches long, each one worth about half a million US dollars). Paul had it all planned out: we took apart the pyramid, hauled it out to Mitzy who was waiting down the snow-dusted street in the van, and rebuilt it with regular house bricks Paul bought at the hardware store and spray-painted gold (this was Erin's "great idea": a sort-of extra *fuck you* to Krasner, I guess). We were so used to being in the Krasners' when we weren't supposed to be, that there was no sense of urgency. We worked slowly, carefully. When we were almost finished building the fake pyramid, Erin took my hand, and I followed her down the hall, up the front stairs, across the kitchen, up the main stairs, and into Stephanie's bedroom. She plopped down on Stephanie's wide bed, popped the jawbreaker out of her mouth and dropped it onto Stephanie's night table. "I bought some condoms," she said, her eyes sparkling. "I think we can afford them now." I hesitated, but she grabbed my arms and pulled me onto her. We melted into the downy whiteness of the bed. I was transgressing all over the place.

The next morning, I woke up a multimillionaire, a criminal, and, seemingly most important of all, newly sexually active.

You can imagine what happened next, can't you? Picture it: Paul was in grade eleven, Mitzy and Erin were in grade nine, I was in grade eight, not even in high school yet! But that didn't stop us from burning through hundreds of thousands of dollars those first few weeks. We threw massive parties. Paul rented a three-bedroom penthouse apartment in the high-rise near the mall where we could keep all of our purchases, had a vault installed in one of the bedrooms to store the gold, which we sold one bar at a time to various shady characters. At first, Erin and I continued our lovemaking.

What can I say? The gold changed me, it changed all of us. We spent with abandon, fuelled our wildest whims. We didn't think of saving any of it. What did we know about long-term GICs, safe investments, real estate? Mitzy started collecting high-end knives and guns, moved to LA before the borders closed and you could still bribe your way into the States. Erin got into rave promoting, always had a gaggle of glassy-eyed, spiky-haired rave girls and boys surrounding her (they called her *Mommy*. It was weird). It hit Paul hardest of all. It wasn't long before the money let his addictive side take over. As for myself, I wasn't much better: without the aid of alcohol, drugs, or a warm body, I could no longer fall sleep; I stopped communicating with my parents; the halcyon days at Kol B'Seder receded into the past; everything I did, saw, or thought, was filtered through the money. At the time, though, I barely noticed. We were kings and queens, riding high.

But I told you this was a story of fear, and it is. By the middle of high school I had bought my way to being among the coolest, most popular kids in school. I had slept with two-thirds of the girls in my suburb, one-sixth of the guys, had everything I could ever want. But we were out of gold. Paul had let his addictions take him into some very dark places, and we lost him to heroin and the teeming underground of criminals and drug dealers that had taken over most of downtown Toronto; the last time I saw him he begged me for a bar of gold, but I didn't have any to give him, I didn't save a single penny, and I'm not too sure I would have even if I could. I was a cold, calculating hedonist. Eventually, of course, I blew it with Erin, and then, like the conceited fool I had become, I blew it even more spectacularly with Stephanie. The second-last time I saw her, at the SkyDome, during one of the first major registration events, she told me that something very valuable had been stolen from her father.

"I'm sure he'll be fine," I had said arrogantly. Stephanie was as vivacious as ever, and talking to her reminded me of my innocent childhood adoration. Shortly after we had stolen the gold from her father, Stephanie had transferred to a private school in New York; who knows what rumours about me had reached her, what she thought. I had heard that since she'd been back in Toronto she'd been working as a journalist for one of the last private newspapers—which, like all the others, had by then been shut down—and I was of course too self-absorbed to ask what she was doing now.

"You don't know anything about it, do you?" she asked.

"What? Of course not!"

She looked at me through narrow eyes. She sighed. "It's really bad," she said. "Really, really bad. Daddy had made, certain, guarantees, and now he's not going to be able to come through on them. And you heard he lost the business, right? We have to sell the house."

"What?! You're kidding!" I was so delusional, I was still gauging my chances of hooking up with her.

Stephanie scoffed.

"Is it really so hard to believe? Look around you, things are not good."

"It's just like one of your stories," I said.

She looked at me like I was subhuman. She spoke, slowly, sadly. "If you can't see the difference between the two, you're more lost than I thought."

"I love you," I said in a burst of recklessness that had become second nature to me. She looked stunned. A long moment passed. She studied me with her narrowed eyes. My mood soured.

"What happened to you, huh?" she said eventually. "You used to be such a nice, sweet boy."

I had a quick retort for her, of course; those days, I had a quick retort for everything (though I would be lying if I didn't say that this was the first time in four years that I started to doubt myself: a tiny little rip, but from then on there was nothing I could do from stopping the real world from seeping in, accumulating).

Unlike Stephanie, Krasner himself never confronted any of us—did he even suspect? In any case, what does it matter, the gold was gone; our fates were sealed. In the end, Krasner had become more complacent than he thought, in his poorly protected mansion, in his brotherhood meetings, in his trust in the rule of law. In a locked room in his basement he didn't bother to check on until it was too late. How angry at himself he must have been when it all came crashing down. A few short months after that conversation with Stephanie, the tanks would be rolling along Rideau, along Robson, along University, and the true terror would begin. But this, of course, is the part you already know, the part we all know all too well.

Let me just say this, then, in lieu of a proper ending. In the coming years, there would be survival. There would be horror. Horror stacked upon horror, humankind finally teetering too far over the very edge of the abyss. There would be hideous compromise. There would be escape—though, of course, there ended up being no one to save us, no airplanes to lift us to freedom, and there never had been. For a very few, there would even be honour (I hope Menachem, wherever he is, managed to hold on to his ideals; for so many of us that was the first thing to go). But it was only after everything else, only after I heard what happened to the Krasners, what happened to Stephanie, that there would be guilt, terrible, body-slamming guilt. Guilt so stupendous, so unimaginably vast, that it drowns out everything else, becomes indistinguishable from the fear that follows me through all the days of my endangered life.

The Streets of Thornhill

ANOTHER MONTH, another board meeting. And somehow, this one was even more excruciating than usual. David Krasner was his typical pompous self. Cheryl had yet to adjust to her role as president. The building committee infighting was as painful as ever; JNF Jimmy and Bert were nearly screaming at each other over the committee's foolhardy decision to buy that land up there, even though they didn't have the money to build anything on it!

Norman Greenski shakes his head. Even though he has spent the past five years on one executive or another of the Reform synagogue he had been a member of since the kids were born, and where he's now acting chair of finances and membership, he still manages to be surprised by the behaviour he witnesses. Like Kol B'Seder, like everywhere, he supposes. Though aren't Jews supposed to make a unified stand against a hostile, indifferent world? Well, not these Jews.

Nothing to do but walk it off, as usual.

The walk from the synagogue to the small but fully detached house he shares with his second wife, Naomi, her teenage son, and occasionally Norman's two daughters is twenty minutes by the most direct route, but Norman would very rarely—in sleety rain, a blizzard, the growing handful of unbearably humid days Thornhill received each summer—take the most direct route.

Today, a perfectly mild late-May evening, he takes Atkinson all the way around.

"Hullo Norm!" It's Julie. A neighbourhood fixture and one of Norman's walking acquaintances. "What's new in the Jewish world?" Julie always gave off an exuberant, infectious energy. Whenever Norman ran into her she had a smile and a story. Today she's wearing a long skirt and a purple sweater, her hair in a loose bun.

"Oh, the usual array of worldly forces against our small beleaguered band. Any interesting sightings lately?"

Julie exaggerates her face into a mask of extreme concentration. "Hmm...hmm...yes! Of course! Phillipe and I saw a scarlet tanager in the park behind Brickshire. They rarely come this far north." Many years ago, Julie had belonged to Kol B'Seder, but left for the Orthodox shul down the street. Norman had heard that she hadn't lasted long there either, there had been some kind of altercation, nobody was sure exactly what. Most people at Kol B'Seder did not care for Julie, but Norman didn't mind her. You never knew what Julie was going to say; you never knew which Julie you were going to get. It was the perfect analogy for bird watching, a hobby they both had in common.

"A scarlet tanager? Well then. I'll have to keep my eyes open."

"Oh, you'll see her Norman, you've got that special Jewish touch!"

Norman leaves the curve of Atkinson for his own street. He notices that the house beside the elementary school hasn't sold yet. Its For Sale sign has been up for nearly two months. They must be asking too much; I wonder what sharing a fence with the school does to the property value. Thinking about the fence, about real estate, brings Norman back to the board meeting. The building committee was in shambles—it's a good thing he declined joining. JNF Jimmy and Bert only calmed down when Cheryl suggested they hold off on making any decisions for now, continue exploring options, discuss it further at next month's meeting. Bert was right: you'd think by now Jews would be good at getting the full potential out of land. But not these Jews—no, we're going to lose all of our money *and* that land up there. We bought prematurely. Norman was in the minority—along with Bert, and, surprisingly enough, the rabbi—who wanted the shul to stay housed at Isaac Babel Elementary, where it had always been. But others—JNF Jimmy, the Krasners, Cheryl—wanted bigger and better for Kol B'Seder. No more sharing space with a parochial school for them!

Norman's mind runs its tongue along the memory of the rest of that day's meeting. As usual, Bert, Norman's lone friend on the executive, serving his second term as vice president, cracked jokes and softened the mood at any chance he got. It was Harold Berman's first meeting as the new speakers' series coordinator (since Sherman's death officially called the Sherman Teitelbaum Speakers' Series). Harold hadn't said much in his committee report, just mentioned that he had some new things in the grinder, ready to start percolating. Norman wonders how Harold would do. Geri Krasner's were big shoes to fill.

That scarlet tanager though. He'd have to remember to tell Naomi.

⦂ Until Norman's mother had died, the extended family would go to her and Norman's father Chaim's apartment every Friday night for dinner—the very last Friday of her life they were there, eating her breaded chicken and green bean casserole, only a few thousand heartbeats left to her. Now they congregated at Norman's to mark the end of the work week and to bring in the (for them, utterly secular) Sabbath. In attendance tonight was his father, getting on in years, though still with a fierce grip on life. Norman's two daughters, Rebecca and Jen, who mostly lived with Cheryl at her house on the other side of the mall. His stepson, Kal, still dirty from his baseball practice. Norman's sister Karen and her daughter Miriam. The only family member missing—except for

Chaim's first family, murdered at Auschwitz—was Norman's brother, who immigrated to Israel fifteen years before.

They were at the table eating dinner. Chaim was fuming about the latest news from the Middle East. "Where does the UN get off? Why is it that the only democracy in the entire region routinely gets the scorn of the so-called international body?" His raised hands were shaking with a combination of age and emphasis. "I'll tell you why. Nazis! Everywhere you look—Nazis!"

Norman was used to his father talking this way, and usually agreed with him, tonight being no exception. But Norman's niece Miriam, recently returned from a two-month spring placement program in Israel for Jewish undergraduates, apparently did not.

"Saba, it's not so simple," she said. "As long as the occupation continues, how could there ever be hope for peace?"

Chaim's hands fell. "Occupation? What is this occupation? There is no occupation! Grow up, Mirala. Those are disputed territories! They're disputed! If anybody's occupying anybody, it is those so-called Palestinians!"

"How can you even say that, Saba?"

Norman watched this exchange wearily, wisely staying out of it, though he did notice that Jen and Rebecca's forks were literally floating halfway between their plates and their mouths—trouble brewing? Norman couldn't understand it: how could Miriam come back from Israel so full of self-hatred? Every single time Norman returned from Israel—the last visit to his brother two summers ago as much as his first visit in the seventies—he was full of clarity, pride, light, hope, resolve. Norman wasn't a religious person, but in Israel he was unmistakably full of *something*. (On certain visits, there was enough of a tug to leave everything behind, move to Jerusalem, walk the sacred streets and ancient alleyways in robes, that Norman had to be careful he didn't actually do it.) To think, an entire country built by people like him, *for* people like him. Yes, the soldiers with their machine guns can be disconcerting, but they are *his* soldiers, their guns are protecting *him*, their cold iron hearts are cold and iron for him and for his family. Norman looked at his father, whose face was red with anger, his usually perfect English slipping into Yiddishisms. Norman wasn't too worried; Chaim could hold his own—how could Miriam even think of challenging his experiences? Chaim had literally been through hell and survived to tell the tale. But it was best to not get involved. Let it remain between grandfather and granddaughter, survivor and teenager. Man and girl.

Before things got even more heated, however, Naomi asked Kal about some ongoing drama taking place on his Double-A baseball team, pivoting the conversation away from the large and political to the small and familial. Her job as hospital administrator often came in handy at the dinner table. She was Norman's rock in a sea of conflict. Love swelled up in Norman like the first colours of a mist-shrouded spring sunrise.

Later, after dessert, Norman saw Rebecca and Jen talking conspiratorially with Miriam in the kitchen. Jen's eyes landed on her father's before flicking away.

Yes, definitely trouble.

: Norman takes in the early Saturday morning light over the suburban houses before leaving his front lawn. He walks towards Clark in the fresh, fluffy air. On mornings like these, up early enough to catch the coating of his dreams and spread them on the warm newness of the day, he could feel each house as a colour, a fluctuating aura. His own house a faint grey, emanating homeness, comfort, the gravitational centre. His neighbour's house a mustardy yellow, the row of townhouses at the end of his block a xylophone of darkening purples. Each house a colour, and every bird a sensation. Red-winged blackbirds, calming red shocks against liquid blue-black shimmer. A pair of blue jays, playing in the leaves of a crimson king maple, sparking bursts of electricity. The neighbourhood red-tailed hawk a sentinel against a chaotic world always churning just out of vision, out of sense, but always, always there. Norman walks through a group of Orthodox families walking in the opposite direction, on their way to shul, fancy black clothes and strollers, dress shoes clicking on the sidewalk. He smiles and nods, happy to live alongside Jewish people carrying on the oldest Jewish ways. If Norman's life had gone differently, he often thinks, if his waning-and-waxing sense of the world as a place of unfathomable beauty and mystery had any element of the religious to it, he could see himself having become Orthodox. A ready-made formula for communing with the divine. He wouldn't even have had to leave Thornhill! On Rodeo Street, kids run to the park with baseball bats and mitts. Above, a lone goose streaks across the sky. The day is here now, solid, absolute. Norman's extrasensory antennae are almost entirely retracted. He passes the park where, late one fall evening, he saw bats swooping and climbing above the slides and swings, his mind more snug with each plunge of their thread. The spot where he first met Julie, years ago; she was watering the trees along Bathurst out of a battered metal watering can with a crude sunflower painted on it. Norman passes the house on Charles that burned down the winter before last. The owners had yet to rebuild. As always, Norman wonders how much the new house will be worth. Probably a fortune. Next month would mark three years into what he and Naomi called his early retirement, even though in reality he was pushed out of his job working in payroll at Masada Assets Incorporated with a not-so-great severance package. Walking the Thornhill streets—the suburbs opening up to him like an orchestra accelerating from silence to crescendo—remained the only way to calm his mind, to fortify himself against the onslaught raging throughout the civilized world: anarchists, terrorists, social justice warriors, all these young people who only want to destroy the order of things, upset the fraught balance of light and dark. What a time to be alive. Norman looks up. The sky utterly blue, laked with possibility. A mourning dove, centred perfectly on a telephone wire strung across Mountain Park Crescent, coos into the open air.

After being out for two and a half hours, Norman heads for home. Above him, a flock of geese distends the fabric of the sky like a comb through water.

: Another month, another board meeting. A busy agenda. First, updates from the building committee, still stalemated. Then Cheryl reported on a new fundraising initiative being put on by the sisterhood for the annual women's retreat. Geri Krasner, back from a month in Israel, gave a presentation on the struggles of the Women of the Wall movement. Bert asked Geri pointed questions about the movement's successes and failures. "Do you really think the Israeli rabbinate are going to allow women more religious freedom?" he asked finally, to which Geri responded "Well, Bert, I hope so. We are all Jews, after all." When it was Norman's turn, he filled everybody in on the shul's finances, the holding-steady membership numbers, plans for selling more high holiday tickets. His presentation over, Norman was finally able to relax. The last item on the agenda was Harold, who was introducing the new season of the speakers' series.

Harold was in his late forties, with trim hair that seemed always newly cut, and a svelte figure; Norman often saw him running in the early mornings, headphones on, shutting the world out. Obviously not used to speaking at a board meeting, he stood up, his swivel chair rolling into the wall behind him with a soft crash. Handouts were being passed around.

"Well, it was more work than I had anticipated," he said to mild laughter. "I have a whole new appreciation for the excellent work Geri had done for so many years." Polite clapping, a hearty "hear hear" from David. Norman glanced down at the list of dates and names in his hands. "Hopefully everybody'll agree that I've managed to put together a stellar lineup for the fall season. We really tried to represent a wide range of viewpoints and interests, both Jewish and otherwise."

Somebody loudly snickered; all eyes turned. It was JNF Jimmy, looking incredulous. Nearly bald, face sunburned to the point of peeling, Jimmy acquired his nom de guerre—which he wore with pride—from non-stop battering for donations to the Jewish National Fund, for what Bert called an "obsequious love" for Israel. His was a frenetic and almost scary temperament; Norman usually tried to steer clear. Now, Jimmy scanned the room, basking in the sudden attention.

"You invited a *Palestinian?*" he asked, saying the word as if it were barbed.

There was a shuffling, an uncomfortable readjustment. Geri Krasner sighed audibly. Bert, sitting next to Norman, suppressed a surprised laugh, tried to turn it into a cough. Norman looked down closer at the schedule. Sure enough, there it was: "November 19, 2011. Jasbir Khalidi. Palestinian scholar/activist."

The room's attention swivelled to Harold, who was still standing. He seemed flustered but resolved, a tree in defiant bloom.

"Yes, Jimmy, we did. Yes we did yes we did. It is part of my mandate to bring in views we don't necessarily agree with. Jasbir is a well-regarded intellectual and I truly believe Kol B'Seder will be better off for hearing her thoughts."

JNF Jimmy smiled, sickly sweet.

"Looks like a showdown," Bert whispered into Norman's ear.

"Okay, Harold, okay," Jimmy said. "We'll see. We'll see."

With that, Cheryl brought the meeting to a close. Afterwards, milling around the bagels and coffee, Cheryl came up to Norman. "So the girls are off to camp. I hear they had an interesting time at Friday dinner last month," she said.

"It's Miriam. Filling their heads with nonsense."

Cheryl put a hand on Norman's arm, held it with the same tight grip Norman remembered from fifteen years of marriage. Cheryl both had not changed and had changed entirely. "I wouldn't worry about it," she said, pouring half-and-half into her coffee, "what's wrong with hearing a different side of the story?" She winked, walked away.

Norman stood stirring his coffee. He was about ready to be away from people, away from Kol B'Seder, to be on his own, walking the streets. But before he could slip away, Bert was slapping him on the back. "Hey there, buddy. Well, this promises to be a zing-dinger. JNF Jimmy squaring off against Harold. Hoo boy." Red-haired, with a gaggle of five red-haired kids, always ready to laugh or lend a hand, Bert was a beloved presence at Kol B'Seder, and was therefore allowed to get away with positions and beliefs that would have had other members ostracized years ago. A fellow divorcé, he was probably Norman's closest friend at Kol B'Seder; at least, Norman liked him more than he liked most of the other members. "Hey, how many right-wing Zionists does it take to screw in a light bulb?"

"I don't know, Bert, how many?"

Bert twisted his face up into a paroxysm of mock rage. A pretty good impression of JNF Jimmy, actually. "'What light bulb?! Light bulbs don't exist. All light bulbs are terrorists!'"

"Very funny, Bert."

Either Bert didn't know how Norman felt about Israel, or he didn't care; Norman wouldn't be surprised if it was the latter. Bert was supremely comfortable in his beliefs, in his worldview, and he didn't mind getting into arguments about it. Still, for most of his life, people had felt safe telling Norman their feelings, their secrets—in the Masada Inc. cafeteria, on an airplane, on the street, people were always spilling their guts to him. Norman, conversely, was usually tight-lipped, kept everything in, confided in no one, not even Naomi. He often wondered what it was that drew people towards him. Was it the same thing that every few months swelled in him, made the world pulse with hidden truths, before receding into the general background hum again?

He looked out the wall of windows, sipped his coffee. A robin landed under the spruce tree. A chipmunk chittered. The spruce tree remained unfazed.

Norman walks the streets. It just rained. The sidewalks wine-coloured, the air thick with earthy odours. The conditions are ideal for a rainbow.

Julie's standing at the corner of Clark and Charles, looking up into a burly oak tree, where a hornets' nest the size of a papier-mâché balloon hangs like a mutant patio lantern.

"Hello Julie."

"Normal Normie, what's happening?"

"Oh, just enjoying the air. Yourself?"

"Things are great Normie, things are truly great." Julie's eyes are bright. "Have you ever heard of the seventh and a half day?" she asks.

"No," Norman says, half expecting a Bert-style joke.

"Do you really think God just created seven days? Of course not! There's a half day, hidden, but always there. I think I finally know how to access it."

Norman laughs, unsure how to respond. Julie's intensity has him nearly swooning.

"Phillipe says I've been watching too many Kabbalah videos, but he just doesn't have the same sight that I have. That *you* have."

"I don't know what you're talking about, Julie." Norman feels himself becoming irrationally agitated.

Julie looks at him shrewdly, before laughing.

"Yes, yes, Norman. Of course, of course."

They contemplate the hornets' nest together. It reminds Norman of a young pine shrub wrapped in burlap to protect it from the cold, even though it was a hot and humid day in late June.

Eventually, Norman starts to leave.

"Stay Jewish, my Semitic cousin!" Julie calls after him.

Outside of his house, Norman looks across the road. The tree in the backyard of the house across the street was now big enough to be seen over the roof of the house, making it look like the house had a bushy haircut. When they moved into the area the tree must have been as thin as a pencil.

How time moves.

⋮ Norman sat at his desk, staring at Harold's list of upcoming speakers. JNF Jimmy had cornered him after last week's potluck, asked him to sign a petition asking for Harold to be removed from his position for daring to suggest bringing in the Palestinian speaker. "It's just not how we do things at Kol B'Seder," Jimmy said, forcing a pen into Norman's hands. "Did you ever have a problem with Geri? Now there's a woman who understands what Jewish programming is all about! Not like Harold, who, I have to say, is exhibiting all the traits of a classic self-hater. And hey, while I've got you, what say you cut me a cheque for the JNF? When's the last time you donated? C'mon, share some of that retirement wealth Ricky Rosenfeld surely showered you with. Those Jewish forests aren't going to plant themselves!"

It was true that Norman had, for the most part, enjoyed the speakers Geri Krasner had brought in. Thanks to the circles she (and David, her big macher husband) moved in, not only here but in the States and Israel as well, Geri had often managed to bring in some big Jewish names. The esteemed Israeli novelist who lamented the political situation in Israel yet still railed against diasporic Jewish weakness—what was his name again? He'd have to ask Naomi—actually going so far as to say that Jews living in diaspora were not "fully realized Jews." The religious woman from a West Bank settlement, Ruti something or other, who spoke movingly about the constant threats to their lives from their unappeasable Arab neighbours. Not that Geri didn't bring in people from the left, because she did. At least once a year somebody from Women of the Wall came to talk about the ongoing inter-Jewish religious tensions in Jerusalem. There was also the Humanist rabbi who spoke with spit-flying excitement about the revolutionary moment they had decided to remove God from their liturgy. There was the professor from the States, Dr. Kevin Klar, who argued that the world was getting better and better every day, and had plenty of slides and charts and graphs to prove it. During the talk Bert had leaned over to Norman and whispered loudly in his ear, "This is what he calls world history? He's left out everything from Magellan to Mengele!"

In the end, though, Norman had not signed Jimmy's petition, saying instead that he had to think it over. Jimmy did not let him go easily, but eventually he got away and now here Norman was, thinking it over. Why not give the woman a chance? Just because she was Palestinian didn't mean she was a hater of Israel and of Jews, did it? Norman really didn't know. He opened his computer and typed "Jasbir Khalidi" into YouTube, clicked on the first hit. There she was. She was younger than Norman expected, pretty, dressed like Rebecca or Jen would dress. According to the synopsis of the talk, she had a PHD in history and was a professor at Ryerson. The talk was on "The Black Holes of Jewish History and the Palestinian Narrative." Norman pressed play, skipped ten minutes ahead so he didn't have to listen to the long-winded introduction from some department head. "As we've seen," Jasbir said from behind her podium, "Jewish history has had any number of black holes trying to consume it entirely. We live in a time when not one, but two black holes exist. The Holocaust and Israel are these two black holes, bending Jewish space-time into their gaping mouths. The question is: which will win? And which will be better for the Palestinians, whose plight depends on the unethical, unhistorical use of the latter and the existence of the former?"

Norman paused the video. What was she saying? Israel shouldn't have been created? It *was* true, that some people he knew were obsessed with the Holocaust. At a mid-town conservative shul for a cousin's kid's bar mitzvah, every third word out of the rabbi's mouth was Holocaust. JNF Jimmy, for one, constantly referred to it in his fundraising attempts. Even Chaim, a survivor, for damn's sake, had managed to somewhat move on from the defining catastrophe of his life, though he mostly filled it with a love for Israel, Norman had to admit.

Jasbir Khalidi was giving Norman a headache. He wasn't sure who to blame for this latest crisis—Jimmy, or Harold?—but all Norman wanted was to do what was right for Kol B'Seder, for his own corner of the Jewish world. And didn't that mean signing Jimmy's petition, regardless of how insufferable he was?

Maybe he should leave Kol B'Seder entirely. But where would he go? He could go to Israel, live with his brother, be there at the gushing centre of Jewish geography. But he knew he would never go; he'd never leave Thornhill, never abandon the synagogue he had given so many years to. Though he rarely would admit it, he loved Kol B'Seder. The potlucks, the people, the commitment to community, the warm capaciousness when it came to religious belief and religious practice. If only all the JNF Jimmys and Harolds would realize that the entire world would be happier if we didn't exist, and stopped this infighting.

If only Norman had never heard the name Jasbir Khalidi.

: Norman leaves the house. The day is mere minutes old. He walks along Clark, the air warm but not stifling. He is more cognizant than ever of the different eras and kinds of fences that separate the street from the cascading backyards he is walking past. Some, but not all, of the backyards have doors in their section of fence. A door with a new padlock. A door with an old, rusted lock. A fence of beige wood. A fence of brick. A fence with a turquoise door. Another fence of brick. Norman crosses Clark, onto Charles. Just like that, the sidewalks end. The modest family homes become obscene mansions with circular drives, gates, gabled four-car garages, turrets, more windows than the airplanes floating above on invisible strings. Rocky ravines draining parallel to the roads. Robins pecking and hopping on the roadside. A field of close-shaved grass. The original bungalows, built in the forties and fifties when this was all farmland, still holding on, delaying the fortune that would be their owners' once they sell. Squirrels jumping from tree to tree. Norman crosses through the parking lot of the church, ends up on Centre. The massive mansion going up behind the pond is almost finished. From Centre, back into the neighbourhood. A copse of red pines that was shoulder-high when he moved into the neighbourhood, now towering, surely to outlive the residents it rooted under and crowned above. The undeniable sensation that all these mornings are adding up to something new, something momentous.

Naomi accompanied Norman on a Friday afternoon walk. They were making plans for their annual fall trip to Pelee Island for the bird migrations. "That's Julie's watering can," Norman said as they walked along Clark. It was sitting under a tree, its painted sunflower unmistakable. Later, a pair of Cardinals swooping from tree to tree on Bathurst had Norman remembering the scarlet tanager Julie had seen. Was it still out there, somewhere, waiting to be found?

Back at the house, he helped Naomi get dinner ready. Only Chaim was coming tonight; all the kids except Kal were at summer camp. Karen and her husband were on a river cruise in Europe. Norman was cutting peppers for a salad, Naomi was stirring her chicken soup. They had met at a birding event in High Park, almost six years after he and Cheryl divorced. Two great horned owls had been seen roosting behind the dog park, and various bird groups from throughout the GTA were on the prowl. They very quickly hit it off. Naomi was a serious, no-nonsense kind of woman. Bert often called Naomi "humourless," but that was exactly what drew Norman to her: her focus, her lack of a need to constantly know what Norman was thinking. Combined with Norman's quiet outward-facing personality, his hectic inner life, they were perfectly matched.

"Did you read the last letter from the girls?" Naomi asked, adding salt to the soup. "Cheryl forwarded it to me."

"Yeah. They seem to be having a great summer."

Norman thought about telling Naomi about Jasbir, the chaos on the exec. He'll tell her later, he decided, when he had more of a handle on it himself.

That night, after driving Chaim home, Norman went right to bed. He dreamed he was paddling a canoe through his flooded neighbourhood. At first, the water was maybe a foot off the ground, just enough to use his paddle to pole the boat along. But soon the water was high enough that his paddle didn't scrape sidewalk or lawn, the streets lost to the gently undulating lake that had taken over the suburbs. There was nobody else around; there was nobody else in the entire world. Norman was exceptionally calm. He paddled along Clark, cut through the pathway to Bevshire, having to duck as he glided under the linden trees. Maple keys swirled in the air, landing in the soft water, which now lapped the tops of the street signs. Still Norman paddled along. Now the houses were indistinguishable roofs. Now the houses were gone, only the tops of the tallest trees remaining, but then they, too, were gone. Now, as far as Norman could see, water. He was safe in his little boat. The sky was a ceiling of low silver light. There were no longer any fences.

Norman walks home from Saturday services. He had woken up with the sun, spent an hour looking at used canoes on the internet. He hadn't been in a canoe in twenty years, but the dream had had a powerful impact on him; its strangeness stuck to him like paint. On his way back from the washroom during the rabbi's sermon, he had overheard some of the bar and bat mitzvah kids talking about the Jewish forefathers. He stopped to listen.

"They lived for hundreds of years, they obviously had super-powers!" one of them exclaimed.

"No way!"

"Way. They were even able to see the future."

"Oh yeah? Did they see the Holocaust?"

"Oh, definitely."

Norman coughed loudly, walked through the youngsters.

Is this how the kids talk these days? They sound like Julie.

Crossing through the park, there she is. Julie. Sitting on a bench, watching the swallows zip and dive. Norman sits down beside her. Julie doesn't seem to notice.

"I saw you abandoned your watering can?"

Julie twitches her head, turns to Norman, beams. "I left it there as a signal."

"Oh. Okay."

"Oh Normathan, do you feel the change coming? Something's in the air. Something is coming. Something to open us. For now, for now I'm still contained, but I feel myself opening. Why should I stay contained?! Who says that's the way we should be?"

Norman, while not entirely sure what Julie was talking about, finds himself agreeing with her. A change *was* coming; Norman couldn't help feeling he would be implicated in it in some way (though at the same time he knew that if he mentioned anything about this to Naomi, she would talk him out of it—which was why he knew he wasn't going to mention anything).

But what was it?

How would he know?

A hawk swoops in from far above. The swallows scatter, their wings alternating almost too fast for the naked eye. But Norman sees.

⁞ An emergency board meeting was called on Tuesday to discuss Harold and the Palestinian speaker. Norman walked over to the shul with Kal, who was going to play basketball at the nets outside of Isaac Babel.

"Looks like Jimmy got enough signatures on his petition," Bert said to Norman in the front hall of the shul. "You didn't sign it, did you?"

Norman shook his head. The two men walked towards the boardroom together.

"Hey," Bert said, "how many liberal Zionists does it take to screw in a light bulb?"

"I don't know Bert, how many?"

"Two. One to loudly proclaim 'two light bulbs for two people!' while behind him the other smashes the Palestinian light bulb with a hammer."

"That's a little harsh."

"Welcome to Jew-o-politics, my friend."

They were in the boardroom now. The air was tense. It was the most crowded Norman had ever seen it for a board meeting; he and Bert got the last two chairs. Norman's had a broken wheel. A bad sign. People were standing around the table, chatting quietly. Norman spotted his father, standing near the coffee machine. Chaim hadn't come to a board meeting in years. A milling nervousness lay heavy in the room.

When Cheryl sat down, looking both concerned and at ease, quiet descended on the room. JNF Jimmy was sitting to Cheryl's left, looking like a general one murder away from completing a coup. Harold was on Cheryl's right, his face set in sour concentration.

Bert leaned in. "Looks like Harold's a head coach and the team is down twenty points but unbeknownst to anybody he's just put in his ringer."

Cheryl started to speak. "As you all know, we are here because of some issues about the speakers' series, issues or disagreements. Or feelings. Anyways, issues. I have here a petition," she said, looking at the stapled pages with obvious disdain, making Norman happy that he hadn't signed it, "asking for Harold's immediate ouster as head of the Sherman Teitelbaum Speakers' Series."

"Hear hear!"

"Shame!"

"Not soon enough!"

Cheryl took a breath. "I want to let both Harold and Jimmy have a turn to speak, then we can open it up for discussion. After that, we'll vote. And remember," she said, looking around at all the extra faces, "only members of the exec can vote."

Everybody around the table and standing behind it signalled their assent, either by nodding or doing nothing. Cheryl nodded towards Harold. He took a breath.

"I don't see what the big deal is," he said. "Jasbir is not only a professor of political science, but she is a Torontonian as well. She has worked tirelessly her entire life for social justice, for what we would call tikkun olam."

Bert leaned in to Norman: "I've never worked tirelessly for anything. Must be exhausting."

Harold continued: "Isn't it in our Reform movement's very DNA to reach towards justice? Shouldn't we hear what somebody with inside knowledge of the occupation and the, the situation in Israel, has to say?" A few people clapped, others nodded in agreement. Norman still couldn't tell where the room would fall.

"Thanks, Harold. Okay, Jimmy. And keep it to the point," Cheryl warned.

Jimmy took a folder of paper out of his satchel. He looked around the room, smiled. "Now, as you know, I have nothing but love and respect for the Palestinians. Twenty percent of Israel's citizenry is of Arab persuasion, after all. But we have to think of the security of our one Jewish state. There's only one. We won't get another. Which is why the more money we raise, the safer that one state will be, the safer we'll all be. There are enemies out there who want to destroy us, and not only out there—but right here, in our very midst!" Jimmy was heating up, his voice rising. "It's really a simple equation. The more Jewish trees we plant, the safer the Jewish *people* are, worldwide! We need forest armies, huge battalions of pines and eucalyptus to defend us against antisemitism! Any little amount helps!"

"Jimmy!"

"Sorry Cheryl." Jimmy sat back. Relaxed. Came forward again. "Now, through my fundraising work, as many of you know, I have plenty of contacts in the Israeli government, in the defense forces, in the Mossad." Jimmy lifted up his folder, shook it for emphasis. "I asked around on this Jasbir Khalidi person, and I received some very disturbing intel." He was talking barely above a whisper now. The entire room was leaning in. "Very disturbing indeed. I myself didn't want it to be true, but, my friends, I have the irrefutable evidence right here."

Jimmy sat back again. He patted the documents. He smiled. He took a breath. "Jasbir Khalidi is a...*terrorist.*"

Terrorist. The three syllables had their desired effect; it was as if a slow bomb had gone off in the middle of the boardroom There's only one other word in the entire Jewish lexicon that could create such an immediate, damning reaction, and "terrorist" was like the hull of a missile protecting the explosive ordnance of that sometimes-hyphenated word. Norman could barely breathe the room was so stiff, so stalled. Jimmy looked like he had just had an orgasm. David Krasner looked constipated. Even Cheryl looked shaken. Norman glanced at Bert, who raised his eyebrows at Norman, a gesture Norman understood perfectly well: Harold was a goner. For an eternal moment, nobody spoke.

"Well," Harold said, breaking the silence, his mouth strained, "she's here."

The tension in the room broke in spectacular fashion. Jimmy's face volcanoed with rage. "You brought her *here*?!"

Harold shrugged. "I figured if the board actually met her, they'd see for themselves how important it is that we let her talk to the congregation."

For a moment nobody spoke. Jimmy breathed nasally. Norman watched the two men to see who would make the next move.

"Boo."

Thirty heads in thirty swivel chairs turned as one. There she was. Jasbir. Norman felt the room drop an entire octave. She looked much like she did in the video Norman watched, except she had a young girl by the hand, an infant in her other arm, and a teenager just visible sulking in the doorway through which Jasbir had entered the boardroom and had been listening for who knows how long.

She walked into the room as if it was a half-empty movie theatre and she was casually deciding where to sit. Still nobody had spoken. Even Jimmy was momentarily cowed. Norman wondered if his dad would have a heart attack. Jasbir was wearing green cargo pants and a white blouse, had an intelligent face, shiny black hair.

Harold spoke first. "Thanks for coming, Jasbir."

Cheryl stood up, and Jasbir sat down in the vacated seat.

"Thanks for inviting me, Harold. I understand there's some questions for me before I am given permission to speak to your congregation next fall."

"Well, yes, that's correct," Cheryl said, having somewhat recovered from the shock of Harold's Hail Mary pass. "Who has some questions for, for our guest?"

"What are your children's names?" Magda, who organized the youth services during the high holidays, asked kindly.

"This is Youssef," Jasbir said, lifting the baby swaddled in white cloth. "The young lady behind me is Claire, and the haunting presence in the doorway is Tanis. Go and play outside if you want, Tanis, we won't be long." Tanis gave her mother a dirty look, and left the boardroom.

"Great to meet you, Jasbir," Bert said, "sorry for the mess, you caught us at a bad time." Bert was obviously relishing this. "Since you're here, can you help us settle something? Do you think we should pour all of our remaining funds—and plenty of imaginary funds!—into a new building miles north of here, or just stay in this perfectly reasonable space?"

"Bert!" Geri admonished. Jasbir laughed.

"I couldn't possibly say. This *is* a very nice space, though."

There was another pause. Norman glanced at JNF Jimmy: his head was down, his eyes focused on the table. His face had lost its agitated glow, replaced by its customary sunburn.

"I have a question." David Krasner. Here we go, thought Norman. "Do you believe in a two-state solution?"

"If there was such a thing, maybe I would believe in it. What I believe in above all is the right for all the people who live in historic Palestine to self-determination. I believe that as long as Zionism is entrenched in the government, institutions, and military apparatus of the Israeli state that this right cannot possibly be achieved. I believe that the refugees of '48, the occupied of '67, have a right to return, or be compensated. I believe my children and I should be able to visit our ancestral homeland, to live there if we so desire."

Krasner's face was unreadable. "Thanks," he mumbled.

Chaim was pushing his way through the crowded room. "Excuse me, excuse me, enough of this nonsense," he muttered, leaving through the side door. Norman looked around. Like himself, probably nobody at this table—except maybe Bert—had ever spoken to a Palestinian before. They didn't know what to do with someone speaking so calmly, somebody that represented their darkest fears manifesting as a normal, everyday person.

"Do you have any questions for us?" Cheryl asked.

"I was wondering what kind of childcare services you provide?" Jasbir asked. The room shifted awkwardly.

Magda smiled. "I'm sure something can be arranged," she said.

Was that it? Norman wondered, glancing at Bert, who raised an eyebrow.

"I have some questions," JNF Jimmy said loudly. He had sufficiently regrouped. He put both hands on the table, looked hard at Jasbir. "You say you believe in rights, yet you obviously don't believe that the one Jewish state has a right to exist. How can you call yourself an activist yet clearly hate the Jewish people so much? Do you know what would happen to them, to *us*, if we didn't have a state?"

"I don't hate the Jewish people at all. It's you who conflate a violent ethnocratic state with an entire religious and cultural people that live the entire world over in a multitude of diverse and dynamic ways."

"Oh yeah? Name four Jewish people you love!"

"Moses. Maimonides. Buber. Kohn. Arendt. The Boyarins. Kafka. This building's namesake. Charles Reznikoff, Philip Roth, Grace Paley. Sarah Silverman."

Jimmy's face was getting redder and redder with each name Jasbir listed. Even the pate of his head had taken on a purple sheen. Norman wondered if Jimmy knew half the people Jasbir had mentioned.

Did Norman?

Jimmy was not taking this well. In fact, he was screaming, his anger monumental, buttery, unfocused. "You're an antisemite! Where do you expect the Jews to go? To drown in the sea?" He turned to the board members, all the visitors. "I have the documents right here! This woman might have a silver tongue, but I have proof. I have fucking *proof*! Who are you going to believe?! Who?!" Having thoroughly exhausted himself, he slumped back in his chair.

Jasbir responded to Jimmy's tirade as if he was an impartial moderator and the question he asked was done so in good faith. "Do I believe the Jews should drown in the sea? Absolutely not. Some things cannot be put away. The state of Israel should never have been created, its crimes should never have been committed. But it was, and they were." Jasbir shifted Youssef to her other arm. "The task before us now, as I see it, is to find a way that everybody can live as equals in a free land, and to find ways where militarized domination of another people is a thing of the past."

The room had taken all it could bear; Norman was impressed the decorum had held on as long as it had. But end it did. Everybody was talking, shouting, gesticulating. Cheryl yelled over everybody that emotions were too high for a vote, we'll have to settle this at our regular meeting next week. Jimmy huffed out, taking his folders with him. Everybody soon followed.

Outside, people were milling around, heading towards their cars. Norman hoped to make a quick escape. There was Kal, playing handball with Jasbir's older daughter against the side of the school. They were talking and laughing. The young Palestinian was very athletic. What were they talking about?

"Are you coming Kal?" he called over.

"Nah, I'm going to stay here for a while. See you at dinner!" Bert and Jasbir came out of the shul, chatting amicably about Tanis's chances of getting into a good university on a squash scholarship. Norman nodded at his stepson and started towards the sidewalk. He had to find his father.

On the walk towards Chaim's apartment he heard robins in the trees, saw a quarrel of sparrows lifting like a blanket from lawn to lawn, felt the neighbourhood hawk, somewhere up above, watching, surveying the streets of Thornhill.

⋮ The streets reveal their secrets, their patterns, but only if you give them time, give them attention. Norman's walking, his mind full to bursting. This situation in the exec, it was worse than anything that's happened since he signed on. What was he supposed to do? Maybe it *is* better for the members of Kol B'Seder to be exposed to somebody like Jasbir. Were there things about Israel that most people just weren't able to see? Then again, he couldn't get JNF Jimmy saying the word *terrorist* out of his head, it stuck to Jasbir like tree sap, poisoned every thought Norman had about her.

Suddenly Julie's beside him. Norman realizes he hadn't seen her since the day of the watering can. She's glowing. Her eyes are on fire; Norman could fall into them. His heart rate picks up.

"Didn't I tell you great things are coming, Norman?" she asks, the question ringing like birdsong. They're walking together along the street in perfect lockstep. Julie's giving off the most intense energy Norman's ever felt. It's like her very essence is enveloping Norman in a warm hug. He's entranced. "Well, they have come. Oh yes, great things. I am the one we've been waiting for, Normie. My whole life finally makes sense. I finally understand. I'm here to lead us all to salvation, to freedom, to golden justice! Since I was a child, I knew I had a higher calling. All of the pieces fit together now. The seasons, the trees, the hornets' nest, the scarlet tanager, you—oh you, sweet, simple Norm! Don't you see?" Her voice is like honey, oozing into Norman's ears. Everything he is is her voice. "We are not waiting for Jerusalem. Jerusalem isn't a place. Don't listen to those warmongers. Listen to me! I am not here to monger war, I am here to monger peace! I will multiply the fishes, I will enter through the east gate, I will sing hallelujah and the seasons will rejoice. Jerusalem isn't a place. Jerusalem is here. Jerusalem is *inside* me. *I* am Jerusalem!"

Without noticing, they've walked right to Norman's driveway. Norman doesn't know what to say. He's bereft of words. He nods, nods again, and goes into his house. Julie waves joyfully and pertly walks on.

⦂ A month after his forced retirement, Norman had found a dead bat in a flowerpot in the backyard. The tiny body, the perfect folded wings, the eyes shut tight in concentration; it had shaken him badly. The little guy had a white substance all over his face, as if he was eating powdered donuts. Norman had gone inside and looked up bats on YouTube, learned about their upcoming demise, the shocking number of deaths, humans' responsibility for the spread of the disease. He was in a funk for fifteen days.

It was the closest thing to how he felt now. The funniest part was that he found himself inclined to believe Julie. Julie as the messiah, come to earth to lead the Jewish people to the next stage of the universe. Not the strangest thing that had happened this week. He could see himself believing her. Why not?

Naomi came home from the mall, two grocery bags in each hand. "I ran into Cheryl," she said as she put the groceries away, "she told me what happened at the board meeting."

At first Norman didn't know what she was talking about. The incident with Julie had erased everything else from his mind.

"I saw Julie just now. She basically told me she was the Jewish messiah."

Naomi sat down beside him. At first she didn't respond. "We should call Phillipe. We should do something, make sure she's okay. It sounds like she's having a psychotic episode."

Norman nodded, knowing she was right. Knowing how badly he wanted to believe, nonetheless.

That night, he called his brother Saul. They hadn't spoken in a few months.

"Norm! When are you coming out here again?! It's been too long!"

"I don't know, I have my plate full with the exec and everything over here."

"Yeah, yeah. You wouldn't believe this country, Norm. We *bend* over backwards to treat these Arabs with more respect than they deserve, and what do the so-called peace-loving Jews who live here say? Not enough! Well, it's never enough!"

"Uh-huh." Norman could feel his brother's smugness, it was sizzling out of the phone like fryer grease.

"I'm telling you, Netanyahu really has to up his game. This country is going down the shitter. You American Jews, you think you understand what's going on here. Let me tell you, you have *no* idea."

"Uh-huh." Not only was Norman Canadian, *so was Saul.*

"Anyways, how are things in Canada? The prime minister still a raging antisemite?!"

"I'm not sure, Saul. I highly doubt it."

"What are you doing out there, anyways, with those maple syrup drinkers? Bring Dad out here, to the holy land! We need you and your accounting skills. Ha! Do we ever!"

"I'll think about it." Calling Saul was a bad idea.

"Alrighty, Norman. Next year in Jerusalem!" Saul laughed.

"Next year," Norman said, hanging up.

Whatever he felt now, it wasn't any better.

⁞ That night Norman was awash in strange dreams. He was sitting at the boardroom table in the middle of a forest. At the table were Naomi, Julie, Jasbir, Cheryl, their daughters, Jasbir's daughters, Chaim, Chaim's murdered family. Huge trees towered over them. They were discussing if Norman should move to Israel or not. Norman could barely pay attention to the back-and-forth debate, massive birds were flying all around them, weaving around the ancient trunks. "I'll follow Julie wherever she tells me to go," he said. That's when Jasbir pulled out the gun, pointed it at Chaim. Norman's sweet, innocent father. Everybody started chanting: "Terrorist, terrorist, terrorist." Jasbir laughed maniacally.

He woke up in a sweat. Got up quietly, put on his pants and a sweatshirt, went out into the streets. It was well before sunrise. His mind was saturated. He had an unbearable desire to run into Julie. Should he call Phillipe and make sure she was okay?

Turning the corner, there was a flash of red, and then, he saw it. The scarlet tanager. It was hovering in some cedar bushes. It was more impressive than he could have hoped. The red of its body ancient, pure, untouched. A bright strong little body packed with impossible life. He stood watching it. The sun rose all around him, over him, in him.

Back at home, he sat at the kitchen table, waiting for Naomi to come down. The coffee was on. He stared at the phone.

⦂ The day of the board meeting arrived. The day of the vote. Norman walked the long way to Isaac Babel. Was it only yesterday morning that he had seen Julie, right here? She was chatting with Harold, who was in full jogging apparel, running in place, one earbud resting on his shoulder like a piece of cooked spaghetti threaded through a chickpea. They were talking about the new traffic lights that were being installed beside the mall when Norman approached. "The neighbourhood is just too busy for stop signs now," Harold was saying. "Hullo Norman!" Julie said when she saw him. She looked like her regular self; at least, her skin wasn't radiating, her eyes weren't endless, her soul wasn't forty sizes too big for her body. From what he understood, Julie had been back from the hospital for a few days. Norman had called Phillipe, who, of course, knew about Julie. "She gets like this from time to time," he had said. So Julie's not the messiah, Norman had thought, hanging up the phone. She's not the messiah. No.

But she is Julie.

"Hi Norm, how's the retired life treating you?" Harold asked. He was probably trying to deduce if Norman was going to vote for his ouster or not.

"You know, pretty good. More time to walk the streets, watch for birds."

"What a wonderful day for it!" Julie said.

"I was actually hoping to run into you," Norman said to Julie, reaching into his briefcase. "I got you something."

"For me? How sweet!"

Norman pulled the painting out. It was on a 12×12 canvas, a lifelike rendition of a scarlet tanager, the colours vibrant and popping. He had commissioned Bert's niece's girlfriend to paint it.

Julie took the painting, held it out in front of her. Didn't say anything. Norman wondered if perhaps this was a bad idea.

"Oh Normal, I love it!" She took Norman into a big bear hug.

Waiting to cross the lights at Bathurst, Norman wondered what it meant that he—for a moment, at least—believed Julie was the messiah. Did he really want the world to end that badly? He didn't think so. What did he want? To do the right thing. To do right by his family. To do right for his people.

Inside the shul, Norman ran into Bert outside the men's room. Bert hadn't shaved in a few days. The orange stubble suited him.

"What do you think's going to happen today?" Bert asked, as if they were talking about a tennis match. .

"I really don't know."

"Are we going to prove as insular and closed-off as ever? Or are we going to surprise even an old cynic like me?"

Norman shook his head. "I truly don't know, Bert."

Bert nodded, thought of something, lit up. "Hey, hey, how many radical anti-Zionist Jews does it take to screw in a light bulb?"

"I don't know, Bert, how many?"

"Nobody knows, they've never been given a chance!"

"That's great, Bert."

The mood in the boardroom was much mellower compared to last week. Whatever happened today, at least a decision was being made. JNF Jimmy was flitting around the room, whispering to everybody, shaking hands. He was wearing a white shirt with a big pine tree on it, some Hebrew writing. Cheryl had—rightly,

Norman thought—declared today's meeting closed; only the executive were present. Norman felt tremendous pride for his ex-wife.

The meeting started a few minutes late. There were other things on the agenda—the possibility of new textbooks for the confirmation classes, the first round of negotiations with the rabbi on his contract renewal, supposedly important news regarding the building fund—but, thankfully, the vote was first. After all that, it would happen quickly; a yea to remove Harold, a nay to keep him on. David and Geri Krasner, Jimmy, and Cheryl—Norman only feeling the slightest pinch of surprise—voted for Harold's removal. Cheryl had to keep Jimmy from making a big speech when it was his turn to vote. Harold, Bert, Sheri, and Magda voted for him to stay. As it happened, Norman was the last vote. All eyes were on him. He was the tiebreaker; the decision was his. He looked at everybody in turn, his eyes landing on the windows. The sky outside was a gentle blue. Who knew what life was out there, behind the screen of the seen? He thought of Jasbir, of his brother, of his daughters. Mostly, he thought of Julie. Julie and her watering can, her burning eyes. If she had been born in a different time, a different place, who knows how many she would have led. The room grew impatient.

Any moment now, he was going to decide.

Rubble Children

IF IT WASN'T FOR BETSY BROWNSTONE, I doubt any of us would have become obsessed with the Holocaust. While other thirteen-year-old girls were into boys and fashion and vampires, Betsy was reading thick terrifying histories, making charts of the numbers of dead per camp, drawing pictures of synagogues aflame, the doors barricaded shut, disembodied mouths laughing mirthfully. Yes, our obsession would soon parallel hers, but she was the one who showed us the way. Without Betsy Brownstone, I can say with confidence, the Toronto Chapter of Rubble Children, our girls-only Holocaust study group—which also happened to be the first and only chapter of Rubble Children—would never have come into existence.

A fat, stringy-haired thirteen-year-old, Betsy was bossy and brilliant, stubborn and loud. She recruited us one by one into the group, quickly proved her mettle, her deep devotion to all things Holocaust, her right to be our de facto leader. It was Betsy who discovered Claude Lanzmann's *Shoah*. It was Betsy who had us read Ruth Kluger's *Still Alive*, with its opening sentence that we repeated to each other for weeks: "Their secret was death, not sex." It was Betsy who had us memorize the name of each and every death camp, their personnel, their killing methods. It was Betsy who came up with our motto, which we chanted at the beginning and end of every meeting. "It happened once. It can happen again." Betsy's intensity drew us all to her, and her brilliance and magnetism didn't let us go; we were in love with her, we respected and feared her, we wanted to impress her, wanted her to like us, to see that we, too, were passionate about the Holocaust. Not only had she read more than any of us, memorized the most statistics and dates and gruesome deaths, but she was the most willing to force the Holocaust into every aspect of her life. While other girls were preparing for their bat mitzvah parties with dreams of centrepieces of summer flowers, embossed dance floors, and hot DJs, Betsy was envisioning something a little different. She wanted her bat mitzvah to be Holocaust themed: each table named after a different notorious Nazi commander, the centrepieces models of famous Third Reich buildings, the dancers wearing striped pajamas. POW rations for dinner. She would enter the ballroom to a military march.

Naturally, this vision did not sit well with her parents. "Isn't this what's important?" Betsy would rail at the family fights that had become a nightly occurrence. "The purposeful extermination of an entire people? *Our* people?!"

Her father flatly refused to accommodate Betsy, so Betsy— "what choice did I have?" she'd say whenever she told us the story—launched a hunger strike and a letter-writing campaign against him. She wrote seven and a half letters, rife with the facts of Nazi malice, drank nothing but water and ate nothing but plain toast for three days. Even under such pressure, her father wouldn't relent, and Betsy, in a rare moment of compromise, decided to drop her suit.

Betsy didn't win that battle with her father, but to us the outcome was clear: she was a force to be reckoned with. She lived her ideals. We held her even higher in our group mythos. We were the rubble children, and she was our rubble child.

Since the core members of Rubble Children—myself, Betsy, Amanda Stein, Sam Bornstein, and Hadas Grossman—met at Kol B'Seder, the Reform synagogue our families were members of, in the early days we'd meet a half hour before Thursday night Hebrew classes in the shul's boardroom. However, once the synagogue found out what was going on in our little meetings, they insisted on sending somebody to supervise us, which is funny when you think about it: wasn't Kol B'Seder partly the reason for our obsession? The Holocaust was an integral part of the curriculum at every grade. Betsy, who went to a Jewish day school before transferring to Brickshire for grade six, had been inundated with it on a near daily basis.

The administration got Stefan Lemieux, a retired French teacher who often volunteered at Kol B'Seder, to supervise us. Poor Stefan; he had no idea what he was in for. Quickly discovering what went on at our weekly study sessions, he told us that he was not happy that such "sweet young ladies" were spending their time talking about mobile murder vans and unmarked mass graves, and tried to interest us in *The Little Prince* instead. Betsy, in response, made him cry by narrating to him the day in the life of a Treblinka death-camp guard. Stefan told Kol B'Seder that he couldn't continue watching us, and our permission to use the boardroom before Hebrew school was revoked. What did we care? If anything, we felt empowered. *Our* Holocaust education had gone beyond the bounds of institutional sanction. We were now in uncharted waters.

We started meeting every Sunday afternoon at Amanda's house instead. In Amanda's basement, we were unsupervised, unfettered, free to dig as deeply into the pit as we pleased. It happened once. It can happen again.

From those humble beginnings, Rubble Children grew.

⋮ Those Sundays at Amanda Stein's house. They were easily the focal point of our week, where we could discuss what we'd read, share every horrifying and unbelievable fact, lather up our anger and our communal disdain for those responsible, cleanse ourselves in sweet rage at the impossibility of ever truly seeking justice. We'd sit on brown leather sofas, yellow plastic bowls of party mix and paper cups of soft drinks on the coffee table, light coming in from the high basement windows. In the winter there'd be a draft from the never-used fireplace. Amanda's dad would make us nachos with black beans and green salsa; I can still smell the hot cheese. He didn't know the real focus of the club, thought we were organizing a fundraiser for Israeli children living in poverty, and, besides the food and drink, left us alone.

But we weren't organizing a fundraiser. Mostly, we were scaring ourselves shitless. Don't misunderstand these no-nonsense reminiscences, don't think of us as just heartless macabre young women: we were deeply, terrifically afraid. The more fear we felt, the further we needed to go, the more we needed to worry this historical event that in its complexity and its unknowability was ultimately unworriable. We'd practise standing in the basement bathroom's small dark closet without making a sound. We'd scream at each other trying to get us to break, name names, divulge. We'd play Sophie's Choice. We were constantly updating and improving our go-bags. We talked about if we had an hour to vacate our homes, what would we bring, what would we leave behind? The heart and soul of Rubble Children, though, remained the horrendous historical accounts, the details, the paradoxes and debates. We'd argue about the functionalist versus intentionalist interpretation of the Final Solution. We'd devote two weeks to the Nuremberg Trials, to postwar Germany. We'd assemble rigorous reading lists. We'd tell jokes; well, mostly Sam Bornstein told jokes. "In postwar Germany, what do they call a Nazi judge who helped craft the race laws?" she'd ask, her face solemn, like she was telling a ghost story. "I don't know Sam, what do they call a Nazi judge who helped craft the race laws in postwar Germany?" Sam would smile, look us each in the eyes one at a time, before delivering her punchline: "*Your Honour.*" We watched the ninth episode of *Band of Brothers* at least once a month (Betsy supplying the VHS, taped over an episode of *The Young and the Restless*). The six American soldiers on patrol in the woods, the war basically over, when one of the soldiers—a new recruit, not fitting in, desperate to see action—stumbles onto a concentration camp. The truth of what the Nazis had been doing behind their lines dawning on them. We'd sit on Amanda's brown leather couches, amazed and angry, the soundtrack of swelling strings cranked loud enough to drown in. Destroyed bodies hanging off of fences, the imprisoned in their hovel barracks, pits of the dead. The inmate trying to get the soldiers to understand: "Juden. Juden. Juden." The soldiers' disbelief, their shock, their disgust, their anger: it moved us to tears every time. Juden. Juden. Juden.

When Betsy discovered, in a seven-hundred-page book called *The Seventh Million*, that in the fifties an elite team of Mossad agents had planned on infiltrating Germany and poisoning the public water supply, we talked of nothing else for weeks, luxuriated in the possibility of revenge, however lopsided. We wrote a play about the operation, acted it out in Amanda's bedroom. Betsy and Amanda were the Mossad agents, talking in ridiculous Israeli accents. Sam was an ex-Nazi, making us almost pee our pants with her satire. She got a big death scene after brushing her teeth and giving a final Nazi salute. I got to play an innocent German housewife, dying dramatically after drinking a beer stein of the contaminated water.

Like I said, we were different from other girls.

⠿ I remember one meeting in particular. It was before we started going to Amanda's house, before Stefan started observing us; we were in Kol B'Seder's boardroom, sitting around the large shiny table in fancy wheely chairs, the chairs' backs looming over us. We were still deciding on the name of our study group. Betsy was unhappy with Holocaust Girls' Reading Club, the original name.

"To start with, *Holocaust* really isn't the appropriate term," she said. She was sitting at the head of the table. The sunlight from the big windows was making her glow, golden and solid.

"Why not?" Hadas asked. Hadas had recently moved to Thornhill from Tel Aviv, still had a Hebrew accent, though by the end of the year it would be gone. Hadas often told us stories of the elderly people in Tel Aviv who talked to themselves, had numbers on their arms, and how her parents told her to just ignore them.

"Holocaust translates to 'burnt offering to God.' What is that saying about the millions of murdered?"

"Is *Shoah* better?" Hadas asked.

Betsy sighed. "Really, the only morally rigorous term is *The Jewish Genocide of the Second World War*."

"So you want us to be called The Jewish Genocide of the Second World War Girls' Reading Club?!" Amanda asked, rolling her eyes. Amanda was the most naturally bitchy of all of us, and was our front-line soldier whenever we had to face the outside world.

Betsy shrugged. "It's the right term."

So far, at these meetings, I had not said much. I was happy just to be there, to have somewhere to vent my teenage obsession with death and cruelty. Also, if I'm being totally honest, I was quiet because I was unsure of my place in the group: all of the girls, as far as I knew, had family who died in the Holocaust, had a material link to the inferno. Whereas everybody I was related to was safely in Canada by the time the Nazis came to power. Did I have the same right to the Holocaust as they did? Our Hebrew school teachers claimed I did, though I wasn't sure. I was terrified of being outed as a fake, an imposter. A usurper. But now, an idea struck me, from one of the books I had recently taken out of the library and was planning on recommending we read for next week, and I nearly surged out of my chair. "What about if we call ourselves the rubble children?"

"What does that mean?"

"It's what Germans call the generation of babies born in Germany in spring '45," Betsy said. I was once again amazed at Betsy; I thought I finally knew something she didn't. She really *did* know everything.

"Yeah, but it, like, represents how we are all children of the rubble," I said. My armpits were soaked, speaking up like this, speaking directly to Betsy like this.

"Wow!"

"Deep, Danielle!"

"Okay," Betsy said, nodding purposefully. "I like it. I like it. Let's put it to a vote. Those in favour of Rubble Children?" Five small hands went up. "It's decided, then. Thanks for the suggestion, Danielle."

I was beyond elated.

What else did we talk about at that meeting where we found our name? We talked about the controversy over the actual number of Jewish dead. Was it six million, or was it three million? Nine million? What, in the end, did it matter? We debated, once again, how we could possibly raise the money to get down to Baltimore for the Annual Girls' Convention of Genocide, Ethnic Cleansing, and Settler Colonialism. Betsy had discovered the convention in one of the journals she read, and we desperately wanted to go. We yearned to go. Imagine: groups of girls like us from all over the continent, discussing the Holocaust! But we had no way of raising the funds. Betsy's dad, the only one who could possibly have enough money to send us, was still mad at Betsy for her "appalling behaviour" in the lead-up to her bat mitzvah.

When I think about my early teenage years, which is more and more recently, this is what I remember. I remember us sitting in Amanda's basement, high off of juice boxes, laughing at Sam's jokes, crying at the countless examples of human cruelty we looked at weekly, talking in low, serious voices. I remember Hadas's comic strips, in particular the serialized *Adventures of*

Primo Lentils, which told, in comic-book form, the story of Primo Levi's time in Auschwitz, except Levi was a can of lentils, sort of a more absurd, less-developed *Maus*; Art Spiegelman was, of course, one of our heroes, almost a god. (I wonder what happened to those comic strips; these days, Hadas could probably easily publish them as a book.) I remember Betsy showing us how to engage with difficult texts, steering our group through the ocean of Jewish Thornhill according to her own whims and desires. We were dark children. We were focused. We were children of the rubble.

Those were the golden days of Rubble Children, when we had our catastrophe, our unimaginable disaster, and we dedicated ourselves to imagining it, to memorizing it, to bearing witness. Before we stumbled out into the real rubble. Before the beginning of the end of our morbid little reading group.

Before Gloria Crosby.

⁞ The decision to not allow non-Jews into the group was made at one of our first meetings with a near-unanimous vote. I'm ashamed now to say I voted with the majority, with Betsy. In any case, Gloria Crosby wasn't the first non-Jewish girl who wanted to become a Rubble Child. Sam's cousin on her Christian side, Melinda, wanted to join early on but was easily turned away. A few boys also tried to join, most seriously Yoni Krasner. He had a big crush on Hadas, especially after she grew breasts.

"What, I thought all you care about is hockey!" Amanda scolded Yoni the first afternoon he came by.

Yoni looked sheepish. "No, not just hockey! I also care about, about this," he said, glancing at Hadas.

We laughed mercilessly. Hadas, who liked the attention, would have let him in, but we outvoted her and Yoni dropped it pretty quickly.

"Fine, whatever," he said, pretending not to be hurt, "I'll just watch *Schindler's List*, same thing anyways," he said.

"You do that," Betsy said, to which we all snickered. We hated *Schindler's List.*

We were a pretty insular group. We lived hard by the rules. No boys, no non-Jews, and barely any adults. The one adult we ever let near our basement meetings was Betsy's grandfather Abe. He had been born in Berlin, witnessed the rise of Hitler, but escaped in the thirties. We loved Abe, had him come a bunch of times to tell us horrifying stories of being a child in a rapidly changing city; it was exactly what we wanted to hear. Abe went above and beyond though: he told us about his anarchist politics, his organizing with the far left in Toronto in the sixties and seventies, his hatred for borders of any kind, his disgust with what he referred to as "the so-called Jewish state." We didn't pay much attention to Abe's feelings towards Israel—Israel didn't particularly interest us, unless it was directly related to the Holocaust. (I wouldn't find out until years later that the reason Kol B'Seder stopped having Abe speak during their Holocaust education weeks was because he refused to censor his views, especially when regarding Israel.) Besides Abe, nobody got through those basement doors who was not a card-carrying member of Rubble Children. Perhaps if Betsy didn't enforce our bylaws with such decisiveness we would have let non-Jewish girls, boys like Yoni, in from the very beginning. But we had Betsy. So when Sam showed up to a meeting one January Sunday with Gloria Crosby in tow, it did not go well.

"What's she doing here?" Betsy asked. Gloria was Sam's best friend from school, and we all knew her from the bat/bar mitzvah circuit and Sam's birthday parties. She wore makeup, had soft wavy brown hair, a Louis Vuitton purse; she did not seem like the kind of person who would want to spend their Sundays debating if the Mossad made the right choice when they kidnapped Eichmann and not Mengele that fateful day in Argentina. While most of us were mildly unhappy—or maybe just uncomfortable?—

that an outsider was here, Betsy was livid. She looked like she had just climbed twenty flights of stairs.

"What's the big deal?" Sam asked. "Gloria is just as into the Holocaust as we are."

"How could she join?" Betsy asked, indignant. "She's not even Jewish! What does she know about the rubble?!"

"Yeah!" Amanda chimed in.

Sam defended her decision to bring Gloria. "She lost a ton of family in the Irish famine!"

As it turned out, Gloria was her own best advocate. Noticing my book on the Warsaw Uprising, she immediately impressed us with her knowledge of the siege and the fight against the Nazis. She and Betsy got into an argument on the technical details of the uprising, which streets were bombed first, which tactics the Jewish fighters should have employed sooner. Betsy, notwith-standing the fact that she had a great-uncle, Abe's brother, who was there, who personally lobbed grenades at Nazi tanks from the blasted-out windows of a former hospital, was not used to being argued with, and she was visibly flustered.

"Do you think they'll ever find the rest of the Ringelblum Archive?" Betsy asked, trying to steer the conversation into more secure waters. "I read through most of the first three milk cans." This was a regular topic of conversation: we imagined a short story, written in Yiddish, in one of the lost milk cans Emanuel Ringelblum hid somewhere in the ghetto, a story that held the horror of the ghetto like a palm holding icy water up to our parched mouths.

"We've only found two milk cans," Gloria said, causing a shockwave through the room. Betsy often talked about the three milk cans in the Ringelblum Archive. How could it be two? What was going on? Amanda ran to a book to look it up.

"Oh my god, she's right!" she exclaimed, after flipping through the index and finding the appropriate page.

Betsy looked shocked. Nobody had ever successfully corrected her before. The room's attention turned to Gloria. Gloria smiled, sat back on the couch.

"Did you ever think about how if the Holocaust never happened, Anne Frank would just be an old lady living in Amsterdam or Frankfurt, and nobody would know her name?" Gloria asked.

The girls—except Betsy—responded with an assortment of wows and whoas.

Betsy, probably upset she didn't think of it herself, scoffed. "What's the point of a thought experiment like that?" she spat. "The Holocaust did happen. Anne Frank *was* murdered."

"Honestly!" Amanda agreed.

I think after the initial shock, and especially after her performance that afternoon, most of us would have let Gloria in without a fuss. I, for one, was secretly thrilled that Sam brought her; with a non-Jewish girl in the group, my claim to the Holocaust suddenly seemed much stronger. But Betsy remained adamant. Did she see Gloria as a potential rival? Did she just not like her? Was it just her combative nature? Or did she really, truly believe that only Jewish girls should be in Rubble Children? Whatever it was, Betsy, from the moment she saw Gloria descending Amanda's stairs, made it her personal mission to not allow Gloria in.

The following week Sam brought Gloria again, and Betsy showed how far she was willing to go to get her way. At the beginning of the meeting, before Amanda read out the last week's minutes, Betsy put forward a new motion to vote on.

"The motion," she announced, "is to repeal the no non-Jews allowed clause."

As you probably guessed, the motion failed 7 to 2. The only ones who voted for it were Sam and Hadas. That was Betsy, always the wily politician.

Gloria left in a huff, tears streaming down her face, clutching her Louis Vuitton. Betsy smiled before leading us in the recitation of our motto. It happened once. It can happen again. At the time, I was happy to have helped her keep outsiders out. I was a dutiful soldier, basking in Betsy's approval.

Betsy, however, had underestimated Gloria. We all had. Three nights later, Gloria started calling some of the girls. She had news: her father, who was VP of finance at Masada Assets Inc., was willing to pay for us—for *all* of us—to go down to the Annual Girls' Convention of Genocide, Ethnic Cleansing, and Settler Colonialism. Even better, he was willing to finance a side trip to the Holocaust Memorial Museum in Washington.

That night our phones rang non-stop. How did Gloria get her father to agree to something like that? What should we do? What will Betsy say? How rich *was* he? We had Sam describe Gloria's house to us in as minute detail as she could. It was our collective dream to go the Holocaust Museum—how could we turn that down?! Somebody had to speak to Betsy. Somebody had to convince her. She would never change her mind. Absolutely not. Betsy was a fortress, and when it came to Gloria, the drawbridge was raised. What should we do?

It was Amanda who eventually confronted Betsy. With Sam and myself listening silently on three-way, Amanda called her, asked what she was planning on doing now that we had an opportunity to go to the conference in Baltimore.

"I wouldn't care if Gloria's father was going to fly us all to Yad Vashem, if he was going to rent out Auschwitz for prom! We don't allow non-Jewish girls into the group."

"Betsy, c'mon. You're being ridiculous. What difference really will it make?"

"All the difference, Amanda. All of it."

"Well, if that's how you feel, then maybe Sam and the rest of us will just go down without you."

There was a pause. I was standing in my kitchen, the hand I was holding the phone with wet with sweat. My heart was racing.

"Fine. Whatever," Betsy said.

"Whatever," Amanda said.

"Whatever." We heard the click of Betsy hanging up.

"Holy. Fucking. Shit," Sam said, the first to speak. "Did you just mutiny us Amanda, you pirate-eyed bitch?!"

Amanda laughed. "Don't worry about it. She'll come around. It'll be just like her bat mitzvah, you'll see."

Amanda was right. At our next meeting Betsy, not acting anything like the hurt party, put forward a new motion to change our bylaws. Non-Jews would now be able to become full group members, as long as their dedication to the learning and analysis of the Jewish Genocide was proven satisfactory.

The vote, this time, was unanimous. Betsy avoided Amanda's eyes the rest of the meeting, but otherwise she gave away nothing. You might think I would have started seeing Betsy as weak, as human, but no: I was amazed at her pragmatism, her ability to shift positions when necessary. As far as I was concerned, Betsy was still our undisputed leader.

The first person to take advantage of the new policy was Gloria. We started planning for the trip.

Six weeks later we were boarding a rented fifteen-person van in the Promenade Mall parking lot. Somehow, we had all managed to get our parents to allow us to go. I was embarrassed when I saw that everybody had brought their go-bags. How stupid of me! All I had was my carry-on, a hand-me-down from an older cousin. Gloria's father and Amanda's mother were chaperoning. We would spend two days in Washington, and three at the Baltimore conference.

I've never been to sleepover camp, but I like to imagine that the van ride to the American capital is what taking the bus to camp felt like. The camaraderie, the growing excitement, the van going over a hundred kilometres an hour on smooth asphalt roads, Amanda's mom feeding us homemade butterscotch cookies as Gloria's father drove and told stories about growing up in New York City. On the ride down we watched our favourite parts of *Shoah*, as well as a documentary on the opening of the Holocaust Museum Betsy found somewhere, all of us swooning when Elie Wiesel took the microphone. We pretended that the border crossing into America was more harrowing than it actually was. We quizzed ourselves on American involvement in the Holocaust: the boatloads of refugees they refused to let in. Their failure to bomb the death-camp train tracks. Their decision to drop the atomic bombs on Japan, one of the only non-Holocaust related events we discussed regularly. Gloria blended seamlessly into the conversation; after a few hours I forgot she was a newcomer, that this whole trip was happening because of her.

That night in our hotel room five blocks from the Museum, we lay in bed, discussing what was in store for us over the coming days. We were giddy with expectation.

First thing at the Museum, Mr. Crosby had arranged for us to hear a survivor's testimony. The man speaking was ninety-two years old; his hands shook while he spoke, but he still had a full head of white hair, wet, kind eyes. We were sitting in the front row, like VIPs.

"I have lived my life with such anger," he started, taking a slow sip of water. "My whole life, I never tell my story to anybody, never did talks like this. Eh, what's the point I would say. But five summers ago I was the survivor-in-residence on the trip The March of the Living. You know this trip? We vent to Poland. To the camps. At the train tracks in Auschwitz, all the young people, they form a circle around me, and we altogether sang 'Hatikvah.' I tell you, I never felt such peace since the war. After that vee flew to Israel. After so many years, I was cured of my hatred. Since then I make talk all over the country. For you. For the young people." His speech wasn't anything like Abe's righteous anger, it was ground we had all trod before, but it still hit the spot. We all cried. When Betsy sneezed Gloria pulled a tissue out of her purse.

Afterwards, we were let loose in the Museum. There wasn't anything in the exhibits themselves that was particularly new to us—we were very good students—but just to be there, surrounded by photographs of Auschwitz commandants and the Righteous Among the Nations, felt like a homecoming. The best part was the special exhibit on the Ringelblum Archive, samples from the thirty thousand extant pages behind glass, pictures of life in the Warsaw ghetto, the names of the freedom fighters. We all searched for Betsy's great-uncle's name, hugged with tears in our eyes when we found it.

That afternoon was probably the pinnacle of Rubble Children. How were we to know we were teetering on the precipice?

It was the night before the conference officially got underway that I met Simone. We had recently arrived at the conference hotel in the outskirts of Baltimore and checked in. I was getting ice for our room, Simone was feeding quarters into a vending machine.

When I turned around with my full bucket of ice, Simone was looking at me. She had an Oh Henry! in hand.

"Hi, what's your name?" she asked. She was a Black girl a few years older than me, wearing a dress, her hair in tight braids. She had a pretty face, eyes that in their depth and humour reminded me of Sam Bornstein's.

"Danielle. Yours?"

"Simone. You here for the conference?"

"Yeah. It's our first time."

"I've been coming for around three years. What group are you here with?"

"Rubble Children."

"Cool name! Yeah, I'm here with the Young Black Activists caucus. We're fighting for prison reform. The amount of Black men in prison is a form of ethnic cleansing and is totally unacceptable. You should come to our panel tomorrow afternoon!"

"I thought the conference was mostly about the Holocaust?"

"Somebody's been lying to you! No one form of systemic oppression gets top billing here. That's what's so great about it!"

I didn't respond right away. I didn't know what to say. Ice loudly fell in the guts of the ice machine behind me.

"Cool. Well, see you tomorrow, I guess," I said eventually, hugging the ice bucket to my chest.

"Stay woke, Danielle!" Simone called after me, biting into her chocolate bar.

I didn't tell any of the other girls about Simone, but I was up most of the night worrying about it. How was it possible that a conference on ethnic cleansing didn't centre on the Holocaust? How could that be! Oh, how little I knew. I finally fell asleep, the phrase *stay woke*, which I had never heard before, fog-horning in my head.

⦂ After a restless night, it was morning. We rode the elevator down to the conference level, saying goodbye to Amanda's mom and Gloria's dad, who were going to go sightseeing in the city. We registered. We were given name tags, pamphlets, and plastic bags with pens and stickers, pointed in the direction of the conference floor. We were here. The Annual Girls' Convention of Genocide, Ethnic Cleansing, and Settler Colonialism. Young women of all colours and sizes were milling around, hugging, laughing, talking in serious, low voices. We stayed close to each other, unsure where to go first.

As Simone had hinted to me, the conference was not what we were expecting. Apparently—I would learn later, at a talk by a young Lakota woman who was president of the conference association—in its first years, it *was* mainly a Holocaust symposium, but that had changed. Other groups had started attending, demanding space. For a few years the conference was a place of battle, contention, girls screaming about their suffering, comparing atrocities. Three years ago, led by Simone's African American caucus, the conference association voted, after an hours-long, teary meeting, to totally revamp its mandate: now, it was no longer about competing horrors, but coming together to fight for a better world, to dismantle the capitalist system that pits sufferings against each other, to demilitarize, to denuclearize. A big banner in the main room of the conference read, "We are not here to compare our suffering. We are here to witness each other. We are here to fight for a better world. Together, we are stronger."

Simone's panel that afternoon was amazing. She talked about growing up in Oakland, about her brothers and cousins and their run-ins with the police, about not understanding why the world was the way it was, until she found an Angela Davis book in her underfunded school library. Simone's life was so unlike our lives in the Jewish suburbs of Toronto yet, somehow, I felt a powerful affinity with her. While the Holocaust was in the past—its horrors fast receding—Simone was living and fighting against a system still very much oppressing her and millions of others. We were so preoccupied with delving into our own people's open wound that we never, not for a second, considered that we could turn our flashlights out towards the world, to our own backyards.

I rarely think about that conference now, but when I do, the feeling of discovery, of shame, of shyly approaching Simone after her panel to give her a hug, still blitzes through me. We learned about settler colonialism, the age of empire, about Indigenous dispossession, the hundreds of years of ethnic cleansing, lawmaking, forced eviction, massacring, and dehumanization that is ongoing to this very day, this very moment. We sat in on panels about the horrors of slavery, of the Middle Passage, of lynchings, of the Jim Crow south and the ghettoized north. We learned of the daily violence done to gay bodies, trans bodies. We learned about the worldwide horrors perpetrated each and every day.

"How are we not constantly talking about all of this?" Amanda asked when we were safely in our hotel rooms after the first day. She was aghast. Betsy looked like she had just found out the planet she had been living on wasn't earth after all, but some other oceany, treed rock orbiting a distant star. Hadas drew a new comic that night, a six-panel doozy where Primo Lentils stumbles upon the canned beans aisle at the supermarket. We lay on our beds, not talking. We were full of wet sandwiches and hot chocolate, our backpacks were full of books, our minds were full of a new sense of the world, an even deeper disgust at the powers that be.

If it wasn't for Gloria Crosby and her dad's money, we would not have gone down to Baltimore, we would not have been shaken from our own particular nightmare; we would not have looked out over the lip of our pit and saw the colossity of the mine field. If this was what being woke meant, I didn't know if I was ready for it.

The next day, the keynote lecture was about the plight of the Palestinians. We knew there were people who called themselves Palestinians, but like I said, Israel only interested us in its relation to the Holocaust. The speaker, a young Palestinian woman who grew up in Italy, told us about the Nakba, about the hundreds of thousands of stateless refugees, about the open-air prison that is Gaza. How the Nazis and the Holocaust were used to justify the attempted erasure of an entire people that had nothing to do with the Second World War. The human ingenuity and creativity when faced with the starkest survival that was shockingly familiar to us. The narrative we took at face value crumbled into dust. The young women we met after the keynote, hailing from all corners of the Palestinian diaspora, were smart, dedicated, kind, lovely. They put us to shame. These girls were actually out there *doing* something. We might have been children of the rubble— though, as we had learned yesterday, we are all children of the rubble—but these women were not just wallowing, they were building something new, fighting for a better world for their own children.

It was an intense weekend. The stories we heard, the friends I made, they'll be with me always. Do you want to hear them? You know where to look. You won't be hearing them from me. They are not my stories to tell.

⠿ That was the end of Rubble Children. The nine-hour van drive home to Toronto was a quiet one. Betsy spent the whole ride drawing furiously in her notebook.

"Hey, what do they call colonizers, ethnic cleansers, and war criminals?" Sam asked. Nobody took the bait. Sam gave her punchline anyways, though she was obviously deflated. "The Founding Fathers," she said, almost a whisper.

"That's not funny," Amanda said.

"I can't wait to tell Zaidy about all this," Betsy said. It was the first thing she said all day.

Though we would still meet once or twice more after the trip, our hearts had gone out of it. We were growing up. We were turning fourteen, fifteen that year, and other things started taking precedence. I've lost touch with most everybody from that part of my life, but I know where some of us ended up. Betsy lives in Silicon Valley, is a VP at Facebook. Sam Bornstein started doing stand-up in Toronto before moving to New York, where she now writes for television. Hadas became a Palestinian activist; I see her on the news from time to time, getting screamed at, called a self-hating Jew, an idiot, a terrorist sympathizer. She takes it better than I would. Simone is also on the news from time to time; the youngest Black senator from New Jersey, her fight for prison abolition and reparations were making serious waves. Surprisingly—or perhaps not surprisingly at all—it was Gloria, fierce Gloria Crosby, Betsy's first real threat, who stayed connected to the Holocaust most of all. She is a professor of history at SUNY Albany, an expert on the representation of genocide in contemporary media. I read her first book, on the Holocaust and graphic novels, and was delighted to see in the acknowledge-ments the obscure sentence "To the ladies of RC."

But that was all still ahead of us. For now, I watched the coun-tryside going by the window. My mood was dark. Darker than usual. Was this so different from looking out the window of a car speeding down the Autobahn? A road to the rainforest clearcuts? Some Israeli highway?

It happened. It can happen again. It is happening.

Holidays, Holy Days, Wholly Dazed

APPLE TREES, FENCES, BREAD

The house was operating on three distinct levels. In the kitchen and in the family room, the adults. In the living room and spilling out into the hallway, the children. Zipping through all the floors of the house, into the backyard, weaving in and out of the adults' legs, stopping without warning to smell or scratch before taking off again, moving to their own invisible pack logic, the dogs. Matt rose from the couch where his father and uncles were watching the football game in their dress shoes and tucked-in shirts and belt buckles of varying silver, went into the kitchen, told his mother he was going over to Jeremy's.

"Be back in half an hour," she said. She was cutting apples, a half-dozen pots boiling away.

Matt mussed Jimi's shaggy fur on his way out the door. He cut across the driveway, walked five doors over to Jeremy's house, stood in the driveway till Friedman's van pulled into the court. Matt slid open the door and got in. They drove the suburban neighbourhood, smoked from the water bottle billy that Friedman kept in the glove, crossed Dufferin to grab more weed from Christian in Granite Ridge. Matt smiling uncontrollably, watching the world outside the windows. Their high school, white and blue, conjuring weekday sensations of highness, desire, fear, boredom. A very tall man on a very short red children's ladder, reaching up to pluck an apple from an apple tree in his backyard, the tree sighing with the red fruit. A new fence going up on Bathurst, a tall post every ten feet, the exposed backyards.

The summer had ended what felt like hours ago, the shifts telemarketing for We Care Lawn Care at Dufferin and Steeles, the evenings and nights in the parks and ravines and basements of Thornhill, the lazy mornings eating egg and ham breakfasts in the broiling backyard heat, given way to a new school year, the routine of class, the annoying comfort of books and homework—and just as Matt was getting used to the new groove, here come the Jewish holidays bashing their way into the calendar. The windows rolled down, the sweet smoky reek of autumn fusing with the watery billy smoke, Matt breathed in, held it, coughed it out.

Friedman dropped Matt off fifteen minutes late. He slipped into the house through the garage, got into the bathroom to wash his hands and rinse out his mouth with burning hot water without anybody noticing. Dinner had not started yet. He stood around with the adults in the kitchen, couldn't get into their conversation, kept sniffing his hands, his shirt collar. He migrated to the kids, playing with Lego on the floor. He knelt down, couldn't find a proper moment in the complex narrative to jump in, assert his teenaged vantage. Upstairs, to find the dogs. They were splayed out on the carpet outside his parents' bedroom door. He lay down with them—here was a cognitive shelf he could slide right into. He fell asleep in their warm group heat, dreamed swoopy dreams until the voice of his mother roused him.

Slightly less high, he started down the stairs, the dogs pawing past him. He sat down at the table. The house smelled of brisket, of his aunts' perfume, of apples and honey. All of his cousins around the table, his aunts, his uncles, his parents. The dogs took their meal-time positions, expectant and worried. The coming two hours of food, laughter, argument, reminiscence its own felt presence in the room. The first night of Rosh Hashanah, the Jewish New Year, celebrated by Matt's family and their ancestors in one form or another, with more or less religiosity, but always close to the harvest, for who knows how many thousands of years. Matt pondered the vastness of human time, started to get afraid, shrugged it off. Tonight was tonight. He reached into the table and ripped a big, meaty chunk off the challah crown, the younger cousins who noticed laughing with shock. The sweet, cakey dough worth whatever would happen next, when his mother returned from the kitchen with the first two bowls of soup, one in each hand, and saw what he had done.

APPLES AND HONEY

Tammy and Shoshana were over. They were in the backyard when Shoshana showed her breasts to Matt. Matt had been in the grass with Jimi, Tammy was facing the house, and Shoshana, in a quick practised motion lifted her top to her neck, looked meaningfully at Matt, then pulled it down. The whole thing lasted less than a second, but it was a second that sizzled clean through Matt's brain. He was stunned. Shoshana turned away, already talking to Tammy, Jimi jumped onto Matt, and he fell into the leaves, an action he hoped would elicit laughter but was met with silence.

Earlier, that morning, they had all been at shul together for the first day of Rosh Hashanah. A bunch of them, mostly fellow six-teen-year-olds, but also some older and younger kids, had snuck out of services and gone out onto the road to get high, crouching behind a parked minivan in their suits and dresses as they hur-riedly passed around pipes and lighters. Back in the chapel, Matt was too stoned, too paranoid, to sit still; he was sure the weed smell was streaming off his suit jacket, mingling with the com-bined force of the congregation's group hatred of him. They had come back in during Rabbi Koffee's sermon, which had some-thing to do with generational approaches to Judaism, or at least the one and half sentences he paid attention to did. Afterwards, Tammy and Shoshana came over so Matt could change out of his suit before they walked to Friedman's.

He had fallen in love with Shoshana when he was thirteen, a few weeks into the bar/bat mitzvah circuit. Her sharp tongue, her adventurousness, her physicality, a blend of vulnerability and perfect abandon—how, in quiet moments, when she'd be looking at something, anything, the DJ with one hand on his headphones, Friedman's dad slow-dancing with his sister-in-law, the sun setting outside of the large Richmond Hill Country Club windows, her eyes would change to such detached, philosophical, inquisitive focus, a look that prompted their Hebrew teachers to tell her to stop staring into space, which is not a proper way for a young Jewish girl to behave. Those first unquenchable waves of love were over three years ago now; things had changed since then—but still, with the slightest effort he could pull those tides back in. Shoshana had, more than once, made clear to Matt— slow-dancing at Shelly Blumenthal's bat mitzvah after two hours of his working up the nerve to approach her, at the annual Sukkot lunch at the Goldblums, smoking weed on the shul roof during the now defunct shul-ins—in no uncertain terms, that she wasn't into him, that they were just friends, good friends, but friends only and just, just and only. Understood? He had convinced himself he was over her, but seeing her bare chest, for, what could it have been, a millisecond, a nanosecond, a milli-nanosecond, had lopped off the intervening three years in one hot, clean swipe of the knife. Who could blame him? He had never seen a girl's breasts before, and, later that afternoon in Friedman's basement, as they passed Tammy's green bong around, Matt, slumped on the shorter of the two white leather couches that were the focal point of the large basement, absent-mindedly punching the bowl whenever it came past, trying not to look at Shoshana, who was sitting with Rob on the longer couch, laughing at everything he said—fucking Rob with his acne and easy-going manner, the *Face/Off* VHS he kept in his knapsack and would put on in the early hours of the morning—held an imaginary conversation with Shoshana. They were in Friedman's basement's small little bathroom, standing bathroom close. Why'd you do that, why'd you flash me? *You tell me.* I don't think it's because you suddenly like me. *No, definitely not because of that.* Was it to torture me? *Matt, you know me better than that!* It's just your nature, it's why I fell in love with you. *Ha ha, Matt, what could you possibly know of love? You're sixteen years old! You're utterly clueless! Here, let me show you what love is.* Having fantasized about being in a bathroom with Shoshana hundreds of times, the scenario was going into unwanted corners—unwanted, at least, in the public of Friedman's basement.

A knock on the basement door brought Matt back. Everybody froze. Noam was literally holding a smoking bong. Like Matt's own parents, Friedman's were usually cool, but Friedman's dad had once screamed at all of them and they scattered out the back door. "Yes?" Friedman said, tentative. The door opened, and the hand of Friedman's mom reached across the threshold, holding a plate with apple slices and two ramekins of honey. Friedman took it. "Thanks, Ma." Ripples of relief, embarrassment.

Shoshana took a slice of apple and popped it into her mouth. Matt took the bong from Noam's lap, cleared the chamber and without exhaling proceeded to punch the rest of the massive bowl, his eyes focused on the warm glass shaft of the bong as the hot smoke osmosed into his body. Three-quarters of the way through the hit, the *pop-whoosh* of the punch too close to stop now, a tripwire in Matt's brain tripped, triggering the screeching, blaring alarm system with its familiar refrain: *you are too high.* He was too high. He put the bong down on the carpet, coughing wildly. Okay. He was too, too, too too high. He was having a heart attack. Okay. His brain was going to burst its casing. Okay. Okay. He floated into the bathroom, which was a bad idea, floated out the back door, up the stone steps, and almost immediately felt better in the afternoon-cool expanse of out-of-doors. Standing in the backyard, huffing the lush nostalgic burn of the autumn air, the oak trees that must have been older than Friedman's house—older than the entire suburban neighbourhood—rustling in the wind.

THE SHOFAR BLASTS, THE BUBBLER BUBBLES

Matt usually refused to go to shul for the second day of Rosh Hashanah, but since it was a weekend anyways and he didn't get to skip school, he acquiesced to his parents. Strange reasoning, but so goes the stoner teenage mind. He woke up still groggy from that stupid bong hit—which had made for a sour, interminable second Rosh Hashanah dinner at his aunt's house on the other side of Thornhill—put on his suit again, got into the car with his parents again. Again drove through the early-morning suburban streets to the shul, Kol B'Seder, parked in the distant lot, walked towards the building in brilliant late-September morning light. The chapel, again. The prayers, again, the standing and the sitting, again, the looking at the crowd, trying to spot Shoshana or Tammy or Friedman, again, the worn siddurs with their prayers and the Hebrew Matt could read well enough but not understand a word of, again, the choir and their singing, again, various members of the congregation called up to blast the shofar, Rabbi Koffee's sermon, on a different topic—something about the commonalities between the new Jewish year of 5763 and the almost finished Christian year of 2002?—and with a slightly faster cadence, but still, again. Again, they went to get high, though this time Matt brought his bubbler, and they walked to the park behind the shul. The world smelled like rotten apples, like rotting leaves, like plastic and wood, like distant campfires, and soon enough it would smell like marijuana. The honks of a flock of geese, an unbalanced V in the sky, being pulled on magnetic strings. The satisfying clicking sound of Matt's bubbler as it went around the circle counter-clockwise, his friends in their dresses, his friends in their suits and kippahs. As usual, laughter. As always, the paranoid return to the chapel.

After the service, the halls outside the sanctuary filled with adults and children like smoke pooling into a bong chamber. Matt was looking forward to getting away from the thronging crowds, to get out of his suit, meet up with Friedman and Todd, eat something, smoke some of the hash Todd was raving about.

It took a moment before Matt noticed Samuel walking beside him. "Were you in there for the shofar blasts?" he asked in a fast, conspiratorial voice. Samuel was a neighbourhood fixture, worked at the McDonald's in the mall. He was older than Matt, but how much older Matt had no idea—maybe in his twenties? Over six feet tall, long oily hair, small eyes, soft melodic voice, Samuel was one of the first people to reliably sell weed to Matt and his friends. Matt couldn't remember exactly when Samuel started showing up at the shul, but he was a regular attendee now, was always asking Matt after Saturday services, "Did you feel anything? Did you feel anything? I *definitely* felt something." Now—was it his first high holiday at Kol B'Seder?—Samuel looked half to fully crazed, like Matt looked the one time he did mushrooms and got stuck in front of Friedman's basement bathroom mirror for what felt like hours. The brown corduroys and Value Village blazer just barely squeaked past the unwritten Kol B'Seder dress code. "You felt it, didn't you? Wild, man, wild. It's like no other high on planet earth. The ram's horn, the fucking ram's HORN! Can you believe it?! Transported right back to Mount Moriah! The first rock concert in human history, with Yeshua himself headlining!" Samuel smiled like he had, in fact, just seen the face of God. It scared Matt a little. "Mount Moriah, brother! All of us, taken through time and space at the sweet sonorous sighs of the pleading shofar. Abraham's devotions, Isaac—fucking Isaac! My god! Wild stuff man, wild!" Somehow, they were out behind the shul, standing next to the rusty dumpsters, a row of young pine trees shielding them from the backyards. Had they walked there? Samuel was carefully lighting a long thin blunt with a match still attached to its box. He tended it gently, smoking contemplatively. He seemed to have calmed down some.

"My favourite time of the year, baruch hashem," he said, speaking much slower now, philosophically, some sort of post-frenzy debriefing. "The sweet new year, the godface of the shofar, the days of awe, the dread of Yom Kippur. Is it not wild?" He passed Matt the blunt and Matt, not even wanting to, took it. The weed tasted like shit, but it mixed like dirty oil in the gas tank of his high, and he shifted from third to eighth. Matt looked at Samuel through eyes each now equipped with their own pounding heart as he continued to smoke the blunt in long calm draws. Samuel was always an oddball—when they had first met he was obsessed with the samurai, was teaching himself Japanese, saving up for a plane ticket. Then it was improvisational rock n' roll music, the Dead, Phish, other bands Matt had never heard of. Then, for a short intense while, it was the fact that we're living in a giant computer simulation run by an advanced alien civilization: he'd ply you with questions about the nature of reality and terrify you with the statistical certainties while taking your cheeseburger and nugget order that you'd share with Friedman, both of you in hoodies that smelled like fresh laundry, in the late-evening food court, the high windows half blocked by snake plants glowing copper, laughing at Samuel's unshakable faith, downplaying your own fear of being a computer projection. And now, this. Judaism. And, of all the flavours and textures on offer in Toronto, Reform Judaism! For Matt, shul had always just been another circuit on the circuit-board of his life, right beside school, home, the mall, the neighbourhood; the transcendence apparently hiding in the congregation's mild-at-best religious adherence had gone largely unnoticed, though Samuel was quickly changing that. Watching him now, Matt couldn't help but wonder how long Samuel would be counting himself as a member of Kol B'Seder: wouldn't it be no time at all before his newfound passion for the Jewish religion propelled him to the

Orthodox synagogue down the street? It wasn't hard to imagine him full blackhat.

Thinking all this, still smoking the blunt with one hand, Matt watched himself as, with his other hand, he took the bubbler out of his tallis bag. He passed the blunt to Samuel and proceeded to load the bubbler with his own ganja, roughly ripped into small green pillows. Samuel flicked a new match into flame and brought it to the mouth of the purple water pipe, and Matt inhaled. "Ta-kee-ah," Samuel sang in a drawn-out, warbling Thom Yorke falsetto, mimicking the shofar prayers. Matt, hacking through uncontrollable laughter, passed the bubbler to Samuel just as his mom started yelling his name. She was standing at the corner of the building, arms crossed.

"Shit, gotta go," he mumbled, already walking away.

"Happy days of awe my Jewish brother!" Samuel responded, standing beside the dumpsters, the blunt in one hand, the pipe in the other, his hair lifting in the wind.

As often happened these days, Matt couldn't tell if his mom was mad at him. His father had a smile on his face, was his usual quiet affableness after doing his Jewish duty and attending high holiday services. Some of the older people definitely shot him dirty looks as they walked towards the car. It wasn't until they were pulling out of the synagogue's parking lot, and Matt saw Shoshana and Tammy in Rob's car, that he realized he had left his bubbler with Samuel.

DAYS OF AW, YEAH; FANTASIES; MEETING PEOPLE

At school on Monday Matt couldn't stop thinking about Shoshana. He saw her lifting her shirt over and over again, as Mrs. Pomeransky drew swooping parabolas on the chalkboard, the swoop of Shoshana's shirt one quadratic equation he could not solve.

By second period English, instead of "A Rose for Emily," his mind had wandered to the first time he saw her. It was a Friday night soon after Matt's parents had joined Kol B'Seder, where his mom's sister had been singing in the choir for years. Their first Friday there, Matt overdressed in a brown suit, sitting beside his mom and aunt, incredibly antsy, bored, angry, embarrassed, shy. He was eleven years old. He had passed a bunch of children as they had walked into the building, and after the short, guitar-led service, Matt nervously approached. Shoshana was arguing with an older boy about the similarities between Hebrew and Arabic. (As Matt would find out later, Shoshana's mother was a Moroccan Jew, and the whole family had recently started taking Arabic lessons together, from an older Lebanese man who lived on their street.) "How can they be related? The Jews and Arabs are eternal enemies!" the older boy said. He exuded confidence, coolness; Matt would have been terrified to even stand next to him. "No they are not!" Shoshana responded. "Did you know that the Jews who lived in Baghdad spoke Arabic, wrote it in Hebrew script?" She counted to ten in Hebrew, then counted to ten in Arabic (was that the same Friday night he looked over and saw her mom combing Shoshana's hair in the chapel, Shoshana's face radiating passive annoyance?). The boy looked cowed. He huffed, shook his head, stomped off. Matt was enthralled. A short animated eleven-year-old, holding sway over her small rapt congregation that Matt wanted to be a part of more than he ever wanted anything ever before.

The bell rang and Matt absent-mindedly scrunched his homework sheet into his knapsack. Lunchtime. They walked over to Todd's, ate pizza bagels and got high. Drew tagged along, with his too-short haircut and too-big ears; as usual, he didn't have any weed of his own. They talked, insulted, begrudgingly shared their herb with Drew, laughed to the fishtank gurgle of the bong.

Fourth period biology, and Matt was adrift within minutes. Shortly after Matt first saw Shoshana, Shoshana first encountered puberty. Matt was not far behind; at the time, it was as if Shoshana's new breasts had triggered his own changes. To wake one morning into a strange new world, slopes of non-discriminating desire, peaks of euphoric release, valleys of dread, emotion, self-loathing, but always a river or a stream or a headwater leading back to the hills. He was masturbating by that mellow spring, was smoking cannabis by that scorching summer. The two biggest firsts of his young sheltered life, so similar and yet so different— more blissful when done together, but also, sometimes, more wretchedly cavernous in the cold dark wake of orgasm. But, oh, those fantasies he would construct. He and Shoshana. Matt and Shoshana. Shoshana standing close to Matt. Whispering something in his ear. Their bodies, clothed, touching. Their bodies, not clothed. Touching. Sometimes they did everything everywhere, but mostly she sat on his lap and their eyes would be bong shafts, trading smoke from their curved bowled centres They would come together in his mind and he would come alone in his basement bedroom.

When Ancient Civ finally rolled around—the cultures of Mesopotamia even older than the Jews!—Matt was uncomfortable, burnt out, his mood gone funky. He sat there slouched in his chair, the rest of the day playing in front of him as if it were a vision: to the park to smoke hash oil, to the mall to eat, score off of Samuel if he was there. To home, to pass out until dinner. Get high, take a shower, glance at his homework. Stay up far too late. Tomorrow so far away it might as well have been another planet.

⁞ Wednesday after school they went over to Joan's house. Joan had only been hanging out with them for a few weeks, had transferred from Fog Hill at the beginning of the year. At lunch, hitting hash oil off the tips of safety pins in the park, she mentioned that both her parents worked and they could hot-knife at her place. So here they were, at Joan's narrow, cramped townhouse in Granite Ridge, a ten-minute walk from school. Matt normally didn't go into Granite Ridge unless they were grabbing weed from Christian, and never on foot.

Joan dropped her bag in the kitchen, which the front door opened directly into. Beside the kitchen was a small living room and the stairs. They followed Joan up. On the carpeted landing there was a twin mattress, a desk, and a dresser pushed up against the wall. "I had to make room for my drums," she said by way of explanation, choosing a key from her overstuffed keyring and unlocking the padlock on her bedroom door.

"Don't your parents care?" Todd asked. Joan looked at him as if parents were an authority in a faraway castle, with no bearing on what went on *here*.

Matt had never been in a recording studio, but his first thought when Joan swung open her door was that it would look something like Joan's room. He had never seen so many instruments! She had moved her furniture out to fit in the drums, but the room also contained guitars, basses, amps, keyboards, mixers, things Matt didn't have the words for. On hooks behind the door hung some pants, sweaters, Joan's black No Frills work vest. The four of them could barely stand in there.

"Where do you *sleep*?" Matt asked.

Joan shrugged. "If I feel like sleeping, I stack the drums and throw down a yoga mat," she said, kicking the kick drum. The only thing in the closetless room besides musical instruments was a worn paperback book sitting on the synthesizer. Matt turned his head sideways to read the title. *Dark Rivers*.

"The river is dark?" he asked excitedly.

"The river is eternal," Joan said in response.

"The river is eternal!" Matt and Friedman shouted, everybody laughing. "Are you excited for the movie?" Matt asked. "Todd isn't."

"I hate that fantasy shit."

"It's not fantasy!" Joan and Matt said in unison. More laughter. "If anything, it's sci-fi, with fantasy elements," Joan added.

"The movie's going to kick ASS!" Friedman said.

, "Speaking of getting your ass kicked," Joan said, dropping onto her knees and starting to rummage under the drums. Matt, Todd, and Friedman looked at each other: who *was* this girl? Joan came back up, holding a scarred-black butter knife in each hand. "Let's get cooking!" she said, grinning.

They tromped downstairs. Apparently hot-knifing hash oil wasn't exactly easy, and after a few failed attempts Joan pulled out an Altoids tin with a little cube of tar-like hash, and they each took a turn heating the knives up on the coiled stove element and pressing a tiny tear of hash between the red-hot steel, whoever's turn it was bent over the knives with a toilet-paper roll fast to their mouth to suck in the rich white smoke.

Back upstairs, Todd slid behind the drums, Friedman picked up a bass, Matt positioned himself in front of a keyboard. Joan plugged in a guitar, strummed a chord as the amp grumbled into life. The overdrive was thick, oceany, loud. Todd and Friedman started a simple 4/4 pattern, and Joan, without easing in, without warming up, just started ripping on top of it. Gorgeously overdriven riffs pealing out of her, her tiny fingers parabolic on the frets. After a few minutes Todd stopped drumming, and after a couple more bars so did Friedman. Matt had yet to hit a single key. The three of them watched Joan, bending back into the onslaught, her small, shaved head glistening with sweat, the music far too heavy for that tiny, cluttered bedroom.

: An hour later, walking to the park to smoke a joint, they ran into Leon, Cali, and Christian. Matt really only knew Christian, their Black drug dealer. They were older, cooler, rougher, grittier. They combined their two circles, passed joints, lit cigarettes, talked quietly, seriously, conspiratorially. Matt was nervous just being near them; he had never been a member of a group like this.

"Hey Matthew," Christian said, pulling on a joint, shaking a dreadlock out of his face, "where's Jeremy been at?"

Matt took the joint, ashed it on the sidewalk. Jeremy, a year older than Matt, had been on the school basketball team with Christian. "He's doing a year exchange in Germany."

"Yeah, but don't tell Matt's mom," Friedman joked.

"Fuck off!" Matt said, smacking Friedman, hoping he wouldn't have to explain. Nobody seemed to care, though. Around went the joints.

The conversation, as it so often does during a smoke session, sloped towards drugs. Where Matt and his friends usually stuck to talking about various marijuana strains, past sessions, former glories, now the subject quickly segued into hallucinogens, MDMA, acid, before landing on the rise of synthetic drugs.

"These factories in China," Leon said, his face contorted as he took a long drag on the joint. He was wearing a faded Guns N' Roses shirt, his fair hair in a long ponytail. "These factories, they just mass produce these cheap LSD copycats, mostly 25C-NBOMe, flood the North American market. It pretends to be acid, but is definitely not acid." Leon exhaled, started coughing madly. "Sorry, sorry," he said between coughs, "my lungs are shit." When he finished coughing he lit a cigarette.

"We got ripped off at the last Shambhala festival," Cali said, taking two quick hits from Matt's joint. Cali was in her twenties, Matt would guess, was somewhere between a raver and a rocker, had brown skin, a wallet chain, wide jeans. Whatever she was, she owned it totally; Matt was in awe. "It was daaark. Eight sinister hours. The maw of the cosmos tried to swallow us whole. It had everything, all of that bad-trip nonsense. Fear. Paranoia. Vasoconstriction. Leon shat himself." Everybody laughed, Leon nodding through cigarette smoke. "The comedown was fucking horrendous," Cali continued. "My brain was fizzy for weeks."

Leon concurred. "It starts off fine, all light and glory, but when it reaches the peak, it turns on you. That's what you get for eating poison. It's lucky we didn't die."

"Capitalism at work," Christian said. Large, friendly, brilliant, Christian chopped from his parents' garage where he was studying for the accounting exams.

"How can you tell if it's real acid or not?" Matt asked. This conversation was terrifying him.

Cali looked at Matt like nobody had ever looked at him before, male or female, teenager or adult. Like what he had to contribute to the conversation mattered. Love for her swooned through him like a perfect hit of hash, and he savoured its released sweetness, pleasant in its fleeting wave that he would never—and that he knew he would never—act on.

"Unless you have a chemical kit in your backpack, you can't with any certainty," she said, almost whispering. "Though clean LSD doesn't have a taste. Fake LSD burns your tongue."

"If it's bitter, it's a spitter!" Leon proclaimed, to a ripple of chuckles.

"But by then, it might be too late," Cali said. "The best thing to do is to know your source." The conversation paused as everybody watched Leon fix the canoe on the spliff.

"Did you see the new trailer for *Dark Rivers*?" Christian asked, and the conversation moved on to discuss how the novel's author, Hera Black, only wrote the one book, in the early sixties, and nobody knew anything else about her. Matt had stopped listening: already terrified yet compelled by drugs that didn't grow in the ground and that you couldn't see or smell or hold in your hand (or put fire to and smoke), Matt was deeply off-put by the news of fake acid. If everything is fakable, copyable, and you can't tell until it's too late, what's the point? What is vasoconstriction anyways? *Eight sinister hours.* Matt laughed out loud, stopping abruptly.

"Shit! What time is it?"

"Five-fifteen."

"Fuck! Fuck! I'm late for the ortho!"

Friedman offered to drive him, they said goodbye, left Granite Ridge, crossed Dufferin, a truck honking as it veered past them, jogged across the soccer field, got into Friedman's van. Friedman dropped him off five minutes later on the other side of the mall, and Matt burst into the office's waiting room. Mothers of young children having their teeth fixed stared at Matt. His heart still pounding from the run to the van, he saw himself from their eyes: mussed hair, red eyes, the smoky reek of bad news. Matt laughed, sitting down in a plush red waiting room chair. Above reception, there was a framed photo of the skyline of the old city of Jerusalem; it reminded Matt of Samuel, his talk of the shofar as time-travel device, his calling the days between Rosh Hashanah and Yom Kippur the days of "awww, yeah." Thinking of Samuel reminded Matt of his bubbler. Who knows what strange spiritual rituals Samuel was conscripting the beloved purple pipe in? Matt laughed again. A mother pulled her daughter close. How could anybody be afraid of Matt? More laughter, this time—he had to admit—probably more than slightly off-putting. Later, in the lowered dentist chair, Dr. Mustard's gloved hands in his mouth as he asked his patient about how he spent Rosh Hashanah—a position Matt found himself in every month for the past two years—Matt felt great. He loved the feeling of having his elastics changed. Shoshana's still undigested action, his new friends in Granite Ridge, the season's hash oil and hash and weed dressed with hash oil filled Matt with promise, and Dr. Mustard with his firm strong rubbery fingers—well, with Dr. Mustard's help, and his parents' financial investment, Matt was going to reinvent himself, re-emerge from the teenage cocoon remade, refashioned, resplendent.

HEBREW SCHOOL

Don't ask Matt how he got so involved in Jewish education, because he wouldn't be able to explain it. It just sort of, you know, happened. The Thursday night Hebrew classes and Saturday Shabbat classes were as regular as school, weekends, summers. Where most of his Jewish friends had summer camp—that alternate world they spent four to eight weeks at every summer and that they assured Matt he could never understand without actually attending—Matt had this.

All of which still does not explain how, at sixteen, Matt was still going to classes that most everyone else stopped going to after their bar or bat mitzvah—confirmation classes, they were called, though what it confirmed Matt wasn't entirely sure. Not only that, but Matt was now *teaching* nine-year-olds himself. He and Rob, for an hour each Thursday, after their own classes, taught twenty-two children about the holidays, some basic cultural stuff, the letters of the Hebrew alphabet, all pre-ordained in the curriculum that was handed to them in a musty forest-green binder the first day of classes. The only other people near their age who were employed by the shul were Shoshana and Noam. Shoshana taught the ten-year-olds, Noam was the "music teacher," went from class to class Saturday mornings, his acoustic slung over his shoulder, played songs in English and Hebrew.

It was a job. It paid. It was pretty easy. And, yes, Matt didn't particularly like Rob—mostly because girls seemed drawn to him, but also because he was a know-it-all, because he had terrible acne and yet was still supremely confident, because he worked at Film Forest so acted like he had inside knowledge on movies and the film industry—but they worked well enough together. Matt found that the higher he was, the better he taught, the looser he was in front of the students, the more laughter he received. But perhaps the reason he was still there every Thursday, every Saturday morning, was that he easily fit in these halls, he knew the codes and patterns, and, though he would deny ever learning anything of substance, still got a thrill from being so close to, from being a part of, the strange and wonderful world of the Jews.

LET'S GO OUT TO DINNER, AND SEE A MOVIE

Film Forest was in a valley bordered on the west by Yonge Street, on the east by an unending succession of big-box stores and parking lots that repeated right to Bayview. At the southern edge of the theatre, Highway 7. A river on the far north side. Situated around the large parking lot like planets in tight orbit were two chain restaurants, a bookstore, a small undeveloped triangle of trees, and the concrete movie theatre itself, the elaborate forest scene erected on the massive building uplit at night by sweeping spotlights. Friday night, Matt told his mom he was sleeping at Jeremy's, Friedman picked him up, Todd, Horito, and Joan already in the van, and they drove to the theatre.

Steak and baked potatoes and blooming onions at The Saucy Aussie (Matt pretending not to notice that Joan only ordered a loaded potato). Pipe hoots in the restaurant's wood-panelled washroom. Wandering the aisles of the bookstore, Joan picked up the new movie-tie-in edition of *Dark Rivers*, read the back blurb: "A mysterious people on an alien planet. A war to end all wars. Visitors from beyond the stars." "Whoever wrote that didn't read the actual freaking book!" Horito exclaimed. A blunt in Friedman's van, Friedman sketching the movie theatre, the fake trees, the restaurants, and the bookstore in his sketchbook. After the blunt, billy hits, the soundtrack alternating between Wu-Tang and Dave Matthews. A hastily rolled joint. Joan leaning in, giving Matt a super. The car filled with smoke. Drew asking if he could keep the roach, ya know, for later.

And finally, after all the preamble necessary and unnecessary, they entered the sprawling movie palace itself. The engorged central area, the vending panopticon ringed by fast food and frozen yogurt booths. The warm aroma of butter, cologne, soda, shampoo, plastic, laughter, sweat, tobacco, marijuana. The trills and sirens of the arcade. The two wide corridors of theatres branching off from the main hub like immobile concrete wings. Matt, so high it felt like he had a wet, translucent washcloth over his eyes, reacting to every body, noise, look, gesture, an integral part of, yet entirely removed from, the sensory overload of the frenzied teenaged commons.

The plan was to see *Broomsday*, the fourth in the Declan Broome franchise. Todd bought three children's tickets and a senior; Rob was taking tickets, a fresh whitehead on his chin, and just waved them through. They were late to the theatre, had to sit in the front front row of the front-most section, crane their necks as they laughed and hit each other. Matt's popcorn bag was so saturated with butter it left a perfect imprint of Declan Broome's rugged face on his jeans. Matt tried to stamp Todd's shirt with the popcorn bag, Todd screamed at him, popcorn tossed everywhere. Down went the lights. The preview for *Dark Rivers* had them whooping and barking.

Another six previews and the movie started. Ten minutes and eighty-five explosions in, the need to pee hit Matt like one of Declan Broome's back-flip-roundhouse kicks to the gut. To get a laugh, Matt fell out of his chair and crawled along the aisle to the exit. Leaving the theatre was like exiting a house of worship, the change from sacred to profane swift enough to leave Matt disoriented, as if he had stood up too fast (which he also had). Matt walked down the hall, past the darkened kids-birthday-party room, cold with sunken memories, and into the washroom, where he trundled up to a urinal, barely getting there in time. Ah, sweet, slightly erotic relief. Leaving the washroom, Matt let himself be drawn to the bright lights of the vendors, where he exchanged coloured dollar bills for colourful candy worms. He stood there, listened to the pleasant cacophony around him, munched on the soft sugary worms. He was alone. His mind had slowed from NFLT to Mach 3. *Broomsday* was momentarily forgotten. Instead, he watched two Goth girls sitting at the tables near Do You Want FRIES With That? make out. They were more early nineties Goth than early two-thousands Goth: spiky hair, dark makeup on powdered white faces, studded black leather jackets and pants, plenty of piercings apiece. They were really smashing their faces into each other's. Matt had never kissed somebody like that; c'mon, man, you've barely kissed anybody at all! He wished he was one of those girls, not for sexual reasons, per se, but to belong like that, to have a human partner like that, to have mouths engaged in the tireless work of being alive, together like that. He felt it viscerally: if given the choice, right then, right there, he would gladly vacate his role as an awkward stoner sixteen-year-old boy with the whirring, spluttering mind, would shed his masculinity and not look back.

The Goths got up, and, giggling, walked into the opposite wing of theatres, and Matt found himself following them, his mind saturated with the sugar of the worms he was still eating. They walked to the end of the corridor and vanished up a flight of stairs Matt didn't know existed. At the top of the short, carpeted flight was a sign for Theatre 7.5, a theatre Matt had never been to. His bag of worms empty, he pushed open the doors and found himself in a small theatre. A movie was underway on the screen; the Goths were gone. A wave of sugar-induced nausea compelled Matt to sit down. The theatre was mostly empty. The bearded man next to him looked like what Matt imagined university professors looked like. The theatre was a dark, warm cocoon.

Eventually his attention was drawn to the screen. Since he had missed the beginning of the movie it took a while for Matt to piece together what was going on. There was a large group of people living in a sprawling, boarded-up warehouse. They were split up into groups, with a lone man in the corner being shunned for some reason. The camera moved from group to group, from face to face, letting everybody tell their story in maximal close-up. A mother and her child looking for the father. A grocer with a paper bag of pearl onions. A young woman from a war-torn country on her way to reunite with her lover. Once Matt got used to reading the subtitles—what language was this, German?— Matt figured out that everybody in the warehouse had been on the same bus, and were now dead, and that what had killed them…was, what? A terrorist attack of some kind? And the man alone in the corner was the terrorist? Matt wondered if the movie started with the attack. Memories of September 11th, a teacher rolling in a TV so they could watch the news, getting high on the bleachers behind the school with some fellow high school kids from Saint E, Horito talking about the end of the US empire. Back to the movie: as it slowly dawned on each character, one by one, that they will be spending eternity with each other, there was a series of surprisingly emotional confrontations, admissions, shouting, breakdowns, consolations, weeping. Matt, for all that he thought he loved movies, had never been so enthralled. His mind was above the clouds. The movie ended with a close-up of the man who Matt deduced was the suicide bomber, his face showing an incredible range of conflicting emotions. The instant something—what? what was it?!—began to dawn on the man's face, the screen cut to black. Soft violin music—Matt realized for the first time the film lacked a soundtrack of any kind—started playing over the slowly rolling credits. Polite clapping from the scant audience.

Matt stood up. He was in an emotional daze. If *this* was what film could be like, what had he been wasting his weekends on? He walked out of the theatre, left the unique world of Theatre 7.5 for the mundane one of Thornhill. Not until he was standing under the bright lights of the arcade did he remember the Goths. Matt's friends started hollering his name, and he turned towards them. He didn't know the name of the movie, he didn't tell anybody about it, and by Monday morning the whole experience would seem a faint, spliff-induced dream.

: As usual, Matt was groggy and grumpy for Saturday morning classes at Kol B'Seder. Since it was their confirmation year (and since there were only eight of them) the classes were held in the boardroom. Their teacher, Michael, was a soft-spoken, large man, a PHD student; the class respected him, and unlike the other Hebrew school teachers Matt had encountered, Michael never had to raise his voice to quiet the class, ask a question, get their constantly dividing attention. The day's topic was abortion in Judaism, based on a chapter from the class's textbook, *Drugs, Sex, and Integrity: What Does Judaism Say?* Matt had forgotten his copy, so shared with Friedman, who drew pictures of babies holding handguns over the text as Michael led a discussion on women's rights, the act of conception, and healing the world through the practice of ethical Judaism.

During the ten-minute break between the English and Hebrew sections of their Saturday morning, Matt sat swivelling in his chair. He noticed that when the light from the large boardroom windows hit his jeans in a particular angle, the outline of Declan Broome's face could still be made out. Meskie, sitting across from him, was reading an old paperback copy of *Dark Rivers*.

"What's that book about anyways?" Kyle, a small quiet boy with wire-rim glasses, asked.

"It's about a diasporic culture that forgets its history," Meskie said. She was Ethiopian; the shul had sponsored her and her family to come to Toronto when she was a baby. Her younger brother Shai was best friends with Matt's sister Rhita.

Friedman interrupted Meskie. "Well, really, it's about this group of nomadic space travellers who travel the galaxy, staying on planets that they're welcome on, trading their gifts of mathematics and storytelling for safe harbour, leaving when they no longer feel welcome. They call themselves people of the Dark River, the eternal spring at the heart of their origin myth, the centre of their metaphysical beliefs. Like the dark river, they abhor any kind of power, dominion over others, or excessive wealth, which is why they are continually on the move. The novel itself takes place after one group of the Dark River have lived on planet Preethor for fifteen Preethorian centuries, and have nearly forgotten their ways, that they don't truly belong. A war's consuming the entire planet and they have to decide if they're going to forgo their pacifist ways, help the slightly better faction win the war."

While Friedman's summary of *Dark Rivers* was correct, Matt felt he was missing something vital about the book. What that vitalness was, he couldn't exactly put into words. It had to do with the Dark Riverites and their permanent exile, their not belonging to any planet, their fierce and beautiful perseverance, their non-violence. Their difference. Dobro Carthy, the protagonist, wanted nothing more than to live well. And while the planet's in a civil war, there is really no actual violence in the book. Yet every time Matt read it, it made him near-feverish with excitement.

"At the end," Shoshana said eagerly, Tammy nodding in agreement beside her, "a contingent of Dark Riverites arrive and remind them of their nomadic past."

"Shh!" Meskie implored, more animated than Matt had ever seen her. "Don't give away the ending!"

After class, they went to the chapel to steal some bagels from the bat mitzvah lunch. They took them to the park, got high. Matt went to the swings, started swinging himself higher and higher. Shoshana sat down on the swing next to him. They swung together in silence before Shoshana stopped herself with her feet and grabbed Matt by the arm. Matt dug his own feet into the sand and came to a stop.

"Why have you been so weird around me?" she asked, her hand still on his arm, strands of hair cutting across her face.

Matt blinked, unsure what to say. "Uh, no reason?"

"Good, because we're good friends, right Matt?"

"Uh, yeah." Shoshana looked at Matt, nodded, as if she had decided she believed him.

"Oh, Matt, do you remember when we were kids, how much easier everything was?"

"Yeah, I think so."

Shoshana smiled, let go of Matt's arm, pushed herself off the swing and walked towards the others, who were standing around Noam, sitting on a bench playing his guitar.

Later, he saw Shoshana and Noam walking back into the synagogue, their hands clasped together. Matt watched them from the hill on the park.

That night, back at Film Forest, back in *Broomsday*, back to being very high, Matt would be unable to stop thinking about Shoshana, about their conversation on the swings. What was she trying to tell him? What was he supposed to do? How was he supposed to act? Matt would sit back, look up at the high, vaulted ceiling of the theatre. If he could swim up there, into that rarefied air, he would.

LET THE FAST BEGIN

Yom Kippur, the holiest day in Judaism's flip-calendar, was on a Monday; is there anything sweeter than a religiously sanctioned three-day weekend? For the first time this school year, being Jewish had a material advantage. The weekend went by in forties and half-quarters. Yom Kippur morning Matt slept in before meeting up with Friedman. They grabbed pizza slices from Pizza Nova, continued their annual tradition of annoying their friends who, out of tradition, belief, parental compliance, or some combination of the three, fasted.

"Wait, whose house is this?" Matt asked, though as soon as he realized where they were he knew exactly whose house it was.

Shoshana opened the door.

"How goes the fast?" Friedman asked, the same thing they had said at each house they had knocked on, holding their half-eaten pizzas. This time though, Matt felt like an idiot. A wave of shame crashed through him. He hid his pizza, now mostly crust, behind him.

Shoshana laughed. She was wearing sweatpants and a baggy camp T-shirt.

"About the same as yours," she said, narrowing her eyes, laughing again. Her dad said something in French from inside the house. Shoshana looked back, then put her head fully out the door. "I'll meet you at the park in twenty minutes, okay?"

Matt's heart started beating fast. At the park they sat down at the bench under the gazebo. Friedman got to work on a new billy. Matt looked around: the park across the street from Shoshana's house was like the park near Matt's house but slightly different. The plastic slides and swings, the trees whose names he didn't know, the baseball diamond, the backyards and kitchen doors of the houses on the perimeter. It was at this same park, when Matt and his friends were first exploring the suburban night-world in grade seven, that Josh Cohen had called out, surrounded by dozens of intimidating, inebriated grade eights and nines, "I'm drunk *and* high!" Friedman passed the new billy to Matt. He hit a small bowl. Leon came through the park, wearing a Rogers Video vest over a Silverchair shirt, looking even more pale than usual, *skin and bones* as Matt's mother would say, told Matt and Friedman that Joan had just been suspended for fighting with some older girls who were making fun of her. "VP McNichols really has it out for our Joan," Matt said. Leon nodded, lit a cigarette, almost immediately started coughing. "McNichols? He expelled me in eleventh grade. He hates anybody from the wrong side of Dufferin. Alright, I got band practice before my shift, gotta run."

A half hour later, Shoshana was walking down the sidewalk towards them. She had put on a sweater, was still wearing the sweatpants.

"Give me that," she said, taking the billy. She bent her head and punched the fresh bowl Friedman had just finished packing.

"It's *so* boring in there," she announced.

The early autumn air, Shoshana's loose ponytail, the electricity crackling off her skin, Matt's mind humming along. Friedman went off to find somewhere to pee. It was just the two of them.

Shoshana looked right at Matt. "Are you sure you're not mad at me?" she asked.

"What?... No!"

Shoshana narrowed her eyes. "Okay. Well, I just wanted to say that…that thing I did was not supposed to be mean. You know?"

Matt nodded. Shoshana looked very serious.

"I did it out of friendship. I wasn't teasing. I wasn't being mysterious. Even though I can't give you what you want, I still felt like giving you something."

Matt continued to nod as he repeated her words in his head—she *wasn't* teasing, she *wasn't* being mysterious—agreeing with them deliriously. He felt, for some reason he couldn't yet locate, relieved.

Friedman was walking back.

"Understand?" Shoshana said, lowering her head but keeping her eyes on him.

"Yeah, for sure," Matt said.

Shoshana stood up. "Cool. Well I got to get back to the family. Happy fasting!"

"Bye bye!" Friedman said. "Weird girl," he said, as they both watched her walk the sidewalk path that led to her street. "Totally hot, but weird."

Matt felt no need to respond. He was luxuriating in what felt like a delicious secret. "Pack me a bowl," he demanded.

A half-dozen bowls later, late afternoon, Samuel walked through the park talking animatedly with two Orthodox men. He had a kippah on his large head, prayer books in his arms. It looked like he had conditioned and combed his long hair for the first time in years.

Friedman called him over, waving furiously.

"Hey, what are you doing?!" Matt had the distinct desire not to interrupt Samuel.

"What?! We're almost out of smokables!"

Samuel said goodbye to his friends, shaking their hands with a full arm embrace, and went over to the boys.

"Moving on from Kol B'Seder to something more Jew-core?" Matt asked.

Samuel smiled benignly. He looked like he was blasted on serious psychedelics, but Matt wouldn't be surprised if he was as sober as a tree.

"Not at all, my Jewish brother. Spent the morning at Kol B'Seder, the afternoon at Chabad. Chasing all the different manifestations of the godhead. I've already been fasting for forty-eight hours. The whole world shelves away, and we're left face-to-face with God, with ourselves. Every atom of my being reaches out for atonement. The holiness is almost too bright to look at. Imagine what it must have been like during the second temple period, to be the high priest, to walk into the holy of holies, commune with the sacred?"

Friedman looked excited. "Yes, that's what I'm talking about! What's Israel, what's Judaism, without its most sacred building?" Matt had heard Friedman talk about the rebuilding of the temple before, had seen his sketches of the third temple in his sketchbook, but had never paid much attention. "If only the Arabs understood that *we* were there first. The third temple should already be standing in Jerusalem!"

Samuel smiled serenely. "Don't misunderstand me, brother. During the time of the temples, yes, there was a conduit to the holy there, locked in time and place. But that has come and gone. Perhaps it was only an aberration. Because now? Now we carry the holy with us. We carry it within us."

Friedman scoffed. "Without Jerusalem we would not be Jews." Matt couldn't understand where Friedman was getting this from.

Samuel continued smiling. "Some would say that Jews are meant to live in time, not in place."

Friedman glared. Samuel beamed. Matt watched the interaction, a strange smile on his face. He felt Friedman changing in real time, before his eyes, at this park near Shoshana's house.

Samuel looked up at the sky. "Well, time for evening prayers, then it's time to break the fast." Samuel started to walk away.

"I really don't like that guy," Friedman said.

Matt didn't say anything, just watched Samuel as he left the park.

"We're too old for this knocking on people's doors bullshit," he said eventually.

"Shit! What time is it?!" Friedman said.

They were both going to be late for the breaking of the fast. Matt's whole family was probably sitting at the table already, angrily waiting. Friedman pulled the billy piece out of the blackened water bottle, tossed the water bottle towards the overflowing garbage can. Matt grabbed the weed. They bumped fists. Ran in opposite directions just as the rain started.

SUKKOT, SIMCHAT TORAH, HALLOWEEN

Sukkot. Visiting family friends, sitting outside, eating lunches and potlucks, getting high under the stars. Samuel had turned the old fort in the woods behind the mall that a bunch of kids from the Saint E made in the late nineties into a marijuana-themed sukkah. Walking out of the Sobeys on the way to visit him with a soon-to-be-billied water bottle, Matt, Friedman, Horito, and Rob were stopped by an Orthodox man. "You are Jewish?" he asked. Matt nodded. "Want to do the mitzvah of shaking the lulav and the etrog?" Fuck it, Matt was feeling reckless. He nodded again. The Orthodox guy—one of the men he saw Samuel with on Yom Kippur, with a long but scraggly beard, fat cheeks, thin lips, black suit, black hat—looked pleased. He handed Matt the items. Matt shook the lulav and the etrog, following the religious man's whispered instructions. He held the odd, shockingly yellow lemon and the green cornstalk in both hands. He shook it up. He shook it down. He shook it to both sides. The Orthodox man's eyes gleamed. Matt's friends managed to hold their laughter until they were halfway to Samuel's woods.

⠆ Simchat Torah. To Kol B'Seder to celebrate the infinite loop of the Torah. Everybody was there and Matt had terrible cottonmouth, was crashing from an ill-advised gravity bong session, his teeth sore from the ortho's (where Dr. Mustard had regaled the captive Matt with the details of his family's latest trip to Israel). They stood in a giant circle in the synagogue's gym and the Torah was unrolled along the diameter, everyone holding a section of parchment. The congregation sang, the congregation danced, Rabbi Koffee strummed his guitar, a beatific smile on his face. Matt was always drawn to this celebration, the book unfurled in its entirety, a story without beginning and without end, that people he knew had carried anywhere they went.

Outside the side doors, Samuel finally returned Matt's bubbler, told a story about the cyclical nature of the universe, his small eyes fiery with passion. Matt was barely paying attention, was thinking about Shoshana and Noam, who he had seen sneak up the shul stairs, hands grasped. Later, at the park, after pestering him about Zionism, Samuel and Friedman got into a yelling match about Israel. Friedman shouted about the Holocaust, about armies, about enemies, about strong borders, Samuel chanting over him "Torah over terrain! Openness over closedness! Movement over stasis!" Eventually, Friedman huffed off.

⠆ Halloween, and the world gets to try something else for a day. In Matt's parents' garage, they turned the pumpkin Friedman bought at Sobeys into a bong. Matt and Friedman knifed a hole in the top, scooped it clean with kitchen spoons as everyone stood around on the bare concrete. Todd, who was wearing a lab coat, carefully, with doctor-like precision, made the incision for the billy piece and jimmied it in. They used the hose for water; Friedman went inside for some ice cubes. Matt got to go first. He placed his entire face into the pumpkin. It was dark, wet, cold, reeked of autumn. After adjusting his face to snug it in as much as possible, he slapped the pumpkin—he was ready. Joan, dressed as Jimi Hendrix, her electric guitar slung on her back, lit the bowl. The orange hide of the pumpkin was too thick for the sound of bubbling to come through, but weaving tendrils of smoke escaped from where Matt's face and the pumpkin's jagged fleshy edge weren't creating an airtight seal. Matt kept his face in the pumpkin for five, ten, fifteen, twenty seconds, Joan's lighter still flaming the bowl, everybody cheering and stomping and losing their collective minds. Eventually, Matt pulled his face up, smoke escaping from his mouth and nose. His hair mussed, orange flesh streaked on his cheeks, face flushed, Matt hacked out unending mushrooms of smoke. The garage gone apeshit, banana-split-with-extra-fudge out-of-orbit apeshit.

A little before dawn, standing under the gazebo at Hilldale Park after egging vice principal McNichols' house, Matt would vomit orange flecked with pieces of chocolate, flecked with pieces of candy.

October was over.

THE RIVER IS DARK

The day was finally here. *Dark Rivers* was out. Matt was jittery with anticipation. He had read *Dark Rivers* three and a half times. They had their opening night tickets since early November. Matt had been excited for a new strain of weed hitting Thornhill, was still sick with longing for his first sexual encounter, but the waiting for this movie was something entirely new. At least with sex there was masturbation and pornography; all *Dark Rivers* had was two ninety-second trailers and rumours. He'd lie in bed, too high to sleep, wonder about how his favourite novel would be transformed onto the screen. And now, the night had arrived. The plan had been set for weeks: since it was a Thursday, Friedman and Joan would pick Matt and Rob up at Kol B'Seder, they'd go over to the theatre, smoke a blunt, submerge themselves in the visual splendour of the dark river. Then back to Matt's basement bedroom to debrief, punch bowls, sleep. The four of them had all pitched in on a half ounce of Jean Guy, a new strain from Quebec that Christian was raving about. Friday was the last day before the winter break, as good as the holiday itself; they were all skipping.

Matt rode the school day on a wave of palpable excitement. At Hebrew school, he and Rob stood in front of their class, teaching about Hanukkah. Matt was looser than ever in front of the students: he and Rob play-acted the Maccabees' fight against the Assyrians to laughter and applause from the kids. At ten to seven Matt saw Joan's face in the classroom door's window, felt momentarily embarrassed to be holding a tinfoil sword, but then brandished it in the air to Joan's usual wicked grin. For some reason Matt had felt the instinctive need to keep Joan away from his Jewish life, but saw now how stupid that was. The two worlds brushed against each other, and nothing burst into flame.

The car on the way to the theatre felt like they were leaving the comforts of home to embark on something big and drastic, a trip around the world, a journey to the moon, a spelunk into the unconscious. Friedman had a billy ready to go and they punched bowls all the way to the theatre. Once there, they had a few hours to kill before their 10:45 showing. They scarfed burgers and onion rings at The Saucy Aussie. They ran from the restaurant to the bookstore, coats in hand, the air icy and clean. At the huge display for the *Dark Rivers* movie tie-in, Rob picked up a book and opened it at random. "The people of Bron have long tolerated your kind here, planet-grazer," he read. "And now you must make a choice," Joan said from memory. "How do you think they'll make Dobro Carthy look?" Rob asked; the leader of the Dark Riverites on Preethor, Carthy was wise, slow to action, contemplative. They went down to the river behind the theatre, slid on the early winter ice, burned the blunt. "The river is dark!" "The river is eternal!" With an hour before showtime, Rob took them up a ladder to the roof of the theatre. Christian, Cali, and Leon were up there, lounging on folding chairs, wearing bomber jackets and toques, exhaling visible breath into the night. They sat down with them. They were talking about a new drug called L. Supposedly it gave you a six-hour trip of feeling nothing but incredible luck for every aspect of your life.

"It was created by the American government to keep the restless proletariat down if they ever got organized enough to rise up," Leon said calmly, "but they had no idea of its radical potential."

Christian nodded in agreement. "I heard the Navy's having great results with it treating vets with PTSD."

Maybe that was just the kind of drug Matt needed: a small, non-active part of him knew how lucky he was, living where he lived, the opportunities he had, but the majority of his conscience was mired in such petty, day-to-day dread, want, worry.

Cali lit a movie ticket, watched it flame out in her fingers. "Yeah, plus it gets you fucking *ripped*!"

"Anyways," Christian said, "there's basically no chance of us getting any of it anytime soon, though Leon claims he has a hookup."

Leon got animated, the most animated Matt had ever seen him. "I do have a hookup! Jolly's legit, man, when has he ever let us down?"

As they argued, Rob stood up, looked meaningfully at Matt, Friedman, and Joan. They started for the exit.

"Enjoy the movie!" Christian called out as, one by one, they descended the ladder.

Loaded with popcorn and chocolate and extra-large cokes, they bypassed the line and got choice seats halfway up the theatre. Not until they sat down did Matt realize how stoned he was. The theatre was wiggling with slugs of energy. He could barely contain the emotion shimmering inside him. The theatre, packed, was calm-before-the-storm ready.

Down went the lights.

Three hours later, the credits rolling, Matt rose from his chair, followed his friends down the stairs, through the high, carpeted hallway in the crush of jostling bodies, out into the sudden light of the outside world.

Everybody was shouting, exclaiming, high fiving.

Matt was reeling.

They waited in line to pee, they walked to the car, they drove out of the lot. The car's conversation passed over him like air.

Back in Matt's basement bedroom, Jimi lying under the desk, the four of them went to work on the remainder of their half ounce. For the first hour, to a soundtrack of The White Stripes— Joan's new favourite band—they packed massive bowls in the bubbler, loudly punched bowl after bowl in Rob's bong, at some point Friedman, in his careful, dexterous way, fashioned a billy from a two-litre coke bottle he found in the recycling upstairs. The sounds of bowls hit, inhaled, imbibed, sucked, popped, punched. Not until they had made a serious dent in the weed piled up on Matt's night table were they sufficiently desensitized to get into it. And then they couldn't stop: Matt, Rob, and Joan rattling off a list of disappointments.

"They butchered the ending! Dobro Carthy is supposed to die! They're totally just letting him live so they can make a sequel."

"They oversimplified everything—made the Brightons too evil, the Preethorns too good."

"And what was with all of the forced romance? Wasn't Carthy, like, gay with Yu-or?"

"And turning Pereon into comic relief!"

"The whole thing was just so, so off."

Matt's throat was sticky with rage. He had never known disappointment like this, disappointment sloshed with disgust, anger, disillusionment. Since exiting the theatre, the world looked and felt different. He was on the outside of a great, massive machine, chewing everything in, spitting everything out. He wanted to get as far away from the whole sickening edifice as possible.

"I kind of liked it." Everyone turned to Friedman, sitting on the floor against Matt's bed, looking sheepish. "What? So it didn't follow the book exactly. The special effects were fucking awesome."

Matt couldn't think of anything to say except that they had butchered it.

"They butchered it," he said.

"It was empty calories," Rob said.

Friedman looked shockingly angry. "Whatever," he said, reaching for the coke bottle billy.

Nothing but the sound of smoke filling the plastic bottle, filling it, filling it again. Friedman opened his sketchbook. Matt caught the drawing on the last page—it was a realistic, highly detailed depiction of a group of armed Maccabees forcibly circumcising Santa Claus. The Jewish zealots were in full armour, two of them holding Santa down, one brandishing the knife, a few others watching by a wall of Jerusalem stone, Santa's pants down at his ankles. It was a fucking fantastic drawing, hilarious and subversive, but Matt didn't say anything. Friedman flipped to a clean page and started to draw scenes from the movie. Matt stretched for the bong.

At some point, Rob, coming back from the washroom clutching his various acne soaps, turned off the overhead light. Joan flicked on the bedside lamp. Matt rolled a joint. More bong hits. Thick white smoke gulped into lungs, released into the subterranean room. Nearly six in the morning now. The four of them in varying positions of supineness on the floor, on the bed. The bong, tall and proud on the carpet, throwing long hard shadows, a wisp of smoke trellising the rim of the shaft. The world, all of it, every last bit, slant. Matt stoned to the roof of his eyes.

⫶ A new day's light appeared in the small rectangular window flush with the ceiling. Matt lolled near sleep. Friedman, who hadn't spoken or moved in a while, bounced up, stuffed his sketchbook into his knapsack, started looking for his wallet.

"Where you going, man?" Rob muttered. Matt raised his head.

"School."

Matt, Rob, and Joan burst into laughter.

"School?!"

"Yeah man. School." Friedman opened the door, and was gone. A moment later they heard his van start up.

Joan started *Elephant* again. Rob's VHS copy of *Face/Off* was in his lap. Matt reached for the bong. The glass shaft was warm in his hand.

⫶ An hour later, Joan and Rob passed out on the floor, Matt found himself in bed, cradling the worn copy of *Dark Rivers* that his father had stolen from his high school library. Matt's mind was a hundred rooms over, every thought freighted with revelation. Movies are overrated: revelation. Why are we so obsessed with turning books into movies? Why is it that when a book becomes a movie, it's as if it is in its true form, but if a movie becomes a book, nobody cares: revelation. Why should books become movies at all? Books are books! Fuck any logic that always must end in movies.

Revelation.

A moment later, Matt was cataloguing the ideas for movies, business ventures, sci-fi premises that were scrolling through his conscience. A huge, deep pool at the airport that everyone had to swim in before boarding their flights. A bed that made ice cream, either soft-serve or regular. A restaurant that only served sons who had lost fathers. Two planets in the same solar system, both with intelligent life, aware of each other's existence, waiting through the eons to communicate, to get there, to touch each other.

THE FESTIVAL OF LIGHTS

The first of the two family Hanukkah parties was at Matt's house. The whole extended family, aunts and uncles and cousins and cousins' children and the dogs. Latkes were fried. Candles were lit. Prayers were sung. Latkes were eaten. Arguments were had. Latkes were surreptitiously dropped on the floor for the milling dogs. Gifts were given, the adults sitting on couches in the living room, the kids on the floor. Matt hadn't smoked since that morning and was in a bad mood, was still in the post–*Dark Rivers* pall, though he was beginning to come to terms with his disgust with the movie. The book had always opened up in him the possibility of living life differently; the movie didn't do that, didn't even try, it was all the same human bullshit, just repackaged on a different planet. At least there will always be the book; at least there will always be Hera Black's imagination. She must be livid, Matt thought, taking solace in the idea of an author mourning the desecration of her masterpiece before remembering that for all he knew, she wasn't even alive.

His youngest cousin asked Matt to help him set up the Lego space city he got as a gift, and Matt got down on the floor and they laid the roads, built the out-stations.

For dessert, chocolate cake and donuts. Matt fell asleep before everybody had left, dreamed of hurtling through space, totally alone, home an unfathomable distance.

NIGHT WALK

After the second Hanukkah party, at his aunt's house on the other side of Thornhill, Matt walked Jimi around the neighbourhood, smoked a persy joint. It was Christmas Eve, the weather a wet wintry mix: freezing rain, hard crisp snow on the lawns, fog, puddles of icy water. Matt felt acutely aware of his surroundings, was filtering everything through some new hardware that must have been installed when he was asleep. How the back end of Thornway, the twisty street behind his own, was all tall flat narrow townhouses that widened out once the street turned into Arvida. On Brownridge the houses were big, fully detached, getting smaller the closer to the Catholic elementary. The open, lighted windows showcased a mixture of hanukiah and Christmas trees. At one window an older Black man was playing the piano. At this time of year most houses they passed declared themselves— Christian or Jew. The houses that weren't decorated with Christmas lights or a menorah in the window or a whole nativity scene or a giant blue-and-white Star of David balloon were, on this night of sleet and icy rain, the exceptions. Matt stopped while Jimi investigated a young linden tree. The street was eerily quiet. Since he was a kid Christmas was always a strange day. He wondered what Joan, what Horito, what Leon, Christian, and Cali, were doing. He felt very far away from them. He belonged here as much as Dobro Carthy and his crew belonged on Preethor. Anyone who said the Jews of North America have fully assimilated have not been Jewish at Christmastime. Christmas, and the void of Christmas.

"C'mon, Jimi." They started walking again. If the world was ever again going to turn against the Jews, Matt thought, it would feel something like the difference he felt during this time of year, though magnified to horrific proportions. The idea moved him deeply.

Matt laughed. Just like *Dark Rivers*, the world wanted the Jewish book to be adapted to the Christian movie, its supposed final form. But no. Matt chose the book. Matt chose being Jewish. The outside. They turned onto their street. The icy puddles and piled-up slush black and gold from the towering streetlights.

PENIS OR ASSHOLE

"The time between Christmas and New Year's is the choda of the year," Joan proclaimed. Matt and Friedman were sitting on her bedroom floor, playing Monopoly. They were out of weed, had to kill the time somehow. Guitars and drums towered around them.

"So which one is the penis, which one the asshole?" Matt said, moving his thimble onto Park Place.

The doorbell rang. It was Rob, looking harried.

"Did you score?"

"Nah man, Christian's dry. He says everybody's dry."

"What about Todd and his idiotic twelve weeds of Christmas?"

"Todd's in Winnipeg with his folks."

"Shit! What are we supposed to do?"

"Let's try and find Samuel. Does he still work at the MacDo's?"

They bundled up, trudged the thirty snowy minutes to the mall, their moods hardening with each THC-less minute. Sure enough, Samuel was behind the counter of McDonald's, his hair in a hairnet. "Happy H to you, brothers and sister! I was hoping to see you before the eight days had run their miracle-scented course."

"We were hoping for a little miracle of our own," Matt said, bringing his pressed-together thumb and pointer finger to his mouth.

"Meet me at the loading docks in ten minutes."

Twenty minutes later, Samuel walked towards them with a menorah in hand. He had Matt light the shamas candle, light the seven other candles with the shamas, and together they sang the blessing. Even Joan covered her eyes with her hands and hummed along.

Samuel took a thin, long joint, still wet with saliva, out of his pocket, and proceeded to light it with the menorah flame. Matt could not figure Samuel out: one moment he seemed deeply religious, the next he was slinging bacon cheeseburgers at the mall, not to mention that since the Simchat Torah fight with Friedman

Matt couldn't square Samuel's Jewishness with his idiosyncratic views of Israel.

"Don't you care about working with all that bacon?" he asked, faintly aware that he would never have asked such a direct question before the disappointment of *Dark Rivers*.

Samuel smiled. "Do you not know the story of Reform Judaism in North America? The first rabbis on the continent who called themselves Reform were itinerant nomads, young Jews with religious yearning and a craving for justice and adventure, carving out a new syncretic religion. Once the movement achieved critical mass, they had a big celebratory party, and, either on purpose or not—nobody knows for certain—the caterers were not told about the kosher restrictions. The Treyf Banquet, as it became known, was a defining moment for our young movement. Had we gone too far? Could we really stay Jewish but discard tenets as central as Kashrut? Well, my friends, we said yes. The spirit of Judaism can live in an infinite number of manifestations. Of course, those who could not stand these changes broke off from our radical experiment, started the Conservative movement. But those of us who were ready to modernize stayed."

Samuel told this story with the same cadence as every rabbi Matt had ever witnessed, yet the story he told was anathema to the usual narratives he was familiar with. Matt couldn't help but notice that Friedman was getting more upset the more Samuel talked. Samuel took a long, wet pull on the joint.

"Have you heard of L?" Friedman asked, obviously trying to change the subject. At least he hadn't started an argument.

"L? That's the stuff of the forefathers, man! They say that shit is as close as you can get to Moses circa burning bush! Tell me you guys have an L hookup?"

"Not exactly." Christian had told Friedman and Matt that Leon had managed to score some of the make-you-feel-lucky drug, and had invited them to try it, but that didn't necessarily mean Matt had a hookup.

They bought a gram of weed from Samuel, all he was willing to part with, and walked back to Matt's house to smoke it.

It was snowing. Matt was cold and warm and happy. His face was wet. They crossed the last set of lights before Matt's street. The world was large and gorgeous and thrilling to be alive in. He was with his friends, heading to a warm dry place. In two days a new year would start. The dark river would continue its endless flow.

"I'm fucking baked," Joan said.

Everybody, every single living thing on the planet, laughed.

Matt's house loomed up in the hard-falling snow.

FIREWORKS

New Year's Eve. Matt and Rob were sitting on summer tires, smoking billy in the garage, waiting for Joan. Tonight was the night: they were going to dose the L. Matt was terrified, even though Cali had assured Matt and Rob that it would not be anywhere near as intense as acid. Christian had invited Friedman, but he had declined, said he had already invited people over to his basement. Matt was happy Friedman wasn't going to be there. They were meeting everybody else at Leon's; his parents were visiting Russia for the first time in twenty years, for the funeral of his dad's brother. The house would be theirs.

At 9:30 Joan's scrawny silhouette showed up at the end of the court under the lone streetlight, and they punched a bowl as she approached the garage. She was wearing her No Frills jacket, had a large bag of walnuts in one hand, a half-peeled banana in the other, a bright pink toque on her small head. She entered the cave of the garage and plopped down onto a tire. Under the bare garage bulb, everything was soft browns and greys.

"You guys ready?" she asked, taking a bite of the banana.

"What's with the nuts?"

"Protein, man! And the potassium is a must for any psychedelic adventure." She offered the nub of the banana to Rob, who laughed, shook his head. She pivoted the banana to Matt. Matt leaned over and sucked the half-inch of sweet flesh into his mouth. He was trying desperately to keep his nervousness from breaking through his chest and flooding his throat, his mouth.

"Let's bounce," Rob said. They jumped up.

Waiting for the garage door to close, their breath puffing into the cold, Matt wondered if he would feel differently about his house, his parents' house, when he got back later that night. Would the L make him appreciate his life in a true, real way?

The walk to Leon's was a little over half an hour. They cut through the grounds of Matt's old elementary school, through the park Matt had played in from grade one on, had smoked weed in ten thousand times, where he had sat under the gazebo in a spring downpour laughing and hitting bong, out onto Clark, past their high school, crossed Dufferin into Granite Ridge. Leon, Cali, and Christian were sessioning at the foot of Leon's driveway. They turned to watch the three high schoolers approach.

Twenty minutes later they were sitting around Leon's Formica kitchen table. On the table were six sugar cubes on an ornate china plate, a vial of clear liquid. Everyone was chill, supercool, the vibe elevated nonchalance; Matt, though, was pretty fucking nervous, felt as he had never felt before the smallness of Leon's kitchen. He could barely listen to Cali explain what they should expect:

"So. Once we take the sugar cubes, we should have forty-five minutes, an hour, before the L starts to do its work. There should be a quick rise to a glorious plateau. And, if Jolly's not full of shit, literally no comedown. Just blissful self-aware joy."

"Let's do it."

They each placed a hand—white, black, brown—over the plate and picked up a cube. The six of them leaned in, huddled around the table. Matt, his heart sounding off every alarm in its substantial arsenal, wondered what Rob was experiencing. Even with the breath-shortening panic, Matt felt the most intense belonging he had ever felt, which was the main reason he shook off the desire to just pretend to eat the sugar cube—here he was, with people who were unquestionably cool, about to go on a journey only a few dozen other humans had gone on before; he was one of them, he was part of something. The feeling of communal bliss peaked as they, as one, raised the sugar cubes to their mouths and sucked them in. Immediately, the edges of the small cubes started to melt.

Leon smiled wildly, wisps of his blond hair lifting off his head.

The uncrossable line crossed, Matt's heart put down its cymbals, its air-sirens. The sugar cube was a half-muddy slug in his mouth. The sugar cube was a bright little tongue-puddle. The sugar cube was gone, melted into sweet air, and Matt felt remarkably calm.

Okay. No turning back.

Ten minutes later, in Leon's room, Joan tuning Leon's beat-up acoustic, Nirvana and Nine Inch Nails posters on the scuffed and marked up walls, Matt started to feel something.

"I think I'm starting to feel something," he mouthed. The drug, so small in its pure undiluted form you couldn't see it with the naked eye, was expanding in his brain. It was as if he had stepped onto an escalator and was steadily ascending, escalated, being escalated. He was being escalated. He looked at Rob, lounging on a heap of dirty laundry, and they laughed. Joan plucked the newly in-tune low E string. It vibrated out into the room.

"Far out," Leon said, and they all laughed. Matt was feeling mighty good. Mighty, mighty good. Was he already higher than he had ever been on marijuana? Was he already higher than he had ever been on marijuana?

Not much later, Christian sat up from where he had been lying on the floor. "Something's...off," he said, slowly, tasting out the words.

Leon and Cali looked at each other. Cali looked slowly around the room, her eyes concentrated.

"It's like an acid come-on," she concluded.

Leon nodded, as if he was tasting a frozen yogurt he knew intimately but that was supposed to be a new flavour of ice cream. "Yeah. Definitely LSD." He paused, chuckled. "Damn good LSD, too."

"Jolly ripped us off again!"

This is where Matt would normally have become afraid, but the drug had assumed the exact shape of Matt's body, from his head and neck through his chest into his fingers and thighs and heels and hair follicles and penis and balls. He felt unbelievable. A glowing creature of warm light. Rob and Leon were making out: if it had happened any other day Matt might have been surprised, but tonight, right now, everything perfectly in tune with everything else, it made the best kind of sense. Joan finally finished tuning the guitar, strummed an impossibly gorgeous chord, every fibre of Matt's being curving into a hook, velcroing onto the sound's golden tautness.

The room moaned through them.

Some time later, the drug breached the limits of Matt's human shape. Now Matt was enveloped, swallowed, consumed, drowning in geysering currents. Panic, a different, new panic, primal, animal, vicious.

Matt took the bong from Leon's night table, every action vised in rank strangeness. He had to try to calm down. He filled the bowl, put the bong on the coarse carpet, flicked the lighter into flame, put the flame to the bowl, placed his dry lips on the hard rim, sucked. The smoke filling his lungs was hot sand; the smoke coming out of his body was chopped into cascading crystal-cut images. Time slowed and slowed and slowed and Matt knew that if it slowed any more he would cease. The word *cease* expanding so fast it nearly took his skin off.

Apparently Matt wasn't alone; Rob was freaking out. "This isn't real," he was saying, "none of this is real." He stood up, started pacing, shaking his hands, talking real fast. "This is fake, pretend, staged. How can this be real? How can any of this be real? This is just somebody's *idea* of a New Year's party. This is a simulation. None of this is real. Something's off, can't you tell? What kind of world have we made where this can be real?!" Cali led Rob to the bathroom.

Matt felt his own panic about to burst through his carefully maintained facade of carefreeness, which even in the throes of an accidental LSD trip had so far managed to maintain structural integrity. He tried to push his mind somewhere else, away from the sinister workings of the drug. He tried to think of Shoshana. Shoshana showing her breasts to Matt, a tiny sliver of the known world that had brought him such comfort. Shoshana, a friend, his first love, not meant to be, showing herself to him. But even that image, the practised lift, her defiant expression, the hot shock of it, was saturated with ominous colours, pulsing with dread, was growing fangs. Leon and Christian were laughing loudly, Joan was making sharp jangly shapes on the guitar, her face concentration stripped of anything else, shorn of personality, of what Matt took to be Joan's Joanness. A dark wave passed through the room. Matt switched to imagining having sex with Shoshana, sweet, loving sex, Shoshana sitting in his lap, facing him, it was helping, but then he lost it, he lost it, it flitted away like a loosed cartoon balloon, leaving only churning horror.

Matt stood up. Leon's room was too small for Matt's ever-expanding shadow. As he passed the bathroom he could hear Rob saying to Cali, very quietly, "There's supposed to be only seven days. There's supposed to be only seven days."

Matt exited Leon's house into Granite Ridge. The streets were alien, unreal, terrifying. He knew nothing but the desire to move. He was crossing Dufferin when he finally, unbelievably, came up. He hadn't known the word *peak* could be experienced so literally. He came up, he *peaked*, he was on top of a mountain range he would never have imagined existed. The houses of the neighbourhood revealed their bones. The salt on the sidewalks was older than oldness itself. The night was big and cold.

He was walking through backyards he recognized. He was approaching Friedman's backyard. People were standing around the basement door, smoking, laughing. Matt approached, walking funny, a monster outside the bonds of community, of understanding, of language, of species. Now he was talking to them. What was he saying? Shoshana? Is that you Shoshana?

By 4:30, he found himself back inside his own house. He wasn't peaking anymore, that much was clear, but he was still not himself. He crawled into bed, shook through a carpet-burny-yet-oddly-pleasant panic attack, eventually pushing off into a light, skimming sleep.

JANUARY THE FIRST

Matt arrived at Friedman's in the midafternoon. Plenty of people were still there, sleeping on the couches, on the floor. Todd had some hash left so those who were awake were brewing hashbots out on the basement back-door stairs. Matt was himself again, though the strange winds of LSD Land were whispering still.

"Yo, you were talking some fucked-up shit last night man," Todd said, pulling the cigarette out of the water bottle as he turned the bottle upside down and shook out the excess tobacco smoke. "Like, some *serious* fucked-up shit," he said, uncapping the bottle and sucking in the paper-white hash smoke in a smooth chest-inflating draw.

"Like what?"

"Fuck, I don't know man, you were talking about the bones of the houses, about how people who think we're living in a giant simulation have never been in a forest at night, had never had the shit kicked out of them. Fucked-up shit like that."

Matt remembered saying those things now. They still throbbed with the half-life truth they were radioactive with last night.

"Have you ever even *been* in the forest at night?" Horito asked.

"Ha ha, maybe once, I don't know."

"What'd you think we have in store for us in the shitty year of our lord 2003?" Todd asked, picking up from the bundle on his cig pack another fleck of hash with the cherry of his cigarette, inserting the cigarette with steady planning-on-going-into-pre-med hands into the hole burned into the water bottle quickly enough so none of the hash smoke escaped.

"Honestly?" Horito asked. "Either worldwide apocalypse or global utopic bliss-out."

"Which would you rather Hori?" Todd asked, passing the bottle to Matt, his thumb over the hole. Matt took the bottle, shook it halfheartedly. He didn't even feel like getting high. He unfastened the cap, gulped in the burny hash smoke, immediately hacked it back out. The bot hit him in a dirty surge, the acid flashing through him like an electrical storm.

"Whichever one gets rid of the most bullshit, obviously," Horito said.

"Hear hear!"

"Hear hear," Matt couldn't help but agree.

Later, Matt was standing in Friedman's large gleaming kitchen, drinking a glass of orange juice, thinking about how he hadn't even spoken to Friedman today, he hadn't asked how the L was or anything, when Shoshana and Noam walked out of Friedman's dad's study, where they had obviously spent the night. Noam was holding Shoshana's hand in his, the other hand grasping the neck of his acoustic guitar. Matt coughed a little but continued drinking the juice, not angry, not upset, not vengeful, not anything, not anything at all except just slightly, bearably alone.

FOREST HILL

Late mornings, late nights. Joints at the park, bong hits in the garage, pipe hoots with Joan behind the No Frills dumpsters. Matt saw Rob daily. They had quickly become best friends; what

Matt mistook for arrogance was just intelligence, an at-home-in-the-worldness that Matt was trying to emulate. They hung out with Christian and Cali at Leon's, whose parents were still in Russia. They saw the remaining blockbusters at the movie theatre, then saw them again. They ate fast food at the mall, talked philosophy and religion and history with Samuel. Matt had an ortho appointment—Dr. Mustard and his dental assistant Crystal talked excitedly about the trip to Israel Dr. Mustard was taking the entire office on in March, as they changed his elastics from green to clear.

On the last day of winter break, Matt's world shifted onto a new axis. Renee and Laura went to Kol B'Seder, were a year younger; neither Matt nor Rob had noticed them before: their attention had always been calibrated towards their own year, the older kids. But on that bittersweet Sunday, they ran into them at the mall. Renee was holding a Music World bag, Laura had on sunglasses that covered half her face, both of them were wearing knee-length parkas and drinking lattes, which struck Matt as a weirdly adult thing to be doing. They chatted outside of the mall's movie theatre, where Matt and Rob had been playing in the arcade, deciding if they should see a movie. "Want to come down to my place?" Renee asked, taking an inquisitive sip from her latte. "My parents are out of town." Matt and Rob looked at each other. They left the mall, piled into Renee's large black SUV and started towards Bathurst. "Do you boys have any weed?" Renee asked once they were south of Steeles, glancing at them in the rearview, both girls giggling. Matt and Rob looked at each other again. Weed they had.

Renee lived in a mansion in Forest Hill. The house was hidden behind large pine trees, had a gabled three-door garage, and the biggest front door Matt ever saw, made out of some kind of dark, glossy wood. Renee took them to one of the backyard's three separate sections, a large patio with wicker lawn furniture and an industrial barbecue. The barbecue was wide enough that Matt could lie down inside of it. "I could lie down in that barbecue," Matt said, inadvertently, relieved when Laura and Renee laughed. They smoked weed until their fingers were frozen, went inside, listened to Renee's new Dave Matthews CD. The sixteen-note doorbell rang, chiming through the house, and more of Laura and Renee's friends joined them, four other girls, similar to Renee and Laura in some not-yet-definable way. Matt and Rob spent the rest of the afternoon overwhelmed with the energy of these young women. They were different from any other girls Matt had ever known. And their names, their names, they rolled around in his head like delicious fruit: Liz, Yael, Evie, Tasha. They were beautiful, stunning, smart. Rich. Matt knew he would fall for one of them, but it took a couple of hours before Matt's female-body-sensory-array homed in on Tasha. Tasha, her room-shattering presence enough to knock Matt out cold; how could it have been otherwise? The love hit him like a bong hit of super-potent weed, leaving him lifted, flustered, wrecked.

They smoked the rest of Matt and Rob's weed, microwaved spring rolls in a gleaming marble-and-steel kitchen and went to sit in yet another room of couches arranged around a humongous TV to eat them.

Tasha sat down next to Matt.

"So how do you know Reen and Laur?" she asked him.

"Uh, shul."

"Do you live up there, in Thornhill?" Matt tried to keep eye contact. Tasha's big face, light brown hair, wide shoulders, breasts whose proximity made Matt giddy.

"Yeah, not far from the mall."

"Forest Hill born and raised!"

"Oh. Cool."

"Do you go to camp?"

"Uh, no."

"A Toronto Jew who doesn't go to camp? I sense a story there! Cool, cool, I respect that. Well, what camp would you go to if you went to camp?"

"Northland, I guess?"

"Get out! That's where I go!" She paused, looked him over, as if assessing some innate quality. "You'd love it there! It's one of the bigger camps, and I'm sure you've heard that the guys' section and the girls' section are far apart, but it's the best camp Matthew, words can't even describe. I'll be a CIT next year. They say Northland is a counsellor's camp—ya know, as opposed to a campers' camp—and I can't wait to find out! I had to leave a few days early this summer because we had a family wedding in Israel. I almost killed my parents, but, hey, it's Israel! What school do you go to, anyways?"

"Vaughan."

"Do you know Sonya Waxman? She would have graduated last year?"

"Uh, no, I don't think so."

"She's a cousin! Do you have any relatives in Israel?"

"No. Do you?" Stupid! She just said that she did.

"Tons!" she answered.

"Oh, wait—Sonya's like tall, and goes out with that guy Evgeny?"

"Yeah, that's my Sonya!"

That ethereal connection to a cousin—way to have almost missed it!—enough to confirm that Matt was smitten.

Laura came over to them with Matt's bubbler.

"Is Tash drilling you with Jewish Geography, by far her most favourite game?"

The conversation was over; Matt was exhausted. Thankfully, he wasn't called on to do much more talking the rest of the afternoon. These girls, lifelong friends, moved to their own burnless energy. When Matt and Rob finally stumbled out of Renee's house, it was dark out. The big well-groomed lawns were iced in hard white snow. A number of chimneys on the thatched man-sion roofs had smoke curling out of them. The blue-black sky held the promise of winter stars. They stood on the icy road, in a daze.

"How should we get home?" Matt asked.

"Fuck it, man, let's walk! I saved a half-dime of weed, rolled it up just now in the bathroom."

They started walking; Rob lit up the pinner. Matt didn't know how long the walk was—two hours, three hours, four?—but what did it matter? He was brimming, he was aflame, he was on acid again, the streets of Toronto were frantic with their own internal, immutable joy. It was the last day of winter break and not even the spectre of tomorrow's early morning, of first period with Mr. Landau, of all the reading he had failed to do, was going to bring him down.

They walked north.

CHANGE, BIRTHDAYS

Matt and Rob were spending as much time as they could in Forest Hill. *From one hill to another; from thorn to forest.* Matt had never learned so much in such a short period of time, had never been exposed to such wealth, had never felt more like he was where he wanted to be. Laura, Renee, Yael, Evie, Liz, and Tasha were best friends since their first summer at camp, dressed and acted like they were in San Francisco in the sixties or New York in the sev-enties, read books and talked politics and were aware of their relentless privilege but didn't feel guilty about it. They travelled the world, excelled at school, were artistic and outdoorsy. Tasha played competitive tennis. Yael and Evie wrote songs together. Laura volunteered with her father at a soup kitchen two morn-ings a week. They wore their Jewishness with pride, and spoke about Israel in a way Matt had never heard before: a beautiful, foreign place that had its share of problems, the worst of which was the terrible no-good occupation of the West Bank and Gaza

Strip, but that they were connected to through family, childhood trips, history, culture. They spoke a basic Hebrew. They talked a lot about the Palestinians—about their suffering, their being on the tragic side of history, about the need for two states. They all seemed to feel the same way, except Yael, who lived in Israel until she was thirteen, and, whenever the talk had reached a point of self-righteousness she couldn't take anymore, would bring up the right of return—the hypocrisy of it for Jews, the lack of it for Palestinians—the refugees, the treatment of Arabs within Israel. And in all this fecund female empowerment, there was Tasha. Matt had never met somebody, not even Samuel, who had so many words, sentences, ideas, and while they may have been of a less cosmic nature than Samuel's, he was hungry for every single one. She had a world-weary sarcasm that only emboldened the sense that positively oozed off of her that the world was a place of wonder and that she had a definitive right to all that wonder.

That January Matt and Rob spent a lot of time at Renee's. They got hammered on tequila in the ravines of Forest Hill, Yael's older boyfriend or Renee's brother supplying the liquor, Matt and Rob supplying the weed. They watched tennis on Renee's big-screen TV, Tasha and Laura providing hilarious commentary. They visited Samuel at his hut in the woods. Yael and Evie's band, The Esthers, wrote songs and rehearsed for the upcoming girlband-only Battle of the Bands at Lee's Palace in March; they convinced Joan to sign up her band as well. One grey day, Samuel wasn't at his hut, the dirt floor was recently swept, the books that used to adorn the shelves were gone. "Probably off somewhere in the desert," Rob said as they turned to head back to the mall.

Once Renee's parents returned, they started congregating at Tasha's, whose parents were off to Hawaii for two weeks (at any given moment, it seemed one of the girls' parents were away). Tasha's house was even more outrageous than Renee's. It was the first house with an actual gate that Matt had been in. Inside, everything was clean, minimalist, shellacked with taste and money. There was an entire room—bigger than Matt's house—that Tasha called the ballroom, with curved white walls, shiny birch floors, and a crystal chandelier, with no furniture except a white baby grand piano. What Matt couldn't get over, however, was the art. On nearly every wall was a painting that floored Matt. A massive canvas with a blue-shaded cityscape. A spattering of Tom Thompson sketches, each no bigger than a slice of bread. And, hanging in a hallway off the dining room, a painting of a sunset by Edvard Munch. The vivid colours, the messy spill-over, the fullness and curve of the life-giving collection of constantly exploding hydrogen atoms, the painting contained everything Matt was feeling. The uncontrollable fullness of life. He would get lost in front of it for minutes at a time.

It didn't take long for Matt to deduce that Tasha was not interested in him, but it wasn't until Joan said something that it really clicked. It was his seventeenth birthday, they had all gotten together at Laura's house before going to a concert downtown, Horito and Todd and Joan and even Friedman present. Joan said to him, "Dude, you're fucking in love with that Tasha girl. I don't blame you, that face, those boobs, that fucking house, but, sorry to say, she is def not reciprocating the affection," and Matt had to admit that it was true. But so what? He loved her, she obviously liked him enough that she enjoyed spending time with him (and his unending supply of weed). That was more than enough. She didn't owe him anything.

Otherwise, his days at school were the same. He taught Hebrew school on Thursdays, went to classes Saturday morning. Shoshana and Noam were officially boyfriend and girlfriend now. Friedman was still being a dick. Samuel had vanished. Every weed-addled day brought another realization about humanity, friendship, the universe.

The winter wore on.

PURIM

In early March a weed drought descended on Thornhill. Matt's suburb, as well as the parts of Toronto they had access to, were out of herb. There was nothing. This was far worse than the Christmas dry spell. This was wartime-level dryness. Matt and Rob had less than a half-quarter left between them when they got the call from Joan, who had run into Christian on the street. He had told her it could last two weeks, maybe three. Even switching to the most extreme form of rationing they were capable of, how could they be expected to make a half-quarter last them more than a few nights?

Their remaining stash lasted thirty-six hours—there were no Hanukkah miracles here. They were doing well enough until Tasha and Yael stopped by Matt's after the mall and wanted to get high. Matt and Rob had just finished cautiously sharing a bowl, but they couldn't say no to Tasha and Yael. Rob rolled the smallest joint he could muster, and they smoked it beside Matt's house, everything wet and flattened from the clinging winter, went back in for a round of bong hits in Matt's small bathroom. Tasha and Yael pretended to play a game of tennis, giggling and jumping around the bedroom. Outside for another pinner. When Tasha asked Matt, her eyes and golden hair dewy from the outdoors, if she could have some weed to smoke with her volleyball team after practice, Matt couldn't say no, especially now that he was, all things considered, rather blitzed. He thought he gave her around a dime, but after the two young women drove off, Rob told it him it was more like a gram and a half. They went back downstairs to discover the worst: except for the half-smoked bowl still smouldering in the bong, they were officially dry.

Over the next few days things went from bad to worse to pretty fucking terrible. Matt and Rob smoked the kif from their grinders, the fine brown powder producing sharp, fleeting highs. They scrounged their bedrooms and Rob's car for roaches, found seven, opened them to get at their caramelized brown guts, smoked teardrop bowls. At school things got tense. People solid-ified around age lines, race lines, language lines. Fights broke out. Rob and Matt shook flipped-over computer keyboards, went through their jean pockets to liberate weed crumbs from pocket fluff, called Joan and begged—*begged*—her to pilfer her dad's stash, in a cigar box next to the tin can of loonies and toonies in his closet. Joan called back with the shocking news that he was dry too. If adults—*ADULTS!*—couldn't even score, what chance did these lowly seventeen-year-olds stand? In a last-ditch effort, Matt invited Drew over. Sure enough, the first thing he did, with-out even being prompted, was to comb through Matt's bedroom, somehow surfacing with enough marijuana dust for a pinner, which they had no choice but to share with him.

Samuel was still missing. He wasn't at the McDonald's, he wasn't at the cabin in the woods, he wasn't around the shul. Matt pictured him hitchhiking through the desert, praying with a prayer shawl over his head at the Western Wall, dead in the rainforest, part of a radical cell that was attempting to bomb an internet data centre in the winter wastes of Norway. Wherever he was, Matt was sure, he at least had weed.

On the third day of the drought Matt woke into a suburb of zombies. School was a war zone. Paranoia and distrust flowed like honey. That first day of total sobriety Matt masturbated five times. He snapped at his students at Hebrew school for not pay-ing attention.

Was he overreacting? Was he play-acting at being a junkie? Was the throat-sweet lust for a perfectly rolled spliff an illusion? Did it fucking matter?! If he only had a hit of weed so he could think clearly!

The night of the fourth day was when the dreams started. He dreamed he was at his uncle's house except there were three and a half extra basements. He dreamed he was in line for a heart upgrade, but then the power blew and the treasure hunt turned into a free-for-all. He dreamed he was seeing a movie at Film Forest except inside it was Tasha's house, but the basement was the shul, each room filled with bright sharp light, they open the doors of the ark to discover Matt's bong, smoking with eternal flame. Matt and Tasha are walking Matt's neighbourhood post-apocalypse. The neighbourhood looks the same—the houses, the sidewalks, the roads, the trees, the mailboxes are the same—but the very fabric of the dream sops with dread, something's wrong, the bone forest that dwells underneath the world clamouring for attention. Now an unspecified evil chases them, they zig through backyards and zag up and down fences—how could Matt have been so careless that he left his go-bag at home?

Matt woke with a sharp breath, drenched in guilt. At school the mood was dark. The smoking pit was a trench. The classrooms were torture cells. Matt was suspicious of everybody; nobody could be trusted. Your neighbour, your teacher, your best friend, any and all could flip, snitch on you, inform, collaborate. Withhold.

Matt sat alone in the cafeteria, eating a peanut butter sandwich. The world was shit. The powerful were garbage. Nobody understood what it meant to be alive in a place like this. We built weapons and electric fences instead of outdoor stages and hiking trails. The world hated Jews and the Jews hated Palestinians and nobody liked Matt. Nobody liked Matt, nobody cared for Matt, nobody caressed Matt. Nobody would ever love Matt. Whoa, Matt, man—calm down.

He laughed, to himself, quietly, in the cafeteria. He wasn't all the way gone quite yet.

⁞ On the morning of the seventh day the whispers started. Todd heard there was weed in the other side of Thornhill; Horito had been told by some friends at Saint E that a big shipment from BC was due any day; Joan said that Granite Ridge was abuzz with the rumour that somebody had a small amount of super chronic, was only chopping to select people. Matt was just starting to feel normal again, his chemical levels returning to equilibrium, but once he heard there was marijuana in the offing, his throat went sweet, his hands trembled, his sole focus was on obtaining some, lighting it on fire, bringing it inside him.

After school that day Matt and Rob called every drug dealer they knew, everyone who had ever sold them a dime, but either everyone was still dry or they were posturing. Finally, Joan called. "Meet me at the mall in thirty minutes," she said.

On the way from the mall to the mystery dealer's house they ran into Friedman. Matt had heard he had started taking classes at Aish Hatorah, but was still surprised to see him wearing a kippah. Matt invited him to join them.

"So, how are things with your new friends?" Friedman asked as they crossed the field beside the fire station. Matt didn't know if he meant Leon and Cali or Tasha and the Forest Hill girls, and didn't care to find out.

"Good good," he answered.

Joan stopped at a big house right next to a small park. "This is the place."

Matt recognized the girl who answered the door right away. She was a regular at the mall, at Film Forest. Her name was Fatima, she went to Saint E, sometimes Matt and his friends would smoke with her and her friends at the park. Didn't Todd and her make out once in the mall family washroom? In any case, Matt was always a little afraid of her and her shiny black hair and defiant demeanour. She took them up to her bedroom, sat down cross-legged on the bed, and pulled out a zip-lock bag, tossing it to Joan.

"Fifty a half q," Fatima said. Incense was burning on the desk. On her wall was a poster of Bob Marley. Behind her, a red banner that said in white writing "From Turtle Island to Palestine, We Will Be Free."

"Fifty?" Matt asked, knowing he was willing to pay whatever the price was. It was a seller's market if ever there was one. Not to mention that this was the choicest weed Matt had ever seen, two huge buds of light green fluffy herb, fuzzy with shimmering crystal. It was fairy tale–level shit.

"May I?" Joan asked, opening the bag and inhaling. She looked up, her eyes glassy. "We'll, uh, we'll take it," she sighed.

They rolled one of the buds up into two fat joints to smoke on the way to shul. It was Purim. Laura and Renee were in the play, had made Matt, Rob, and Joan promise to come. Friedman, it seemed, was tagging along.

"What was with that banner?" Friedman asked angrily once they were on the street. "What is Palestine? Palestine doesn't even exist!"

"Dude, relax," Matt said. Rob was lighting the joint and Matt was jittery with anticipation, nervousness, anger at Friedman, disgust at the fact of their lifelong friendship. "You don't know what you're talking about."

As the joint burned, the stranger the argument became. Friedman spewed what sounded quite clearly to Matt's ears like clichéd racism, and Matt tried his best to echo what he thought Samuel would say, what Yael would say, but nothing was coming out right. By the time they got to the grey-bricked shul, Matt was walking in slow motion. He couldn't stop laughing.

"Friedman, man, shit, why so much hate?"

Friedman looked aghast. "Hate? I don't hate! I love! I love the Jews and the Jewish soul and Jewish suffering and the Jewish army and the Jewish fist!" He slammed his own fist into his palm. Matt, Rob, and Joan burst into laughter.

"Are you coming in?" Rob asked. They were standing at the front doors. Adults with young children in costumes were coming up the walkway.

Friedman looked at the shul, looked at Matt and Rob. "Nah, man. Have fun with your appeasers." He started walking towards the park.

Inside was pandemonium. Children dressed as Esther, as Maccabees, as miniature Israeli soldiers in camouflage face paint, ran and screamed down the hall. About half of the adults were dressed up too, wearing a silly hat or holding a sword. They were drinking straight from bottles of red wine. "Shit! We didn't even dress up!" Rob said. Tasha—why didn't Matt think that Tasha would be there?!—was dressed as a mummy, distressed strips of cloth wrapped tightly around her arms, legs, butt, and chest. Her boobs looked amazing. Matt could barely look at her, was uber paranoid about the marijuana stink that surely was emanating from him.

Shoshana and Noam were both dressed as butterflies. Noam's guitar was slung on his back. The play was a fifteen-minute retelling of the Purim story, with contemporary jokes worked in. It ended with a big dance number. To Matt, it was a swirl of colour and sound.

Up on the shul's roof, adults and kids alike smoked and drank. Matt had never seen anybody older than twenty-one smoke a joint. Matt imagined what Samuel would say if he were here, his small eyes bright with revelation: *Tomorrow, Purim will be celebrated in walled cities.* What? Had he heard Samuel say this before? Had he made it up? Where *was* Samuel? Matt walked to the edge of the roof, looked out over nighttime Thornhill. These suburbs were pretty much all he knew. The sheer girth of human experience in all those houses and apartment buildings and strip malls. The plant and animal life, the June bugs on the blinds in July, the rabbit Matt had startled while biking through the unfinished housing division, the humans and their roads and their roofs, the layers of sediment and mineral, the seasons and their conditions, the rivers that supposedly still held beavers.

They ended the night in the boardroom. Noam was sitting on the floor, playing guitar. Everybody else was sitting around the long table. Matt was playing with a noisemaker. "What a fun holiday!" Shoshana said. "A real celebration of living in diaspora."

"I like it because it allows us to reveal the irreverence that's always just under the surface," Renee said.

"A real celebration of humiliating our enemies," Rob said sarcastically. Matt noticed for the first time that Rob's skin had cleared up since he started on Accutane.

"What's wrong with that?" Tasha asked. She was drinking a glass of grape juice, her mummy wraps beginning to loosen. "Wherever we are, people want to kill us."

"Not everywhere," Yael said.

"Pretty much!"

"Not here, not in Canada."

"Well, not right now, fine, but who knows what will happen?"

Yael shook her head. "You're crazy, Tash. I'd rather be vulnerable than have power over people. Trust me."

"Who said anything about power?"

"We all know what you're talking about."

Tasha made a sad face, jumped on Yael and started tickling her. The night moved on. Matt thought of Dobro Carthy, the decision he had to make to join the world of Preethor or to remain separate, aloof, not a part of the war destroying the planet. Thinking of Dobro made him sad, which made him realize that he was already coming down. He had been as high as one of the first times he had ever smoked, what made him think he wouldn't come down just as hard? He motioned towards Rob, who nodded, took out the weed, started breaking it up on the glossy table.

MARCH BREAK

Saturday. After Hebrew school, Matt and Rob met Todd at the mall food court so Todd could chop them a brick of hash. The drought had ended, and a deluge had taken its place. Matt and Rob made a pact to smoke the whole thing by break's end. Eight glorious days.

Back in Matt's basement, they carefully broke a corner of the hash up into five little mountains of powder. Matt took the first hit. The hash was smooth chocolate. Leaning back, exhaling the fine smoke, Matt felt the marrow in his bones turn into golden light. He passed Rob the pipe.

It was going to be a fantastic March break.

⋮ Sunday. Matt slept over at Rob's, though out of habit he told his mom he was at Jeremy's. He woke up on the floor of Rob's room around noon. The night before was the female-only Battle of the Bands. It took place downtown, at Lee's Palace. Joan's band, The Racist Textbooks, got third place. Joan absolutely shredded her guitar solos, had had Matt gel and spike her hair, thrashed and scissor-kicked her away across the stage like a born rock star. Matt had screamed himself hoarse. Yael's band, The Esthers, with their quiet, dreamscape songs about lost loves and long roads and purple sunrises, got fifth place. Matt tossed and turned on the floor of Rob's room, not ready to get up, remembering the look of pure joy on Joan's face as she held her trophy.

⋮ Monday. They smoked hash in Matt's basement. They smoked hash in Matt's bathroom. They smoked hash in the park. They smoked hash in Todd's apartment stairwell. They smoked hash behind the mall. They smoked hash at Leon's, where Christian was celebrating his top percentile on the accounting exams. They smoked hash in Matt's backyard before dinner. They smoked hash. They smoked hash. They smoked hash.

⋮ Tuesday. Matt was greening out. Too much hash. He was lying on his bedroom floor, feeling stupid; every mental faculty he'd always depended on was obliterated, down for repair, experiencing technical difficulties. What could he do? He could smoke more, which for once didn't seem like the answer. He could eat some food—but how would he get upstairs, open the cupboard, dialogue with his mother? What he really needed was sleep, sweet, restful, forgetful sleep. He pulled himself up onto the bed and, somewhere after the sensation of falling enveloped him in sweet vertical acceleration, he passed out.

: Wednesday. Matt was in the ortho chair. He hadn't smoked since yesterday, was lethargic and grumpy. Last night's snow had turned to rain and his pants were wet from the walk over. The office staff were abuzz with their recent return from Israel. Suzy, the receptionist, was badly sunburned. The assistant, Crystal, leaned over Matt as she got ready to assist Dr. Mustard. She was wearing large, dangly silver earrings, the silver beads worked into blue-and-white Stars of David. "You're so lucky," she said, "to have a marvellous country like that waiting for you." Dr. Mustard, his rubber hands in Matt's mouth, was the most animated Matt had ever seen him as he railed against Saddam Hussein, the Arabs, Arafat. Matt had no choice but to sit there, take it. Dr. Mustard started telling Matt about the trip to Israel. "It was fantastic. What a country. What a country. We visited a base in the West Bank. I have a picture of me with an Uzi, ask Suzy, she'll show you. Hah. Suzy and the Uzi. By the way, have you started thinking about university, Matthew? I hope you're not considering Concordia. It's a hotbed for antisemitism. Remember when Netanyahu was supposed to give a speech, but those Jew haters shut it down? What do they think? You know who I blame? The administration. These people should be in jail! Though," he said with a flourish, popping an elastic out of Matt's mouth, "York University is no better, from what I hear. My girls are at McGill." Matt made muffled noises, hoped it would suffice.

: Thursday. At Hebrew class they had a guest speaker, a representative from the Women of the Wall movement. Matt thought back through all the guest lectures he had attended through six years of Hebrew school. He remembered: a Catholic priest; a female Protestant minister; an imam from the Islamic Friendship Centre; a Bahá'í speaker; an Anishinaabe woman who taught them about the four cardinal directions, the Two Row Wampum Treaty. The administrators had thought it would be a good idea to bring their class of fourteen-year-olds to the chapel to sit through an interminable debate between Rabbi Koffee and a rabbi from the Orthodox synagogue down the street.

A skinny older woman with black hair and big colourful necklaces, Elise was loud, fast-talking, physical. "Who here thinks women should be able to pray at the most holy site in Judaism without being hassled by big hulking security guards?" she asked animatedly. "Who here thinks women should be able to wear tefillin and read from Torahs?" She was pacing now, gesticulating with her wrinkled hands. "Who here thinks Judaism should be for everybody, regardless of their gender?! Israel is our country as much as it is the Orthodox's. Why should gender equality not extend to the Wall?"

Matt started off enthralled at Elise's rhetorical flourishes, but still managed to fall asleep for the last ten minutes.

⠿ Friday. Matt's basement bedroom. Rob, Joan, Renee, and Tasha were over. They were smoking bong and exhaling out of the small window. There was still nearly half of the hash brick left, so Rob and Matt had decided to bring in reinforcements. Bending down to pick up a spilled piece of hash, Joan found Matt's Hebrew school textbook under the bed. "*Drugs, Sex, and Integrity?* This is what you've been doing all those Saturdays?"

"Give me that!" Matt said, lunging for it. "I thought I had lost it."

Joan got away from him, sat down on the desk chair, flipped open the book. She started to read the table of contents. "'Alcoholism and drug abuse: does Judaism sanction getting high?' 'Premarital sex: Rabbi, may I?' Uh-huh, uh-huh. 'Intermarriage: why does it so upset Jews?' Intermarriage, what's that, like when Jews marry their cousins?"

"Not exactly."

Joan turned to the drugs chapter, started to read. "'The "why" of alcohol and drug abuse remains a mystery.'" Laughter. "'A release from tension, a cheap "high," a pleasurable feeling, a new experience, peer pressure—'" laughter— "'these are some of the reasons offered by young people who subsequently became hooked.'" Lots of laughter.

"Help, help, I'm hooked!" Tasha yelled, pretending to have a hook lodged in her neck.

Rob took the book from Joan. "I've never really even looked at this thing. Look at these pictures! Ha ha, yeah right, this girl writes to her rabbi to ask if it's okay for her to have premarital sex."

"Well?" Tasha asked, "is it?" Laughter.

Matt finished rolling the joint he had been working on. It had a base of Joan's weed, an obscene amount of hash on top. They went outside.

Back in the basement, Rob picked up the book again. As they continued smoking hash, talking about where Samuel could be, Rob read.

Eventually, Rob looked up. "Isn't it weird that in the whole chapter on violence in Judaism, they don't mention modern Israel once? It's all stories from the Bible."

"Why is that weird?"

"Because Israel's violent."

"Israel has to be violent," Tasha said. Matt turned to her. "Like, I feel for the Palestinians, you know that, but it's their fault they're in this situation. They had plenty of opportunities for a state of their own. They're always the ones to start the violence. What choice do we have but to respond violently?"

Matt wondered if Tasha would be speaking this way if Yael was around.

"Listen to this," Rob said. "'When the Jewish people dream its collective dream, it looks forward to that time of perfect peace.'"

Matt couldn't help thinking of Dr. Mustard. He didn't seem too interested in peace. He thought of Friedman, his argument with Samuel on Yom Kippur and Hanukkah, with Matt on Purim, his drawings of the third temple. The textbook and its evasions couldn't be more wrong: the Jewish people's collective dream, for the time being at least, was of another vintage entirely.

⠆ Saturday. Matt was walking Jimi. The thaw had reverted back to a freeze, and everything that was wet was now frozen. Matt thought of the near-infinite network of puddles and streams and rivulets, transforming from ice to water and back to ice. Mostly, he thought about Tasha. In a moment of hash burn-out clarity, he saw that for now he would have to wait for love to find him, if it ever would. He knew, too, that he would continue falling in love until someone, somewhere, reciprocated.

Jimi nosed him on the leg, they turned onto their street, the road's black ice caught the light from the streetlamps, the whole world shimmered.

⠆ Sunday. Matt and Rob sat in his bedroom, staring at the chunk of hash sitting on the table. "We're never going to do it," Rob said. "We made a pact," Matt said. "Let's go over to Leon's, I'm sure there'll be people there."

It wasn't until the sun had gone down over the Granite Ridge park where they were smoking and drinking, that Matt remembered tomorrow was school.

PASSOVER

Matt was helping his mom get ready for the Passover Seder, bringing food to the basement fridge, lugging the vacuum upstairs. Each floor of the house was a different temperature: the basement was freezing, the main floor was hot, the second floor hotter. On the radio the representatives of the United States agitated for war with Iraq. Rhita and Shai were playing Nintendo in the family room.

Matt's mom had him shelling the hardboiled eggs that would be eaten during the Seder. "I ran into Jeremy's mother at Nortown yesterday," Matt's mom said, chopping carrots.

"Oh yeah?" Matt said, not looking up from the eggs.

"Can you believe we haven't seen each other in so long? She told me Jeremy's been away all school year, doing an exchange in Germany."

"Oh really?" Matt said, cornered, caught, waiting for the axe to drop.

"Must be nice, to be so far away from one's parents." Matt's mom put her hand on Matt's face, turned him to look at her. "Eh?"

"Yeah, guess so." Matt's mom shook her head, released Matt's face.

"When you're finished with those eggshells, throw them out and wipe down the counter."

"Yes, Mom." Matt breathed an inner sigh of relief.

⁝ The main conversation during that night's Seder was Bush and the impending war. Afterwards, smoking bong in the bathroom, Matt replayed it in simplified form. Bong hit. Uncle 1: The economy! The economy! The economy! Bong hit. Uncle 2: Our security! Our security! Our security! Bong hit. Aunt 1 (married to Uncle 1 but obviously in love with Uncle 2): The Arabs! The Arabs! The Arabs! Bong hit. Why was it—Matt couldn't help thinking with spluttering anger—that he seemed to be the only one saying, quietly, maybe too quietly, but saying it, saying it nonetheless: Human life! Human life! Human life! He poured the brown bong water into the toilet. He rinsed out the bowl. He flushed the toilet.

As usual, Matt refused to keep Passover but joyfully ate the matzah brei his mom made in the morning, with heaps of maple syrup. Stumbling across *The Ten Commandments* on television,

Matt sat through the whole thing, suffering through the endless commercials. The story of a vengeful god, of hideous violence, of wandering, of redemption—what could be farther from Matt's daily life? Matt couldn't help feeling bad for the pharaoh though, for the loss of his son. How was that fair? When the Jews mark the doorposts of their houses with blood to signal to the angel of death to pass over their house, Matt thought of his drives with Friedman before the holiday dinners. For the first time since the fall, he missed Friedman, missed Friedman's van, missed Friedman's basement. Remembering that drawing of the Maccabees circumcising Santa, Matt couldn't help but laugh.

The fourth day of Passover, looking for a place to smoke, Matt and Rob trudged through slush and mud to Samuel's shack. The floor had been swept, the pipes of various size and vintage arranged neatly on the camping table. Books in English and Hebrew were back on the shelf, next to orange boxes of matzah, kosher-for-Passover macaroons.

"Samuel!" Matt said excitedly. Rob opened a macaroon tube. Sure enough, not fifteen minutes later they saw Samuel walking through the trees, a gentle long-haired giant returned from the underworld.

"Shalom, chaverim!" He pulled Matt up, gave him a massive hug, did the same for Rob.

Once they were seated again, Samuel told them his story. "I've been travelling North America. The places I've been! The Manhattan docks. The Lower East Side. I followed the routes of Jewish migration: to sunny Miami, to sunny Los Angeles. I visited Jewish summer camps defunct and still going. I stood at the actual site of the Treyf Banquet! Why was I visiting these places, you ask? I was getting ready. I, my young friends, have been accepted to rabbinical college." The whole time Samuel was talking, his hands were busy. He took out of his satchel a Seder plate, started rolling joints and putting them on the plate's various slots. For the shank bone, a fat blunt. For the charoset, three thin hash joints. For the bitter herb, a stubby with the weed barely broken up, meaning it would smoke and singe. For the egg, a fat two-gram spliff. For the matzah, a piece of matzah.

"You don't mind being Reform even though you don't agree with their politics?" Rob asked.

"The essence of Reform Judaism is to change, adapt, to take the grand metaphors of religion and to use them to channel cosmic awe, to work towards justice in the here and now. What better place to make *new* politics?"

"You'll be a great rabbi," Matt said, truly meaning it. Samuel lowered his head in thanks, before removing the first joint from the Seder plate, putting it in his mouth, lighting it.

THINGS BECOMING CLEAR, IN THE BATHROOM

Late spring meant the annual Kol B'Seder retreat, a May weekend at Sacred Mountain Conservation Area. Matt was thinking of not going, but Laura and Renee convinced him to come: "We'll get high in the woods for two days, commune with nature!" Plus, Tasha was going to be there with her parents, who were thinking of switching synagogues.

Laura wasn't wrong. They smoked in the woods, put Visine in their eyes and spray deodorant or perfume on their clothes, sat by the river. The meals were held in a communal dining room, the adults, teenagers, and children sitting at round tables, a hundred and fifty strong. At night they sat around a big fire, singing songs with Rabbi Koffee.

In his room the first afternoon, Matt was lying on the top bunk, his eyes closed. Tasha and Renee were sitting on Rob's bed, talking about Matt. "He'll be cute, maybe, in three or four years. He is funny, though." Did they know he was awake?

"He's cute, I guess, but not *cute* cute, you know?"

"Totally. You know he's in love with you, right?"

Tasha didn't respond; what kind of face was she making?

Later, the sixteen- and seventeen-year-olds congregated in one of the centre's classrooms to have a discussion with the rabbi. The classroom was also a lab: fossils and rock samples in glass containers, science equipment, posters detailing the orbits of the planets. The rabbi led them in a workshop on personal versus group responsibility. Afterwards, Matt went up to investigate the samples. There was a stuffed hawk, looking fierce and beautiful, and two stuffed beavers. In a fishtank-like case on the shelf under the beavers were different sized beaver skulls and a small placard. "The beavers were almost hunted to extinction during the fur trade," Matt read. "But, since then, they have made a strong comeback, and humans are only now realizing the benefits beavers bring to their surroundings, through their damming and manipulation of rivers, streams, ponds, and forests." Matt pictured a family of beavers let loose in Thornhill, pulling buried rivers out of the ground, creating ponds, turning the suburbs back into forest. Tasha came up beside him. "Gross!" she exclaimed, poking the stuffed beaver. She turned Matt to face him. "Come with me," she said. Matt's heart now racing, Tasha took Matt's hand and took him outside, beside the building. Nobody was around. She dropped his hand. She was so beautiful, wide shouldered and big faced.

"Look, Matt," she said, "I just wanted to say, that, you know, I know you like me."

"I don't!"

Tasha looked at him skeptically. "And, although we won't be hooking up, I really feel that once you start having sex, you won't stop."

"Okay..."

"What?! I mean it!" She hit Matt on the arm playfully.

"Okay, okay," Matt said, giving in to whatever it was he was giving in to.

They went to find the others. They were behind the dining hall, had found some pieces of plastic sheeting, were sliding down the north-facing big hill, still patchy with snow. When it was Tasha's turn, she asked if Matt wanted to slide down with her. She looked at him like she was daring him. He shrugged, got in behind her. It was the most they've ever touched. Renee gave them a big push down the hill and they were off! They were going fast, they were flying, they were out of control, Matt's hands on Tasha's stomach, her warm thereness. Tasha was whooping, Matt was concentrating, trying to take it all in. The plastic sheet hit a patch of dry grass, and they tumbled off. Matt's face smashed into the back of Tasha's head as they rolled down the rest of the hill. No longer moving, they both lay in the wet grass in head-achey shock. Matt could feel his lip puffed up and bleeding. Tasha moaned and then started laughing. Their friends were running down the hill towards them.

⁝ The next morning at breakfast, Matt accidentally locked himself in the dining hall bathroom. The door wouldn't unlock. He tried to open the door again, but couldn't. It wouldn't open. He stepped back, panic swelling up. The lock was jammed. He was trapped! He could hear Rob and Tasha just outside the door, but couldn't get to them, couldn't call out to them. He looked in the mirror, saw the fear on his face, his bulging lower lip. He was destined to die alone in this tight, confined space. The fear, especially considering he hadn't smoked yet today, was overwhelming. His heart was going to combust.

He was trapped.

Matt took a moment. The next action would determine if he was going to die in this bathroom or not. He breathed down the fear. He put his hand on the handle. He turned the lock. It clicked open.

Matt left the bathroom, rejoined his friends.

AFTER THE PROTEST, THE BUS

One last crest to ride. The lead-up to the Iraq War was barrelling towards its still-not-inevitable start date, and large segments of the world were vigorously protesting it. During that late spring, Matt and Rob spent their Saturdays at the antiwar marches downtown. They'd congregate at Queen's Park, in the shadow of the provincial legislative buildings, and march down University, hospitals and their claims of triumphant humanity flanking them on either side of the wide avenue intersected with statues to who knew what. They sang, they cheered, they danced, they marched. The second time Matt went, he saw Fatima and some of her Saint E friends, holding the red banner from her bedroom. Matt was immersed in the creativity, the energy, the camaraderie. He was growing his hair out. He felt the possibility of change. If enough people took to the streets, things could actually start to shift. They could stop this war, they could stop all war, tear down the borders, turn the weapons factories into guitar workshops, the barracks into libraries. It was like the ending of *Dark Rivers*, when the Dark Rivers emissary arrives on Preethor and implores Dobro Carthy and his people to leave the planet before they get sucked into its hierarchical maw. Dobro responds by saying: "We will not leave. Nor will we stay." (It was only a few nights ago, stoned after a solo bong sesh in his basement bathroom, that Matt realized they had cut the scene from the movie entirely.) To not leave, to not stay, but to reconsider, to refuse, to remake. Marching in the heart of Toronto, it seemed more than possible.

On this particular Saturday, they had spent the morning at Joan's, hot-knifing and baking weed food for the afternoon's march. Matt's time in Forest Hill was behind him; he realized that, for now at least, he much preferred hanging in Joan's cluttered bedroom than in Tasha's immaculate ballroom. They had baked two loaf pans of blueberry muffins, with a quarter of blueberry haze split evenly between them. Out of all the myriad ways to ingest marijuana, Matt had, believe it or not, never just eaten it. Baking, even baking with ganja, seemed like a very adult thing to do. The loaf tasted like mealy garbage, but they stood at the round kitchen table and gobbled it down, ripped chunks out of the two pans until they were empty.

From Joan's house it was a short walk to Steeles, where they could grab a bus to Finch and subway downtown. The days of having access to Friedman's van were gone, part of another life. Not only did they not hang out anymore, but Shoshana told him that Friedman had sold his van to finance a trip to Israel. He was going for the summer, was thinking of staying, making aliyah, enlisting. Matt didn't know what to think of this news, so, for now, he didn't.

Today's protest was the biggest one yet. University Avenue was packed with bodies. It took a couple of hours before the weed loaf hit him, but hit him it did, as if the loaf was short-range cannon-punched into his chest. Matt smiled in the heavy euphoria. It wasn't long, however, before the edges of the euphoria hardened. The crowds, the people, the hundreds of conversations, the slogans, the noise, the edges of the buildings, it all overwhelmed him. He felt claustrophobic, furtive, unwell. He wandered off from the crowd, leaving his friends, making his way on side streets to Queen. He took a roach out of his pocket, smoked it down. The entrance to the subway filled him with fear, but he pushed through and descended.

On the subway that was tunnelling him north, towards home, towards merciful sleep, he was totally beside himself. The thoughts were coming at intense speeds, bursting in his head like lobbed grenades. The slogans from the march ricocheted off the walls of his brain. A different world is possible. A different world is possible. Matt laughed out loud, alone under the city of Toronto, a strange Jew full of revolution and desire. At Rosedale, the subway exploded into sunlight. As a Jew, he belonged; as a Jew, he didn't belong. And somewhere in there—Matt knew with startling clarity—was the ability to transform. He wished he had something to write it all down on. Never had he felt so strongly the need to catch these thoughts, these epiphanies, as they shot across the mental firmament, to catch them and somehow figure out how to perform the work of turning them into planets. Matt closed his eyes as the subway rumbled back underground.

He knew what was coming next, and he relished it. He would get off the subway at Finch, the end of the line. He would ride up an escalator to a bank of pay phones. He would call his mother from one of the phones, ask if she could pick him up at Steeles and New Westminster. He would ascend into the spring sunlight of the bus terminal. He would board the bus with its exposed bright-yellow bones. He would look out the windows, which in the winter or during rain would be so fogged that they'd be opaque, but now were siphoning off heaps of afternoon sunlight. The bus will wait at Steeles for four red lights before making the left turn off of Yonge; he knew that for the rest of his young life he would always remember waiting for that turn at the top of the city. Centerpoint Mall to his left, the other side of Thornhill to his right, the entire country, all its light and all its darkness, northwards.

He saw it all. Matt would be laughing as the bus turned, wholly dazed but entirely with it, the momentous thoughts roiling through him giving him the unmistakable sensation of riding the infinite skin of the world.

"TEL AVIV–TORONTO RED EYE"

A Dialogue

Dear Stephanie:

Congratulations! We've decided to accept your short story "Tel Aviv–Toronto Red Eye" for publication in Moose and Seal. *One of our senior editors will write you shortly with some minor editorial suggestions.*

> *Sincerely, Chelsea Smith*
>
> *Fiction Editor*
>
> Moose and Seal: *Canada's National Magazine*

Dear Chelsea:

This is great news! I'm thrilled to have my story appear in the magazine. I've been tweaking and submitting this particular story for a long time now. After all the rejections, all the doubt, having it accepted in a journal like *Moose and Seal* really means a lot to me. I look forward to the edits. Please let me know if there's anything else you need from me in the meantime.

> Excitedly,
>
> Stephanie

Dear Chelsea:

Hi. It's Stephanie again. I've been walking around in a state of nerve-tingling excitement ever since I got your email. This will be, by far, the biggest publication I've ever had. But then I realized that I never submitted "Tel Aviv–Toronto Red Eye" to your magazine. I double-checked in my submissions notebook, and it's true; I never submitted it. Needless to say, I'm pretty confused. Did you hear about the story from somewhere else (though where that somewhere else could be I have no idea)? If you could fill me in, I'd greatly appreciate it.

> Best,
>
> Stephanie

Dear Stephanie:

Milton Green here, senior fiction editor. I'm looking forward to working with you on this story. Does it really matter where we first encountered it? The fact is that we love it, and can't wait to publish it! Can't beat that. Before we embark on the dark and perilous journey that is known as the editing process, I do have one small niggling question about the story that we should get out of the way first. Why, on page 3 of the story, does your narrator—who we assume, of course, is a thinly veiled version of yourself—say that she feels "more Jewish when on a plane flying home to Toronto from South Florida than when she's flying home from Tel Aviv?" I can't quite grasp what you're getting at here. Please advise.

    Cheers,

    Milton

Hi Milton:

Thanks for writing. I'm not really sure I understand your question, but I'll try to answer. For starters, it's meant to be a joke, commenting on the complicated network of movement between Jewish communities worldwide. But, on a deeper level, I suppose, it's about the deeply diasporic, deeply American, nature of Jewish South Florida, which is quite different than the national, macho Israeli culture. The whole story is meant to interrogate this tension between Israel and the diaspora, which is one reason it takes place on an overnight flight between Tel Aviv and Toronto.

    Hope this helps!

    Stephanie

Thanks for your quick response. I'm sorry to say that we're still not understanding the "joke" as you put it. Are you saying that South Florida is more Jewish than Israel? Why would you have a character say such an obviously false thing? It basically implies that the narrator of the story, and therefore you yourself, don't think Israel has a right to exist as a Jewish state. Is that true, Stephanie? And another thing. Why, in the climax of the story, does your Palestinian-American character have sex with your Jewish character in the washroom—both of them women, might I add—while everybody waiting in line calls them derogatory names? Why have a Palestinian character in a story about Israel at all? And one that takes place on a plane, nonetheless? Isn't that extremely triggering for your story's potential Jewish readers? I found it triggering. Quite triggering.

Pardon my language, but what the fuck is going on here? The whole story is about how false the borders are between Palestinian and Jew, Israel and Canada, settler-colonialism here and settler-colonialism there. And in answer to your last question, no, I do not think having a Palestinian—who is a human being just like any other human being—on an airplane in a story is triggering, and frankly, I'm surprised you would say such a thing.

No need to get testy. We just don't like, nor understand, this scene at all. In fact, we're recommending that you alter it/remove it entirely. There are things that a Jewish writer should not write about. You know this, Stephanie. You should know this. We gave you the benefit of the doubt, but it seems that the antisemitic tendencies we located in the story are more than just a writerly flourish.

Milton, I'm sorry for swearing in my last message, it's just that I'm pretty frustrated. This has turned from an excellent week into an exceedingly strange week; never before have I felt like my fiction has come alive, tripped me as I walked down the street. Does writing about the complexities of the Jewish experience, does acknowledging the existence of Palestinians, really make one an antisemite? Not to me they don't. As a Jewish writer who happens to live in Canada, I deeply believe that my fiction should go to these uncomfortable places, should say what has for the most part remained unsaid, should expose in order to move towards something better. I've always loved the fiction in *Moose and Seal* for this very reason.

So, you admit that you're a self-hater? We had our suspicions. What do you know about Israel, anyways? What, you think because you've read a couple of Tom Segev books you're an expert now? Well, I'm afraid if you are not willing to remove the following items from your story, we're going to have to retract our offer of publication, and the *very handsome* payment that would have gone along with it. Not to mention the Canada-wide exposure. Please excise from the story:

1. *The aforementioned scene in the bathroom.*
2. *The Palestinian character.*
3. *The discussion of Israel's nuclear arsenal.*
4. *The argument between the Orthodox man and the secular woman about messianic time that ends with them giving each other handjobs.*
5. *The contention that living in diaspora could possibly be better than living in a utopic country such as Israel.*
6. *The daydream about the ethical potential of intermarriage.*
7. *The entire ending—and most of the beginning—will have to be rewritten as well.*

We actually recommend that you change the entire plot. Why not have it be about a young Jewish man afraid of commitment falling in love with a tough-around-the-edges Israeli sabra? And have the pilot a raging Israel-hating antisemite? Now there's a recipe for comedy and romance! Or, instead of it taking place on a plane, why not at a Bedouin tent during a birthright trip? Now that would be a story!

What? What are you talking about? Why would I change the whole story?

Because you are a good Jewish writer and you want to write good Jewish stories.

Wait a minute. You accepted the story for publication. Why did you do so if you don't even like the story? I've been speaking to some of my writer friends (and non-writer friends, not to mention my therapist), and you are behaving very unprofessionally. Normally, I would probably just go along with it, but "Tel Aviv–Toronto Red Eye" is very important to me. I'm seriously thinking of pulling the story.

Now Stephanie, don't get excited. You think you know how you feel about Israel, but do you really? Remember the nights awake, full of doubt? Remember your own time in Israel, thinking, maybe it's not as bad as all that? Remember how you felt when you saw that Palestinian man at the Nakba Day rally wearing a shirt that said "The Zionists Did 9/11"? Think of that man whenever you want to write a story that extols the virtues of intermarriage.

What does that one sad, crazy man have to do with anything? And no, I will not make those changes. I refuse to soften my writerly vision for your fear of upsetting your Zionist readers, or whatever the hell is going on here.

Well then, Stephanie. Sorry to say. You will never publish at Moose and Seal, *or any other major Canadian magazine again. I'll see to that, believe you me. Enjoy being on the wrong side of history.*

Fine.

That's just fine.

No big deal.

No big deal at all.

…

Wait.

Wait a minute!

I've changed my mind. Okay? I'll do it. I'll make the changes!
You're right, setting it at a Bedouin tent makes much more sense.
I'll do it all! Just please, please, *please*, publish my story.

Hello?

Milton?

Hello?

Hello?

...

Hello?

A Handful of Days, a Handful of Worlds

MAY 2, 2018

When the Truth and Reconciliation hearings began in Israel/ Palestine—alhaqiqat walmusalaha in Arabic, emet v'peeous in Hebrew, "the hearings" to most English speakers—Brenda and Kate were in the slow, bittersweet process of breaking up. The big world goes through yet another tectonic shift; two small lives coast apart. Or so it seemed to Brenda.

As usual, Brenda woke up to the radio, set to go off three hours after Kate's own alarm went off, two hours after Kate left the house. "You're listening to CBC Radio. It's May second, 2018, the time is 9:30. Stay tuned for the news." The following news segment, like the news segments for the past who-knows-how-many days, was about the hearings. Brenda lay in bed, her thoughts circling around the biggest news story of the century like rushing water approaching a drain. Peace in the Middle East. Real, actual peace. It was like living in a box of bold text in a high school history book, and Brenda didn't know how to feel about it.

She turned over, bringing the blankets with her. Brenda had never consumed so much news; watching the hearings had become the one regular thing she and Kate did together anymore. The last hearing they watched was similar to all the others: a table on a wide dais. Six speakers: three Jewish Israeli, three Palestinian.

One of them was an Israeli general in his army fatigues, with a pudgy face, a scraggle of grey hair; he looked like every Israeli general that had ever been a talking head on CNN, that had ever been a sympathetic yet ruthless father figure in a Hebrew movie. In front of them, in descending order, were the examiners—a mixture of international observers and Israeli and Palestinian human rights activists—the translators, talking into their headsets, the press, typing on their phones or writing in their notebooks, and, finally, the general public. Like all the hearings they had watched, it appeared to be standing room only. A class of what looked like grade eights sat in the back row.

"He looks exactly like your grandfather," Brenda had said about the Israeli general. Kate had laughed.

"If Zaidy's parents had decided to join a kibbutz instead of boarding a boat bound for Chicago when they left their shtetl, it could have *been* my grandfather."

"What do you mean, Chicago? Didn't he grow up in Montreal?"

"I never told you this story? My great-grandparents disembarked early, in Quebec City, because my great-grandmother went into labour."

"So you were supposed to be an American?!"

"I was supposed to not exist at all, I guess."

Brenda put her arm around Kate. It felt like old times, but she knew it wasn't. On the screen the Israeli general that could be Kate's grandfather was shouting in Hebrew, his face reddening, his fist pounding. According to the subtitles, he was saying: "Were we innocent? No, we were not innocent. Were we evil? No, we were not evil. They were our enemies. And yes, we were their enemies. Oh yes. We were at war, we acted as if we were at war!"

One of the Palestinians, a man with a thin face and a two-day beard, tapped his microphone. "We were at war, sure. But now that we are not at war, we have to look at what happened during the war, at what the war was, at who brought war."

Brenda had looked over at Kate. Kate was staring at the screen; concentration filmed her eyes, the slight downturn of her mouth setting off pangs of longing deep in Brenda's gut.

The remembering was almost unbearable. She sat up. Kate had forgotten to open the blinds. The room was still dark, stuffy, thick with uneasy dreaming.

Time to stand up, Brenda.

Time to start your day.

⦂ Unlike in Canada, where the Truth and Reconciliation Commission on the country's treatment of the Indigenous peoples—whose land the state was built on—took place without the mistreatment actually ending, just changing form, and where the government and institutions and corporations continued to do the same things they had done for hundreds of years, the hearings in Israel/Palestine were the result of deep structural change. The Israel Brenda had known growing up, the Israel Kate learned about in Hebrew school, simply no longer existed: there was now one single state for Jews, for Palestinians, for everybody. There was no hierarchy of ethnicity, no occupation, no occupying army. Equality and justice were being enshrined into law. The country was transforming at every level, in every nook and cranny. The combined forces of external pressure, internal protest, and ceaseless Palestinian resistance had cracked the situation wide open, tipping the country into state-level change. The Israeli government toppled, an interim coalition took over, with a Jewish Israeli and a Palestinian as joint leaders. Peace wasn't just declared, it was being built. Palestinians, Jews, Christians with a Jesus complex, people with knowledge and expertise—as well as, of course, those without—were pouring into the country. Towns were springing up overnight, designed and built by Palestinian engineers and contractors who had learned their trades in the Gulf States. The refugee camps were emptied out. Reparations were being reparated. The accountable, for once in the long, sordid history of nations, armies, and bureaucracies, were being held to account. Israeli and Palestinian were getting to know each other as if for the first time. Those who were against what was dubbed "reunity" were being drowned out by the sheer excitement of what was taking place. It was like a wild, unforeseen dream, but it was real. The twinned histories of Israeli Jew and Palestinian Arab were not being swept under the rug, ignored, or sugarcoated, but acknowledged, looked at, talked through. The hearings, though difficult, were a necessary part of acknowledging what had happened, what had taken place, and making sure it did not happen again.

Later that afternoon, Brenda was at her studio, getting ready to paint. Her routine never varied. Turn on the kettle. Arrange the brushes. Put on the only pair of jeans she painted in, that she had bought the summer before grade ten at Jean Machine in the Promenade Mall, the smock she replaced a couple times a year. When the kettle started to whistle, she poured a mug of tea, waited twenty seconds before plucking the teabag out and placing it into her second mug. Everything in order; time to paint.

She was slowly chipping away on a new set of paintings called *Joining the Party*. She had three finished, was working on a fourth, and had another three and a half sketched out in her notebook. The one on her easel was the biggest in the series, on a canvas six feet wide and four tall. It was a hospital scene, rendered in vivid realism. There was an elated mother in bed, family members huddled around, a doctor handing the squawking newborn to its mother, nurses cleaning up, the hospital machinery with its toggles and gauges. Everybody was wearing white VR goggles, sleek protruding eyewear. Even the newborn was sporting a newborn-sized pair, still splotched with vernix. Brilliant golden light was flooding in from the large window that looked out onto sky and trees. (Other paintings in the series included a canvas with four famous sex scenes throughout human history, every eager participant wearing the goggles; a Victorian-era woman fingering another Victorian woman who's holding her skirts up, both in the goggles; scientists watching a nuclear bomb testing, goggles shielding them from the blast.)

Today Brenda was finishing the fine details of the sky outside the hospital room window. As she painted, she thought over her relationship with Kate. They had started dating so young—Kate was only fourteen! It took Kate's parents a few years to accept Brenda, but once they did she was a part of the family. Their third date, eating Nutella crepes on Queen Street, running hand in hand to catch the streetcar. The year they spent in Victoria. Brenda painting in the bedroom as Kate lay on the bed writing a university paper. The fight they had in Barcelona about where Brenda should do her MFA, walking the streets, the beach, screaming at each other. The nights that for no particular reason blossomed into holy hours of conversation, discovery, laughter, love. They had promised to be together always, but then always shrunk from the infinite to the surprisingly finite. When Joyce and Kerry broke up last year, Kate and Brenda discussed often how that would never happen to them—and yet, here it was, happening. It wasn't that they didn't love each other anymore; it was that the love had changed. Their ideas of their lives had changed. Brenda wanted to stay in Toronto, continue building her art career, teach classes at OCAD. Kate wanted to travel the world, even go to Palestine and be a part of the renaissance taking place over there—just a few days ago Brenda had found Kate working through one of her old Hebrew school textbooks. Though, if Brenda was being honest, it was Kate that was really following through on the split. They had declared they would never be apart countless times, and now the idea of them living separate lives on separate continents wasn't just okay. It was comforting. Bitter, but comforting.

They hadn't told anybody yet. For now, they were sitting with the knowledge. It's funny: knowing their relationship was ending, they were spending more time together than they had in years, weren't getting together with their friends, were barely leaving the house. Kate hadn't even told Sandra, her best friend. They were seeing Kate's parents on Friday. The plan was to break the news to them then.

Just like that, Brenda decided to change the sky out the hospital window from robin's egg blue to cerulean. She looked at the nearly finished painting. She was happy with the hundreds upon hundreds of decisions that had brought her here.

They were listening to the radio that night, packing boxes, diverting the river of their lives into two separate streams, when they heard Stephanie Krasner being interviewed by Georgia Talcum-Ross on CBC's *Books and Talk*. Stephanie was there to promote her new book, a collection of short stories called *A Handful of Days, a Handful of Worlds*.

"Can you believe I used to go to shul with her?" Kate enthused, her hands flat on a box she had just finished. "Her whole family were pretty serious bigwigs at Kol B'Seder."

They stopped packing and sat down on the floor to listen to the interview.

—The title of your new collection is quite elusive. Would you care to explain its meaning?

—No, not really. I'd like to keep it mysterious, if that's okay, Georgia.

Kate and Brenda laughed.

—Of course! The title story is also receiving pretty extensive backlash. Similar to the story from your first collection, "Austria 1933."

"I read that story!" Brenda said. "Remember, the whole thing takes place in Vienna, and is about Jews arguing if they should leave Austria or not, and the whole time you're going, *Yes, of course you should leave! Of course! Don't you see what's coming your way!* And then, in the end of the story, Hitler gets assassinated, the Nazis disband, the war never starts, there's no final solution, the Holocaust just disappears."

"Yeah, I remember. I remember thinking that her fiction is actually a lot like your art, in a way. Taking the familiar and tweaking it just enough to shock."

Brenda's instinct was to disagree with the compliment, but she shrugged it off. "What a story. It stayed with me for weeks. What's this new one about?"

"The early Zionists colonize Iceland instead of Palestine, or something, create a Jewish state up there. I heard people talking about it at work, didn't realize it was one of Stephanie's. But shh! Let's listen!"

—The Iceland story is reminiscent of Michael Chabon, wouldn't you agree? The frozen chosen, and all that?

—Chabon, yes, partly. I'd say Lavie Tidhar and Neva Semel were more of an influence, to be honest. And, of course, Hera Black, the author of *Dark Rivers*, looms over all of my work.

—Why write a story like this at a time like this, Stephanie?

—Well. Who knows why a writer writes about what she writes about? I had recently gone on a trip to Iceland, and with everything happening in the news, all the changes happening worldwide, the hearings, the story just sort of erupted in my head. I couldn't write it out fast enough as we were busy touring waterfalls, geysers, and volcanic rock fields.

—Yes, but why make the situation so extreme? The Zionists in the story force nearly all of the Icelandic population into a small strip of land in the remote mountains.

—Have you not been listening to the hearings? This is very real. These things really happened. Really *do* happen. Maybe not in Iceland, but in Palestine, not to mention right here, in Toronto, in Canada. Settler colonialism, in this instance Jewish settler colonialism, is not just a single event in the distant past. It's a mechanism, and the main thrust behind this novella is, what if I took that mechanism and moved it somewhere else, somewhere that would shake readers out of their historical complacency?

"'Well, everybody knows that Custer died at Little Big Horn. What this novel presupposes is, maybe he *didn't*?'" Kate said in her best Owen Wilson.

"Shh!" Brenda exclaimed, though they were both laughing.

—...and, for whatever reason, Iceland presented itself to me as the perfect place to do this. The ethnic cleansing, the dehumanizing, the replacing of one people's narrative over another, the historical and archaeological erasure, the militarization of an entire society, the devastatingly powerful mythology, I thought: why not try to burn it all off in the cold clear light of Iceland, so to speak?

—Would you like to read us a passage?

—Definitely. So, this is just over seven pages into the story, and the third-person narrator is giving a little potted history of Jewish Iceland, which they call Jewsland.

—Great. For those of you just tuning in, this is Stephanie Krasner, about to read from her new book, *A Handful of Days, a Handful of Worlds*.

—"As everybody now knows, the first modern mention of Iceland being the true home of the Jewish people is in a small pamphlet published by Baruch Greenberg in the early eighteen hundreds. He is the first to suggest that the Sagas are actually the creation of Jews, and hypothesizes that the Icelanders were actually one of the lost twelve tribes of Israel. Once the Christian Zionists in Britain got a hold of Greenberg's pamphlet, they publicized it to no end; it was they who declared that all the Jews needed to be in Iceland for the rapture to arrive. 'Only through ice will the fire come.' Now we know that, in fact, in the tenth century a flotilla of Sephardic Jews sailed to Iceland from Spain and started a small Jewish community near Selfoss. This, however, wasn't the first time Jews were in Iceland. As the early Zionist movement proved without a doubt, Iceland is mentioned in the Bible a shocking three hundred and two times.

"It was at the second Zionist conference that Iceland was presented as a possible solution to the Jewish problem; everybody, including Theodor Herzl, the great man himself, was skeptical. Nonetheless, by the third congress exploratory parties were being dispatched to see if a mass colonization of the island was possible, and excited Zionist sympathizers were presenting detailed plans for accessing the untouched natural resources of the country—one, an engineer named Gottfried Beringer wrote Herzl detailed letters with his plans to harness Iceland's untouched thermal energy, plans that proved prophetic. Shortly after the third congress, Herzl wrote and published a novel that imagined a thriving Jewish utopia on the plains, mountainsides and coasts of Iceland. 'It was like no other period of my life,' Herzl wrote in his diary. 'The imaginative spark, the six weeks of harried creation. The dream of a Jewish Iceland came to me wholecloth.' (Herzl, as we all know, emigrated to Iceland in 1915, retired shortly thereafter, and died a happy, fulfilled man.) The first pioneers arrived at the turn of the century, and by the onset of World War I a healthy Jewish population was carving out a land for themselves. The Icelanders, a simple farming people, unequipped to understand what Jewish immigration would do for their livelihood, were aghast, and resorted almost immediately to violence. Snorri Ben-Dalvik—born Guri Mendelsohn in Poland—quickly became the main architect for the settling of Iceland, the driving force behind reclaiming the Jewish right to their ancestral land and the overseer of the resettling of the natives. It was Ben-Dalvik who held the first truly Jewish Althing in almost seven hundred years. With the UN's help, Iceland was soon declared the official home of the Jews.

"The rest, as they say, is history. Now Jewsland is a proud, independent Jewish country, famous for its thermal energy, geologists leading the fight against climate change, mountain climbers, artwork, jewellery, and revitalization of Jewish religion and culture. Jewothermal power heats more than half of Europe. The one thing the Jews of Iceland want above all else, of course, is peace. But with the indigenous Nords refusing to put down their weapons, what choice do they have but to keep them locked in the mountains like the vagabonds and common criminals they are? If their leaders truly wanted peace, they would accept the Jewish nature of Iceland. Until then, Jewsland will continue to maintain the biggest standing army in the Northern Atlantic."

Brenda turned the volume down. "We should buy this book for your dad. He'd get a real kick out of it."

Kate looked thoughtful. "*I* want to read it," she said eventually. "Stephanie Krasner. Wow, who could believe it."

Brenda smiled. Listening to Stephanie read her work, this woman from Kate's childhood, gave her the same sensations of joyful sadness she experienced when finally finishing a painting.

: They rode the subway to Finch, end of the line, and Kate's father picked them up at the kiss and ride. "What a time to be alive, eh?" he said as they drove towards Thornhill. This wasn't the first time Brenda noticed that one way people were dealing with the tremendous changes taking place at the world level— Israel and Palestine reunified, reparations underway, the failures to confront the changing climate—was pithy sayings, repeated aphorisms, Kate's father's *what a time to be alive*. Though, yes, Brenda would agree, it was indeed a time to be alive.

Instead of the World War II documentaries or hockey games that were the mainstays at Kate's parents', both usually with the volume muted, there was another hearing on the television. They sat with Kate's parents and her uncle Bert watching it, Bert's five red-haired children playing on the floor. An elderly Palestinian woman from Gaza was telling her story. She had lost three children, two siblings, many cousins in the repeated bombings and awful living conditions. Her husband was paralyzed from the waist down. "It is okay, now though. We have what we have been waiting for. The land returned, admittance of guilt. Peace. To my Jewish brothers, sisters, cousins: let us join hands after a hard hundred years. Let us celebrate together!" The video cut to an Israeli government official talking calmly, candidly, about the bureaucratic planning that allowed Israel to maintain its Jewish majority for so many decades.

"Disgusting," Kate's father said. "How could we all have been so stupid?" Brenda remembered, not all that long ago, when Kate's father was an avid Zionist. Brenda thought about her aunt Jill, her family's resident antisemite. At the last dinner Aunt Jill attended, she had said, just come out with, "I don't trust these Jews and Arabs. They're up to no good. You'll see." Nobody said anything, though Brenda's brother Frank had made a disgusted face at his plate. Like all tense moments at Brenda's family table: eyes down, cutlery noises, until the moment passed or something else came up.

"I still can't believe it. I never thought I'd see something like this. It's like a dream," Kate's uncle said. Brenda had never seen Bert not trying to turn everything into a joke. What a time to be alive, indeed.

Kate's father changed the channel. It was another news report, this time about the few groups who have rejected the new reunity government in Palestine. Right-wing Jewish settlers and right-wing Arab Islamists had momentarily put aside their differences to declare in a joint signing that they would never put aside their differences. As far as they were concerned, the land would always be contested, violence would always be the answer, ethnic superiority the very air they breathed. The tide had shifted so far out, though, that they were suddenly left far, far away from the water. And hopefully they would soon asphyxiate.

"I feel sorry for these people," Kate's father said. "Why not accept something good for once?"

The news shifted to a montage of the global ripple effect the new accords in Israel/Palestine were having: borders collapsing, crowds celebrating, city-wide protests brewing. Scared politicians making placating speeches. It felt like anything was possible. It felt, at times, like too much to take in. *Was* any of this real?

Later, after dinner, Brenda found Kate upstairs, in her childhood bedroom, sitting on her neatly made twin bed. Brenda sat down beside her. Kate was crying. Brenda figured it was because they hadn't mentioned to Kate's parents they were splitting up.

"Is the world really going to change?" Kate asked. "Or are we just kidding ourselves, like always?"

Brenda thought for a minute. "It seems pretty real to me. What can we do but be along for the ride, trust in the arc of the universe? Things *can* change, things *can* be better."

Kate stopped crying, rubbed her eyes. "'And they rode on, in the friscalating dusk light,'" she said. Brenda laughed, shook her head. Kate jumped up, suddenly brimming with energy, started rummaging through her closet. "Look at this," she said, turning around, holding up her childhood sleeping bag. It was faded purple, had starfish and seahorses on it.

"I haven't seen this in years!" She put her face in it. "It still smells like camp!" She unrolled it on the bed. Looked back at Brenda. Took off her pants and wiggled in.

Brenda hesitated. She stood up. Shut the door. Wiggled in after her.

MAY 2, 2018

Brenda's alarm went off. She turned over, reached for Kate, even though she knew Kate had left the house hours ago. "You're listening to CBC Radio. It's May second, 2018, the time is 9:30. Up next: the prime minister responds to criticism of his government's support for the Birthright Act." Brenda's arm shot out and hit the snooze button. Not today, world.

Brenda biked the Toronto streets in the cool spring air. This was one of her favourite times to ride in the city; without destination, pedalling through the world as it lazily sloughs off the last sticky textures of winter. From Queen's Park, where she was sketching trees, along Harbord—the Harbord Highway, her painting teacher used to call it—down Ossington, through the residential streets, towards Dufferin, the stretch of Dewson that always reminded Brenda of Fernwood Village in Victoria, where she and Kate had lived for a year after university, which made her think of other parts of the city that reminded her of elsewhere, the houses at College and Dufferin Montreal, Bright Street in the east end Britain, the air was cool and sweet, what is it about the city at this time of year, Brenda wondered as she pedalled harder and harder, approaching home, leaning into her bike, finally turning onto Dufferin, no longer any need to pedal, gliding downhill, the swampy realization she had been putting off for days: she and Kate were breaking up.

Brenda locked her bike up on the street, the first time she was going to leave it outside this year. She stepped back, took in the sleek black road bike, only a year old, the first bike she had bought new. The shape of the bike, the tires, the gleaming hardware, struck her as utterly compelling. Maybe she should base her next project off of it. The aesthetic of bikes. Walking up the stairs, Brenda shuffled through all of her major paintings, something she did whenever a new idea was rising up from the unknown. Her first solo gallery showing, *Factory Farm*, was a series of paintings that brought together industrial animals with the larger world of capitalism. In one painting chickens birthed iPhones, in another mother pigs suckled Nestle water bottles, in another a cow's udders were hooked up to a gas pump that was filling up a shiny SUV. The exhibit got excellent reviews—the painting with the cow and the SUV was reprinted in the *Star*!—and she had sold all of the paintings.

Brenda paused at the door. The new project was taking over. A familiar, welcome feeling. Since finishing *Joining the Party* a month ago, she had been planning on doing something to do with trees. But now she couldn't shake the shape of her bike, it was multiplying like a zygote. What if she combined them in some way? The trees and the bike. Yes. Yes!

Aflame with creativity, Brenda shucked the key into the lock and opened the door. She was far more taken aback than she should have been to find Kate sitting on the couch, the television on, crying.

The new project sucked out to the walls of her mind, and her troubled homelife flooded in from the cracks in the floor.

"What's wrong?"

"Oh, it's the fucking news. The fucking country's going to collapse."

It took Brenda a minute to figure out that Kate wasn't talking about Canada. She was talking about Israel. Brenda sat down beside her. Ever since the increasingly beleaguered country had passed the Jewish Peoples Birthright Act, Kate was obsessed, her eyes glued to the television, her fingers scrolling through Twitter. Brenda had never seen her so political; she had become a real news junkie. Not to mention that it must have been all they talked about at Kate's work. Since Kate was assistant head of Jewish programming at Kol B'Seder, the synagogue she had gone to growing up, how could it not be? Brenda couldn't help feeling that this new obsession was unhealthy, but felt she couldn't say anything.

"The world is fucked, Kate. What more can we do but try to be good people?"

"I don't know, Brenda. Peace has never felt further away but also, somehow, closer."

The news segued into a three-minute primer on what was happening in Israel/Palestine. Brenda had seen it a thousand times the past few weeks, but plopped down and watched it anyways.

The international pressure against Israel's treatment of the Palestinians had been showing dividends for a few years. Instead of giving in to the pressure though, bolstered by the mainstream Jewish institutions in America and Canada, who seemingly grew more reactionary with each passing week, the Israeli government battened down the hatches, passing the Jewish Peoples Birthright Act, which granted Israeli citizenship to every Jewish person the world over. The idea was that this would suppress the rising chorus that Israel was artificially maintaining a Jewish majority through force. Now that every Jew was a citizen of the country, they outnumbered the Palestinians two to one. No more democratic threat; no more sanctions; no more singling out. Or so went the reasoning of the talking heads on CNN.

So far, the plan was backfiring. Badly. Leftists, Palestinian and Jewish groups across the globe, were protesting, demanding Palestinians be given citizenship, the right of return, be treated as equals. There was daily chaos at the Knesset. The prime minister was barely holding on to his coalition; if an election was called, nobody knew what would happen. The joint Jewish-Palestinian list responded with their own bill, the Binational Peoples Bill, which they framed as an opportunity to rethink the ethnic nationalism that the current government, that the entire state, was built on. As the bill gained momentum, the reactionaries on both sides started to join forces. Islamic Jihad and the Jewish Defense League had signed, in a highly publicized event, a non-non-agression pact, committing to fighting each other no matter what happened at the Knesset or on the world stage.

The news anchor was reading from a new joint statement from the two radical groups. They were advocating for endless war.

"This is unbelievable," Kate said.

"We should do something."

Kate opened her laptop and started typing.

"Look, there's a protest tomorrow at Nathan Phillips Square. 'Canadian Jews Reject Birthright Legislation; We Want a Free and Equitable Middle East.' We should totally go!"

"If you don't think it'd be weird for me to be there, I'm in."

Kate looked at Brenda. It was the same look whenever Brenda brought up not being Jewish. Though Brenda didn't consider herself Christian, she did celebrate Christmas, and some of her family members—like her aunt Jill, ugh—exhibited some of the worst traits of the hegemonic religion. "Don't be silly, Brenda! At best you're an honorary Jew, at worst a fierce ally."

"Okay, whatever you say."

"More importantly, what if I see somebody from work?"

"Wouldn't that mean that they support the protest too?"

"Yeah, things have just been so tense there. Half the staff support the new measures, the other half don't. We had a meeting in the boardroom yesterday, it was rough."

Kate snuggled into Brenda. Even though they were in the process of ending their lives together, Brenda couldn't help but feel good.

"I forgot to tell you," Kate said, "the dentist wants me to get a nightguard for my jaw pain."

"We'll marry our nightguards together," Brenda sang. "Seriously, though, you'll love it. It's like a nightly hug for all your teeth."

"Everyone I know is getting one," Kate said. "They're prescribing it for every ailment under the sun. Teeth grinding? Nightguard. Headaches? Nightguard. Jaw pain? Nightguard!"

"Constant anxiety? Nightguard!"

"Fear of impending death?"

"Nightguard!"

"Sleepless nights due to the planetary collapse of life as we know it?"

"Nightguard!"

They fell into each other, laughing, touching, belonging.

Like it used to be.

⠿ Brenda was at the studio, trying to paint. In the past week the new project had changed, settled, and changed again. At first it was going to be one gigantic painting, then a series of drawings, and now she was turning over the idea of moving into sculpture. The basic concept had remained the same: a bike that was also a tree, a tree that was also a bike, a tree stuck halfway in its metamorphosis into a bike, a bike caught at the moment of its transformation into tree. She had been obsessively reading up on the evolution of the bicycle's shape, its design.

Brenda hadn't sculpted since university. One moment she was sure that's what was needed, at the next she was racked with doubt. What was she missing? Tired of going back and forth, not used to not knowing intuitively what form any particular project should take, she turned on the radio. A woman was talking, reading a story of some kind.

—"It was Lavie's turn at the mic. The student council chambers went deadly quiet. Delilah's heart was pounding. 'What is Iceland?' Lavie asked. 'Iceland doesn't exist. Iceland is the invention of antisemites used to delegitimize the one Jewish democracy in the entire world! Have you read the Sagas? The Eddas? How could a backward, isolated people like the native inhabitants of Jewsland have created such masterworks of literature? No. They must have been written by Jews. As a proud Jewish campus organization, we stand with all the downtrodden everywhere. We stand with the Indigenous peoples of Turtle Island. We stand with our Palestinian cousins fighting against a hundred plus years of unjust British occupation. But don't be confused. The Icelanders are terrorists, controlled by shady European antisemites to destroy the first truly Jewish nation in two thousand years. Not to mention all the other Scandinavian countries that refuse to take the Icelanders in. They're axe-wielding murderers, every last one of them. If they always cared as much about the island as they claim, why did the first Jewish pioneers find nothing but tundra, impassable mountain passes, untamed rivers? No, they won't be happy until all the inhabitants of Jewsland are frozen solid in the North Atlantic! Don't believe the Icelanders and their grievance fireworks. Go on an Iceright trip, watch your tune change. You can't possibly deny the open, flourishing, democratic Jewish nature of the island.'

"Delilah felt sick to her stomach. How could this be the same Lavie she once was in love with? How could he twist himself into these pretzels of justification? How could everybody lap it up? Was Icelandic life really so cheap compared to Jewish life? Delilah put her head between her knees. She could taste the bile charging the gates of her esophagus. She was going to be sick.

"The next speaker was Leif Svendson, leader of the Icelandic Rights Student Group."

All at once, Brenda saw it. Bikes that were constructed of tiny pointillist trees, each painting a different style of bike, a different kind of tree. A white pine road bike. An oak mountain bike. A cedar hybrid.

Brenda glanced at the clock on the wall. She was going to be late for the protest. She turned off the radio, changed, rinsed her mugs, left the studio, went down to her bike.

If she rode fast and didn't hit too many lights, she could make it.

MAY 2, 2018

Kate's parents' house. They were sitting in front of the television, watching the news. Even though they had talked frankly and openly about breaking up the night before, they were holding hands. They were rapt in front of the screen. Scenes of destruction, of war, of suffering, of smug spokespeople. Impending nuclear apocalypse. Hadn't they seen this all before?

"This is too awful, Brenda. Turn it off."

Brenda reached for the remote.

The day was so grey, so wet, that Brenda had forgone her bike, a rare occurrence, and rode the bus to the panel on writing grants for collaborative art projects that her department at OCAD was putting on. The last time she had taken the bus was in the fall; she remembered because it was when she first knew, without a doubt, that she and Kate were going to break up. A woman was talking to her friend in the seats in front of Brenda and Brenda had overheard her say, "Sure, I mean, I love all his friends, the sex is *great*, and he's a killer doubles partner, but I *have* to break up with him." And that was the moment that, as if she was being doused in cold water, Brenda knew. She could hear that anonymous woman's voice, even now.

When Brenda got home, damp, but not soaked, the rain having let up, Kate was sitting on the couch in the dark, wearing the bee antennae from last year's Halloween costume. Brenda felt a wave of emotion. On Saturday they had returned from their first trip to Palestine. They had made the plans, bought the tickets, booked the hotels and hostels, all before they decided they were breaking up. Since they were still getting along, more or less, once the trip was upon them they decided to still go. The country was amazing. The Jews and Palestinians who lived there had built a thriving, vibrant country. Everywhere were the signs of coexistence. The inhabitants were proud of the history, of the near misses that led to the Arabs and the Jews coming together in the early thirties, taking a unified stand against Nazism, the British, and the Jewish ideologues who wanted the land exclusively to themselves. It's a history everybody knows well; Kate would hear it every year at Kol B'Seder on Unity Day. They had gone to a talk at the joint Islamic-Jewish university in Jaffa given by a professor of Hebrew-Arabic literature about how important it is to keep up the work of maintaining Palestine. "There are dark forces in the world who would rather see the region torn up, destroyed, shucked open," he said. "Even now, there are fringe parties in the

Knesset, Jewish and Palestinian, who want to destroy what we have built here. We must defend against them." On their last day, they swam in the sea, showered the salt off in a beachside change station, ate hummus and pita under the stars.

"Kerry called," Kate said as Brenda took her shoes off. "She wanted to know where we've been, says we haven't seen her in months."

"I guess it has been a long time," Brenda said, going to the kitchen, turning the lights on, starting to take ingredients out of the fridge. She had told Kate yesterday that she would make dinner tonight. Like old times. Kate even came into the kitchen with her computer and worked while Brenda chopped, sautéed, boiled. Tired of the indie rock station on the radio, she switched to the CBC.

—If you're just tuning in, this is Georgia Talcum-Ross, and you're listening to *Books and Talk.* Today we're speaking with Stephanie Krasner, Canadian Jewish author, about her new short story, "A Handful of Days, a Handful of Worlds."

"Holy shit, Stephanie Krasner! Didn't she go to Kol B'Seder with you?"

Kate grimaced, continued staring at her computer screen. "Yeah. Remember, I told you about her new book yesterday? The shul is thinking of trying to get her to come speak."

"Oh, right." Brenda turned back to the sauce.

—Thanks, Georgia. Don't forget, there's six and a half other stories in the collection as well! The plot of "A Handful of Days," or "That Jewish Iceland One," as most people seem to be calling it, follows Jewslander Delilah Snorridottir as she discovers the Icelandic narrative while in college in Canada. She tries to start an Icelandic Allies chapter at the university but meets fierce pushback from pro-Jewsland factions led by her ex-boyfriend Lavie. In the end, she gives up, and heads back to Iceland to try to enact change from within.

—The story is just full of such delightful invention. Explain to our listeners what an "Edward" is.

—Ha ha, I was proud of that one when it came to me. An Edward is somebody, somebody in the story, that is, somebody on the left who has a blind spot when it comes to the Jewish settler colonization of Iceland. At first they were called PEIS: Progressives Except Iceland, which became Prince Edwards, and then, finally, just Edwards.

—Yes, but why write a story like this at all? The Jews and Palestinians have a lasting peace, that any history book will tell you was won through Arab and Jewish organizing in the British Mandate in the twenties and thirties, through intense organizing from the Jewish diaspora against the Zionists, through collective horror at the Holocaust and a commitment to lead by example. With so much of the world except Palestine falling apart, why imagine what would have happened if the defeated early Zionists colonized Iceland? Some of your critics are saying it is an irresponsible thing to write about.

—Thank you for that question, Georgia. As you alluded to, peace was not a foregone conclusion in Palestine. Far from it. What else is fiction, what else are stories, supposed to do, if not break us from our sense of historical certitude? Fascism is on the rise the world over. There are people in Palestine, Jewish, Muslim, and Christian, who are trying to corrupt that country's robust democracy. We are busy actively forgetting the very real colonial history of this planet, not to mention this very country of Canada, only so we can do it all over again on other ones. I thought to myself, what better way to remind us all of what could have been, of what, indeed, was—what better way than a totally imagined scenario?

Brenda turned off the radio. "Dinner's ready," she said, trying to sound upbeat, though as she cooked and listened to Stephanie, the more despondent she became.

They sat down at the small kitchen table and started to eat. "Do you really think it could have ended up differently in the Middle East?" Kate asked. She was in one of her blunt, combative moods.

Brenda chewed her pasta. "I don't know, maybe. Why think about that, outside of fiction?"

A pause. "Do you think it could have worked out differently for us?"

Brenda sighed. She had been thinking the same thing. "Maybe. Maybe not. Maybe certain relationships only have a certain amount of love. Why should love be forever or not at all? If Palestine were to fall apart tomorrow, at least it had nearly eighty years of peace, right? Should we just forget about those? Anyways, why think about it now? What happened, happened."

Kate's face looked small, fragile. The bee antennae were still on her head, probably forgotten, sitting askew, loose strands of hair floating as if trapped in the antennae's electrical field. There was a dab of pasta sauce under Kate's left eye, a spot Brenda used to love to kiss. "We'll still be friends, right?"

Brenda didn't answer right away. She looked down at her food. The way her plate was arranged made her want to paint for the first time in weeks. All through their trip, seeing the sights, the wonders of coexistence, Brenda and Kate pretending to be a couple to the outside world, hardly talking in their hostel rooms, Brenda's creative urge, usually barely containable, had been at its lowest-ever vibration. Since they got back, she hadn't been to her studio, just spent her days biking the city, along the lake, up the river and through industrial side streets.

Her studio. There was a stack of newly stretched canvases, propped against the wall, just waiting for colour and pattern and shape.

Maybe tomorrow, she'd go.

Brenda was biking home. Pedestrians, cars, other cyclists, traffic lights, the streets, the city, the world, Brenda felt out of sync with all of it. The whole of Toronto seemed to be performing sloppy U-turns, backing into spots without looking, opening doors into bike lanes, the city one long red light. By the time she pulled up to her apartment she felt like she had survived a war.

Upstairs, Kate was making chili, the radio blasting sharp-edged rock. Brenda came up to Kate from behind; Kate, focusing on the pot, shrugged her off.

"Can I change this while we eat?"

"Sure, go ahead."

Changing it to the CBC, they caught the tail end of the weather before being returned to *Books and Talk*.

—Thank you, Stephanie. What a great scene.

"Holy shit, is that Stephanie Krasner?!" Kate said.

"Probably. I thought I heard something about a new book."

—Can you explain the epigraph to the story?

—It's from Leon Uris's novel *Exodus*, which sold in the millions of copies and was a very problematic telling of the founding of the state of Israel which glorified Jewish violence. It's taken from the—very long, ha ha—scene where all the countries at the UN vote on partitioning Palestine, and Uris's narrator judges them for it. The quote I used for the epigraph is right after Iceland votes for partition, and reads "The world's oldest republic had worked to make the world's newest republic."

—Speaking of, what kind of reaction do you expect from the Icelanders themselves?

—I've already gotten responses, and not just from Icelanders. From Jews, from Canadians, from sweet little old ladies in Alberta with filthy mouths.

—...You've gotten a lot of hate mail.

—Yes, people love sending me emails telling me why I'm not a real Jew, what I don't understand about history, how it's the Palestinians' fault that three million of them are trapped in Gaza, that all Jewish people, especially soldiers, are saints, that the West Bank isn't actually occupied, that Jerusalem should be a hundred percent Jewish, calling me all kinds of names I can't repeat on national radio.

—It's not only individuals, is it? Lots of Jewish institutions have responded harshly. We have the Union for Reform Judaism's response here. Let me read you some of it. "We find Ms. Krasner's fictional flight-of-fancies very dangerous and damaging to the Jewish people. Reform Jews believe in a strong, well-defended Israel—we always have and we always will—and while we are the first to admit there are problems with how the country is run, is that not the case everywhere? What Ms. Krasner has done here is make a false equivalency. How could the early Zionists conquering the sovereign nation of Iceland have any bearing on what happened in British Mandate Palestine, in the real world? All it serves to do is feed ammo to our enemies. We do not accept any fiction that questions Israel's fundamental right to exist as a Jewish state." Your response, Stephanie?

—Hey, we're not all perfect.

There was an awkward pause.

—No, seriously, this institutional fear of fiction that challenges the Jewish mainstream is exactly why such fiction needs to be written.

—That's all the time we have. Thanks so much Stephanie. I'm Georgia Talcum-Ross, and this is *Books and Talk*. Stay tuned for news.

The news opened with the American president's plan to visit the Temple Mount in Jerusalem on his first official visit to the region. The announcer read a quote from Jasbir Khalidi, a Palestinian activist, saying the president visiting the contested Temple Mount was an ill-considered idea, and would be seen as an affront by most of East Jerusalem's Arab population. Remember, Khalidi said, that the Second Intifada began when Ariel Sharon visited the Mount.

"No shit!" Brenda exclaimed, turning off the radio.

"Some people from work are going to a protest on Saturday about this," Kate said.

Brenda nodded. "We should go."

"Totally."

Brenda took the plates to the sink, and turned on the tap.

⫶ Brenda and Kate went to dinner at Brenda's parents'. Meals with Brenda's folks were often awkward affairs, the opposite in many ways to meals with Kate's family: quiet instead of loud, everything loaded with subtext instead of blaring with text text, no talk of food instead of constant talk of food, which was one reason they didn't visit Brenda's parents so much. But since the latest US presidential election, things had taken a decidedly tense turn.

Brenda's brother Frank was there with his girlfriend, Blair. When Brenda's family had found out Blair was trans there had been a minor scandal, but that was last month's intrigue. Brenda's aunt Jill, the only one still not okay with it, was sworn to silence, or no more dinner invites. Frank and Blair seemed oblivious, though Brenda knew they were not. They were laughing, whispering in each other's ears. They both stunk of marijuana.

During the soup course nobody spoke.

"Did you know that one of the most at-risk non-human species in coastal zones affected by climate change are dogs?" Frank asked, he and Blair laughing.

"How interesting, Frankie," Brenda's father said. Brenda knew that Kate often had trouble determining if Brenda's father was being sarcastic or not. This time Brenda herself was stumped.

"Yeah, we've been reading about how many puppies are put down every year," Blair said.

"It's really a moral catastrophe," Frank said, nodding in agreement with his girlfriend.

Over the main course they talked about the weather, traffic in Toronto, Brenda's mom told a circuitous story about a woman in her church choir who had lost a lottery ticket. When Frank brought up how a lot of dog toys and sex toys are interchangeable the room shifted into slightly more dangerous waters.

Jill, who had apparently held her tongue long enough, took the opening. "What do you think of the president's plan to visit the Temple Mount, Kate?" Jill was an outspoken supporter of the president.

"Uh, I think it's probably a bad idea."

"Well, I'll tell you what I think. I think, as a so-called gentile, that this obsession with the Jews has gotten out of hand. Why should the president continue placating these people?"

Silence. Everybody ate without talking.

"Here's what we need to do," Frank said. "We train ten, twenty dogs how to play Ultimate Frisbee, and we tour the world's refugee camps, bringing canine joy to the masses."

"Frankie, enough."

"Those Jews need to be knocked down a peg or two," Jill said.

"Aunt Jill," Brenda said, "I really feel like you should shut the fuck up."

"Brenda!" Brenda's mom exclaimed, aghast. Kate was trying not to laugh.

"Well I never," Jill said, putting her napkin to her mouth.

It felt like the worst of it was over. The tension had broken.

"Anyways, Blair and I are getting a puppy," Frank said.

"Kate and I are breaking up," Brenda announced.

Everybody kept eating. Nobody looked at each other. Jill had a slight smile on her face. Kate got up and went to the washroom. Brenda felt nothing but relief.

That night, Brenda and Kate were in bed. They hadn't spoken much since dinner. Both of them had stayed on their phones during the subway ride back downtown.

"I haven't stopped thinking about what Stephanie was saying on the radio yesterday," Kate said. Not what Brenda would have guessed had been occupying Kate's mind. "I know the occupation, what's going on over there, all of it, is messed up, but I never really thought about it. It's fucked, Brenda. It is so fucked. I don't know what else to say. Fuck! What's wrong with everybody?"

"There's just bad people out there," Brenda said, unsure of the proper response.

"Let's buy a copy of her new book," Kate said, thoughtful, determined.

Brenda turned over, held on to Kate, and they stayed like that for a while, for as long as they could.

MAY 1, 2018

The lights in the bookstore go down. The author takes the podium, makes a joke, drinks from her water glass. She opens the book to the tabbed page and she reads.

"The sun skimmed along the shimmer of the horizon. Delilah Snorridottir stood watching it. Jewsland could be better. Jewsland could be a home for everybody, for Jews, for Icelanders. For everybody. The land could be open to all. Fuck the one-sided narrative of the Iceright trips, of her father, of the American Zionists. Of Lavie. Things do not have to be this way. It's like Leif said: every moment a hundred thousand worlds are possible. After what she witnessed in Canada, it was harder to imagine, yes, but a dream was still a dream. Jews lived in diaspora for thousands of years, it kept us strange, open, wonderful. What happened? Why did we land in Iceland? Let's lead by example. Let's tear down the border walls. Let's throw away the nuclear codes. Let's invite the Icelanders to our Friday night dinner table, eat challah and cod stew together. If it fails once, let's try again. And again and again. Let's get rid of all this shit! Let's replace it with something better. This is *our* collective dream, after all.

"Delilah had a moment of doubt. What in the history of the Jews, in the whole history of this messy, mistake-prone species, could lead one to believe that something so beautiful could ever be obtained?

"Delilah wasn't sure, but that wouldn't stop her from believing nonetheless."

Acknowledgements

My deepest thanks to University of Alberta Press, and everybody there. Michelle Lobkowicz, my acquiring editor, Douglas Hildebrand, Duncan Turner, Alan Brownoff, Cathie Crooks: thank you for taking a chance on these stories about the suburbs, Jewishness, teenagers, politics, and cannabis. Thank you to the two peer reviewers who gave their time and expertise to these stories, and to Kimmy Beach for her excellent, generous copyediting. Thanks as well to the Canada Council for the Arts, whose funding allowed me time and space to complete this collection.

Some of these stories appeared in journals and magazines, often in altered form. My forever gratitude to *This Magazine* for publishing "Tel Aviv–Toronto Red Eye" (and for the excellent accompanying illustration!); to *X-R-A-Y* for publishing "The Krasners"; and to *The Temz Review* for publishing both "Temples" and "The Streets of Thornhill."

Deepest love and thanks to my first readers. David Huebert, who read many of these stories at various phases of existence. Tyler Ball, who read the collection in its infancy and its entirety and went through it page by page with me at Future Bakery. Thank you to Asha Jeffers and her indispensable feedback on "Rubble Children." A special shoutout to Dan Sadowski: I'll never forget reading a draft of "The Krasners," the earliest story from what would become *Rubble Children*, aloud to you that autumnal day as we drove around Toronto running errands. I knew from my excitement and your laughter that these stories were worth pursuing.

The ideas and images of these stories came to me in one original burst of colour and sound that I could barely transcribe into a notebook fast enough. And then the hard work began. As with all fiction, each story's admixture of truth, memory, imagination, improvisation, and reading came from somewhere; I acknowledge those somewheres, wherever they may be.

I worked on this collection at the Banff Centre, on Spadina Avenue, on Gordon Street, in cafés indoor and out, at York University, at Robarts Library, in Iceland, on Kahshe Lake, in Thornhill (of course). The land and landscapes where I wrote left an indelible imprint on these pages.

My friends and family are everywhere in this book. Myra Bloom, Toby Gottlieb, Alex Smith, Sam Blostein, Jeff Ebidia, Nick Kiverago. This book is dedicated to my parents, Cathy and David Kreuter, whose support for my work and politics has been a huge catalyst. Steph and I often tell people that our siblings are our best friends, and it is true: Ben and Becca, Rachel and Sam, Jenn and Jon, Daniel and Dana, what would Toronto be without you? I'd be remiss not to mention the dogs in my life: Piper, Daisy, Louise, Beanie.

This collection has existed in one form or another since before my daughter, Noa, was born. I love you more than anything. Moving through this world with you is beyond words in its delight and meaning.

As always, Steph, my best friend, life partner, and laughter coach. Here's to that moment early in our knowing each other where I mimed the "cool" way to smoke a joint, and we nearly died from the ensuing hysterics.

Finally, this book is for all the children who live and who die in the rubble; may we be held accountable, may we build a world without borders, without bombs, without rubble.